BRODY

A HOPE CITY NOVEL

KRIS MICHAELS

Detective Sergeant Brody King stared down a Hope City back alley at the dented steel exterior door that wore the scars of collisions it had survived. He and two of his men were assigned to cover this entryway. He listened intently to police comms via an earwig. Thanks to an undercover agent wearing a wire, the conversation inside the building was being broadcast to his team. Twenty-two men and women, permanently assigned to the Hope City's Joint Drug Enforcement Team, or JDET, waited in position for the undercover DEA agent to give the signal. At the undercover agent's predetermined code words, they would storm the building and take down the participants, including the undercover officer. His arrest would keep the man's identity from the rest of the scum currently exchanging cash for a shipment of drugs. His team was highly trained, briefed with the latest available intel, and ready to take down a major conduit of cocaine into the city.

"Standby, we may have new players inbound." Through the comms, DEA Agent Amber Swanson's voice slapped his ears in a hard, professional clip; gone was the soft, quiet voice he remembered.

A lot of shit has changed in the last ten years. The ten years since she walked away... and left him down on one knee holding a diamond engagement ring in his hand. Brody's muscles tightened with anger, confusion, and embarrassment—emotions he'd thought he'd put behind him. He drew a steadying breath. His past had nothing to do with this moment, and his focus needed to be on his team, this raid, and the takedown of a major player in Hope City's drug scene.

Brody held still while listening to the drug deal going down inside. Colt Rayburn nudged him and motioned down the alleyway. A blacked-out SUV drove into the tight alley. As one man, he, Colt, and Derek Watson, slid back behind a dumpster. The smell coming from the industrial sized garbage bin could choke a maggot, but it was the only place they could still see the doorway and be shielded from the SUV's direct line of vision.

"Juliet Three. Black SUV. Unknown occupants pulling up to the back door." He whispered the license plate number and shut up when the doors opened. *Wonderful.* The bastards were carrying Uzis.

He keyed his mic and barely breathed, "Four. Armed. Heavy."

"Are you in position to take them?"

He clicked the mic twice. It was their team's way to confirm without talking. Once for no, twice for yes. They'd be able to flank the bastards.

"The deal is almost done. On my count, move in." His captain's voice cracked over the comms. He motioned to Derek to go to the front of the vehicle. Colt nodded to the rear. He agreed with a slight movement of his head.

When they were ready, he keyed the mic three times, giving his captain the signal they were ready. It was a dance the team had done too many times to count.

"On one." Captain Terrell counted down. "Three... two... one!"

Colt and Derek sprinted at the same time he did, except he didn't round the vehicle. He sprinted to the hood, used the bumper as a step and launched onto it. The sound of his weight landing on the hood swung all four men to his position. Derek and Colt yelled, "Police!"

"Drop your weapons!" His Desert Eagle Mark XIX leveled on the man closest to him. Looking down the barrel of the massive handgun would clench anyone's ass, and it worked almost every time. Their free hands went up, and all four leaned down and placed their weapons by their feet. Derek kicked the guns away as Colt spun the gunmen and zip tied their wrists.

"Clear!"

"Get down!"

"Police!"

"We got a runner!"

A door slammed; in the distance, he heard Amber's voice yell, "Halt, DEA!"

"You got this?" Brody jumped down from the newly dented hood of the SUV.

"Go!" Derek dropped one of the restrained men to his knees.

"Runner heading down Marlin Avenue!" Amber yelled into her open mic.

Brody sprinted through the alley and across the street, running full tilt down an alley the next block over. Marlin Avenue curved, and if the runner didn't duck into a building, he'd be coming around right where Brody would exit the alley.

Pounding against the asphalt, he saw the man flash by the alley entrance. He sped up and flew around the corner. He launched at the guy's knees and tackled the man as he ran full speed. The cement sidewalk stopped their fall.

Brody scrambled on top of the bastard and had him cuffed before Amber made it to their location. She glanced at the man and panted into her radio, "We need an ambulance at Marlin and..." She glanced around.

He keyed his mic. "Marlin and Pier Drive. Perp has abrasions, needs to be cleared by medical before we transport."

She nodded and dropped her hands to her knees, her service weapon still grasped in one hand. "Damn, he's a fast son of a bitch."

Brody stood and glanced at the perp. They both were going to be sore, but they'd both okay. He wished he was as resilient as the suspect appeared to be. Guess the cement wasn't very forgiving today. He pointed to the man and for the first time looked at Amber. "You got this?"

"Yeah. Thanks." She stood up and holstered her weapon. "Look, Brody, we should probably talk."

Wisps of her long red-gold hair fell from the ponytail she'd cinched it into, and the strands perched against her high cheekbone. Her face was flushed and her eyes, damn those blue-green eyes of hers, threw him right back to the moment he'd last seen her. She was still as beautiful as he remembered, perhaps more so now. The confidence she was rocking looked damn good on her. He shook his head. "Little late for that."

She flipped her ponytail to her back and put her hands on her hips. "We're going to need to talk eventually. I'm permanently assigned to this team, and there are things I need to say, that I should've told you--"

"Let's cut through the shit. You're a member of my team. We work together. Nothing more. I'm your sergeant and in your chain of command. If you can't deal with that because of our past, you can report directly to Lt. Anderson or Captain Terrell." He turned as the ambulance rounded the corner on Marlin with a black and white behind it. He looked back at her. "Your refusal ten years ago said more than enough. I wasn't what you wanted."

"I was scared! I didn't want my life to pass me

by!" she hissed as the ambulance stopped at their position.

He pointed at the man. "Deal with him. Radio in when you're clear."

He spun on his heel and headed back down the alley. The road rash and ache in his shoulder from tackling the suspect was nothing compared to the pain her words recalled. *She didn't want her life to pass her by. As if he was going to weigh her down and stop her from living.* He'd loved her with every cell of his being. She was *the one* for him. She always would be.

He'd almost died when she'd fled from him. Literally. No, he hadn't been willing to let her go without a fight. When he'd recovered from the shock of her refusal, he'd driven to her sister's house. On the way there, he'd been t-boned by a delivery truck. The accident had put him in a coma for two weeks and then shit got tough. Surgeries and physical therapy distracted him from the rejection that caused more pain than any doctor could inflict. When he came out of the coma, he realized that while he'd gone after her initially, he wasn't going to beg her to love him. As he crossed the street, Colt shouted down the alley, "Brody, Captain wants to see you inside!"

Colt was obviously in charge of processing the SUV. All the doors stood open, and the forensics team assigned to their department was digging into their kits.

"Roger that. Derek and the perps?"

"Perps are in the wagon. Derek's heading down to the precinct with them. He'll sit on them until we get there."

Making sure their perps weren't "accidentally" released wasn't a joke. His father, the Hope City Police Commissioner, had made huge strides in rooting out the systemic corruption which had riddled the department as few as five years ago, but there were still those who "lost" paperwork for a few hundred dollars.

He made for the first door and entered the skanky smelling bar. His eyes adjusted to the darkened interior, and he headed toward the sound of voices. He entered the main seating area of the bar in time to hear his captain.

"What did you say?"

Oh hell, that couldn't be good. When Captain Terrell's voice got low and growled like that, he was one step away from flaying someone alive.

"What's up, Cap? You wanted to see me?"

His boss turned. Oh, hell yeah, he was pissed.

The man's face was lobster red, and his jaw was tightly clenched.

"It seems the DEA is declining to share the bust even though my team effected the apprehension and saved their undercover agent's ass."

He walked forward, planted his feet shoulder width apart, and crossed his arms, as he glanced at the smug DEA agent who was pointedly ignoring his captain. "That so? Well, hell, if they don't want to share the collar, let's call off our team. Let DEA process the scene."

He turned his back on the agent and lowered his voice. "We've got the four perps from the alley. They were loaded with Uzis. This was a hit. They will have intel. If the DEA bastard wants to play it that way, let's take the ancillary busts which have nothing to do with the drug deal. We can push this up the chain. The DEA will be persona non grata for years."

His captain released a huff of air. "Still stuck with one of the sons of bitches on my team. She'll feed info to her agency."

"Not if she doesn't have access to it. She can earn her wings and our trust like everyone else on the team."

"You know her. Do you trust her? She seemed

to have her shit together in the van. Tore out of it when the runner darted." The captain turned his head and stared at him.

He sighed. "I don't know. Haven't seen her for ten years. I have no idea if I can trust her or not. The person I used to know? Yeah, I'd trust her, but..." He wasn't going to sell Amber down the river because of their personal relationship. He wasn't that type of person.

"But, like you said, you don't know her now."

He nodded.

"Follow me." His captain glowered at the DEA Agent. "Degrassi, you've got the scene."

The DEA agent whipped his head around to gape at them. "What?"

"Your scene. We're taking the four men we arrested. They aren't a part of this bust."

"No, they're mine." Degrassi put his hands on his hips.

"What are you charging them with?" He angled his head back to his boss.

"Whatever charges you've booked them on." Degrassi's forehead furrowed. The man resembled a Shar Pei dog with all the folds smooshed together.

Captain looked at him. "Are we charging them?"

"Nope." Brody rocked back on the heels of his well broken in combat boots. "They were in the wrong place at the wrong time."

"Bullshit." Degrassi shook his head. "You're working an angle. I can feel it."

Captain Terrell lifted his radio and said, "Juliet One to all Juliet teams. DEA has the primary scene. Let's go home."

All movement around them ceased. "Your police commissioner guaranteed your assistance."

His captain shrugged, "You guaranteed him we'd be credited with a portion of the bust."

"That's fiction." Degrassi sneered.

"Really? That's not what the Commissioner told me when I saw him," Brody sneered right back.

"Right, the Police Commissioner happened to have the time to talk to a piece of shit sergeant."

Brody shoved his hands in his pockets so he wouldn't be inclined to deck the son of a bitch and let loose with a fake laugh. "That is so funny! Damn, I'll make sure to tell my dad you think I'm a piece of shit sergeant, and he can't trust the DEA."

The man looked from the captain to him, confused.

"Oh, sorry, I was late to the briefing, and we

weren't introduced. King. Brody King." He saw the moment the DEA agent put two and two together.

Amber strolled into the bar, brushing off her black jeans. She stopped short and glanced between the three of them. "Degrassi, what's going on?"

The man didn't acknowledge her. The DEA agent's stare still focused on him.

"Degrassi here is saying the DEA will take full credit for the bust," Captain Terrell said, but didn't move.

"For this collar? Nope. It's fifty-fifty. That's what we were briefed at DEA headquarters, and that's what was relayed to your Police Commissioner." Amber glanced from Terrell to him to Degrassi.

"Oh, for fuck's sake, were you making a grab here, Degrassi?" Amber raised her phone and waved it at the man. "One call and you're doing support work on the coast of the Bering Sea. You've been warned about this shit before."

"There's no problem here. We're sharing credit." The man spun on his heel and stalked to the back of the room where three members of the JDET team and two of the DEA's people were certifying a count of money.

"He'll be arresting polar bears for smoking pot if he keeps this shit up. I'm sorry about him. I'll include his actions in my report to my superiors. It will be the last report from me they'll get until I'm released from this task force, by the way. If I work for you, my loyalty is to you and only you." She slid her phone back into her pocket. "I'd like to debrief our undercover agent with Degrassi, in case he has anything we can work from a Hope City level. Has the cocaine been tested?"

Captain Terrell held up a small ampule. The light blue color of the tube testified to the content of the packaged white powder. "It's legit according to the street kits. We'll have it tested in the lab." He crossed his arms and rocked back on his heels before he spoke. "We have Jorgenson and Estrada for conspiracy to distribute. First count on the cash was fifty thousand. They are doing a second and third count to validate the first pass. Weapons charges are in line for the muscle inside with Jorgenson and Estrada. We'll be able to roll some of them."

She nodded and turned to Brody. "Do you have any intel on the four you arrested outside?"

Brody kept his gaze focused on the count going on at the back of the room. "Not yet."

"King, you and Swanson head to the precinct. I need you to make sure the team gets their shit done. Go through the reports, and then we'll start with the suspects. Having them sit and wait until our interview specialists go after them won't harm anything. I'm not leaving until *that* asshole is gone." Terrell nodded toward Degrassi.

He nodded his understanding while he watched the people counting the money. "Derek is sitting on the four from outside. How many do we have from this mess?"

"The two primaries, Jorgenson and Estrada. There were four meatheads with iron who were cuffed too."

He finally flicked his eyes toward Amber. "Which one is your guy?"

"One of the meatheads. Estrada's right-hand man. He's been working in the family for almost three years now."

Brody wanted to question her about the amount of time the guy'd been undercover, but he wasn't about to initiate a conversation. The less he talked with her, the better. He nodded to the side door and headed out. She'd either follow or she wouldn't. Actually, he'd prefer it if she didn't.

"All in all, the op went well." Amber commented

as they drove north heading away from the harbor area.

He grunted in agreement and was met with an exaggerated sigh from her side of the vehicle.

"How are your parents?"

"No." He refused to open that door. His family was *everything* to him, and when she'd dumped him, she'd dumped them too. His mother was heartbroken, not because Amber had left him, but because of what had happened to him afterward.

He watched her with his peripheral vision. She turned her head toward him and gawked. "No? Just no?"

"That's right. Just no." He glanced at the clock. Five more minutes in this truck and he'd be clawing at the windshield to get away from her.

"What the hell happened to you to make you such an ass, Brody? You were never like this before."

He pulled over suddenly, and she grasped onto the 'oh-shit handle' on the side of the truck. The gear shifter slammed into Park, and he spun toward her. "*You* happened. *You* are the reason I'm like this. *My* family, *my* life, *my* friends, everything I care about is *off limits* to you. I have to work with you. I don't have to like it." He threw the truck back into gear and forced his way back into the flow of traffic.

She had the decency to keep her thoughts to herself until they reached the small outbuilding located on the grounds of the Central Precinct. The squat cement block building had a badge-controlled entry and exit. JDET had their own armory holding their tactical equipment and radios, five small holding cells, a bullpen, two conference rooms, and offices for him, the lieutenant, and the captain.

He jammed his truck into a parking slot and slammed his door closed as he stalked to the building. He drew a deep breath. Was it just yesterday he'd bounced into the building wearing a tux? Yeah, yeah it was. He hadn't been home since yesterday morning. Hadn't eaten since the wedding yesterday afternoon, or slept since the night before last. They'd spent the night planning the op, reviewing the plans, and working assignments. He'd managed to avoid talking directly to Amber for damn near twenty-four hours. Now he was back at the precinct, where if he was lucky, he had every intention of avoiding her again.

She yelled at him from beside the truck, "Brody, wait!"

He stopped and glared in her direction. Luck wasn't on his side. Obviously.

"What?"

"I really do need to talk with you."

"Amber, there is nothing you need to tell me you haven't already said. Why did you come back here? Why? There are hundreds of places you could have landed. Did you know I was assigned to this team?"

"No! I had no idea until I walked in that door yesterday."

"Right. How long have you been back in Hope City?"

"I... I never left."

He stared at her for a moment and internalized the razor-sharp syllables which sliced his soul into tiny pieces... again. She'd dumped him to fulfill her grand plan of a life that didn't pass her by, and yet she'd never left Hope City. So, it was him she didn't want. Had she been playing him the entire time they'd been together? What a moron he'd been. He turned and headed into the building.

"Brody, it's not what you think."

He didn't dare stop. He'd been raised to respect women, all women, even the one who had ripped out his heart on her way out the door. Stopping now would be a *very* bad thing. He'd say words he couldn't take back. Words which would be meant to shred her as deeply as she'd lacerated him.

"Brody!"

He swiped his badge and walked into his building, leaving her outside. She had a badge; she could get in.

Derek pounced as soon as he walked in the door. "Sarge, I separated them. The guy in number three is the weakest link. He's sweating bullets and glancing around. His knees are bouncing. The other three are cold as ice." Derek fell into step with him. "When are we talking to them?"

"Captain wants them on ice while we clean up a bit. Have you started your report?"

"Yep. I hate paperwork, so I get it done and out of the way. Man, the leap to the top of the truck was fucking awesome. One day, though, you're going to land on your ass."

"Nah, that's what all those box jumps at CrossFit are for." He motioned Derek toward his desk in the bullpen. "Send me the prints for these guys, and I'll see if I can get some magic help to identify them."

"Dude, who do you know? No one else can get anything pushed through quickly." Derek plopped his ass behind his desk as Amber entered the bullpen.

He pinned her with a glare. "Do you have a desk yet?"

She shook her head no. Her jaw was clenched shut, and from the flush on her cheeks, she was pissed.

"Derek, put Agent Swanson at Harrison's desk. He's on vacation for the next two weeks. By the time he's back, we'll have a computer for her, and we can pull a desk up from the basement next door. Get her logins and show her how to print."

Derek's face lit up. "Absolutely, I've got her covered."

He didn't doubt it. Derek was a notorious flirt, and if you listened to the man's claims, he never slept alone, although he wasn't strapped down with a relationship. *Whatever*. He spun on his heel and headed to his office. He needed time to breathe without looking at the woman he loved. *Used to love.*

CHAPTER 2

Amber stopped in front of her sister's small Craftsman style cottage and put her crossover SUV into park. She pushed the remote to open the garage and watched it slowly roll to the top before she turned off the engine and slumped back into the vehicle's seat. The last thirty hours had been one shock after another, Brody King being the biggest surprise. She'd known he worked as a police officer in Hope City. She should have stalked his mother's social media. It would have kept her up to date on most of the King family's notable moments, but she'd unfriended all the Kings after everything that had happened.

She'd been so very careful not to be noticed by his powerful family, and he'd disappeared from her life, but nothing would ever eradicate him from her heart. Oh lord, why had he been wearing a tux yesterday? He'd changed so damn much. Not physically, although he was bigger, more muscled, and his hair was longer, but he used to be so happy, open, and approachable. Now? The man she'd tried to talk to today was closed off, bitter, and angry.

She sat in the SUV and closed her eyes. Brody King. Of all the people in the city, why did Brody have to be on this elite team? She opened her eyes and stared sightlessly at the back wall of the garage. It seemed like yesterday. The emotions were as raw today as they had been when he'd asked her to marry him. His proposal had come as such a shock. *Shock?* That day was like being at the epicenter of an 8.9 earthquake. Devastating, confusing, and absolutely terrifying. They'd never had serious talks about marriage. She'd had plans. Plans she'd described to him in detail. Marriage? Maybe, someday, but she hadn't been ready. She'd had her entire life in front of her, and she was getting *out* of Hope City. She'd wanted to experience things her mother never could. With her education, she'd had the world at her fingertips.

Enough. She grabbed her purse and headed into the garage where she locked her service weapon in a small handheld gun safe. The small safe entered the house with her, but only after she locked it. Safety wasn't something she'd ever compromise.

"Long day?" Dawn's voice came from the front room.

She kicked the door shut and put her purse on a hook in the small kitchen. "Exhausting." Her fingers dragged the elastic band from her hair and she slipped it onto her wrist so she wouldn't lose it. "Where's Gage?"

"He's at Johnny's. Birthday sleepover, remember?" Her half sister strolled into the kitchen and headed to the refrigerator. "Wine?"

"Please." She glanced at her watch and sighed, "Damn, it is Saturday, isn't it? I'm sorry. This case went down so fast, and there were complications..." She grabbed two wine glasses from the cupboard and sat them on the counter for her sister to fill.

Her sister's head snapped up. "Was someone hurt?"

"No, not those type of complications." She grabbed the glass of chardonnay and waited for her sister to put the bottle back in the fridge before they both headed to the sectional. She sat down and toed off her boots, wiggling her toes in relief.

"What type of complications?" Dawn aimed the

remote and muted the program she'd been watching.

"I met my new team." She took a sip of the wine and shook her head.

"What? Are they misogynistic assholes?"

"No, everyone except the sergeant was very welcoming." She leaned forward and put her wine on the table.

"What crawled up his ass?"

She chuckled at her sister's comment. She was the office manager at one of Hope City's largest trucking companies, and the woman had learned to swear from the best.

"I believe that would be me."

"Huh? What are you talking about?"

"The sergeant? It's Brody."

Her sister's mouth dropped open and then snapped shut. "No. Oh, hell." Dawn stood up and started pacing, her hand clasped over her mouth. "What are we going to do?"

"Nothing. Sit down, Dawn. I'm too tired to watch you pace."

"But he could--"

"He could, but I'm not going to let it happen."

"How are you going to stop him?"

"By telling him the truth and working with him?"

"Right, okay. So, what? You're going to walk up to him and say, 'Oh, hey, listen after I walked away from your marriage proposal, I discovered I was pregnant with your child, and oh… gee whiz, I decided to keep it from you. Sorry, I was young and frightened and didn't think you'd mind not knowing you had a son!'" Dawn's voice reached glass-shattering levels by the time she'd finished her rant.

"Wrong! I went to that hospital. Over and over. I had to wait until after his family left—they weren't exactly welcoming—but I sat with him until the ICU nurses forced me out of the room. You know I did. He was the one who refused to see me after he'd regained consciousness. I was standing in the hall outside his room when he told his brother there was nothing left between us, and he didn't want to see me! Months later, I went to his house. His mother told me he'd contact me *if* he wanted to talk.

"What was I supposed to do? Should I have pushed myself on him because I was pregnant, *after* I ran out on his proposal? *After* he'd almost been killed because he was chasing after me? *After* he told Brock he never wanted to see me again? Yeah, that's a hell of a way to start a family." She leaned forward and ran her hands through her hair.

"You should have told him, Amber. God, this is horrible."

"I tried; you know I did! I broke us when I freaked and left, but I had to have time to think. I love Brody, but when I saw the ring, I saw my dreams grinding to a halt."

"*Love* Brody?"

Her sister's question sent her mind through what she'd just said. "*Loved*. Past tense." Oh, God, their relationship was very much a past tense. Ancient history.

"That other shit was your mother talking. The woman messed with your head."

"I know. I thought I explained it to Brody. No, I *know* I did! Why did he spring the proposal on me? God, I was such a mess. Then when Gage was born... I couldn't lose him. Family has always been everything to the Kings—and Hannah King's first grandchild? I couldn't risk Brody would try to take him away. We were so broke. I didn't have a job, and you were still in school. We had so much debt. Hell, if it hadn't been for your mom's insurance paying off this house and your student loans buying food, we'd have been living on the streets. You know how powerful his father was, even back then. He'd just have to show up in a courtroom, and any judge would have given the Kings custody of Gage. They would have taken him from me. The Kings had money; they had status. They still have all of that, but now I can fight back. I'm a damn good mom. I'm doing well, and he's a great kid. Well adjusted, smart, and so damn much like his dad." She shook her head. "But I do agree. I've made mistakes."

"Yeah, and they're all coming back to bite us in the ass." Dawn dropped back onto the couch. "What are we going to do?"

"I don't know. I mean, it isn't like we'll be visiting. He won't come here. He doesn't even want to talk to me. Maybe I won't push the issue and not even tell him?" She rolled her eyes. Yeah, like it would be so easy. She was going to have to face this.

Dawn shook her head. "You're the smartest woman I know, but in this, you are absolutely, one hundred percent, wrong. You owe the man a full-on explanation, and he needs to meet his son. Like you said, you tried to tell him. Gage deserves to know his father and his side of the family." Her sister grabbed her wine and downed the contents. "I love that boy, you know I do, but you're hurting everyone in this situation if you do nothing. It's time to face the music."

"I know! I did try to talk to him today. Several times in fact. He won't even look at me. I think he hates me."

"Then get to him through his family."

Amber crumbled back into the couch cushions. "They'll close ranks."

She'd gone to his childhood home. Brody's mom had met her at the front door.

"Hi Amber." Mrs. King came out onto the porch and pulled the door closed. The fact she hadn't invited her in spoke volumes.

"Hi. Would it be possible to talk to Brody?" Her voice cracked, and she blinked back the tears she had in her eyes.

Hannah wrapped her arms around her waist and smiled sadly. Then came the look. Pity. Sadness. Disapproval. And all wrapped up in a motherly concern that almost gutted her. "Honey, I know you will probably have a hard time understanding this, but I do think it would be better if you waited until he was ready to talk to you. He's just home from his second surgery, and he's in a lot of pain. Now really isn't a good time for him. He'll come around." She couldn't prevent the tears that brimmed over her lashes. *"I'm so sorry for... everything."*

"Honey, you didn't cause the accident, but what happened before that? One day when you're a mother, I hope you understand. He didn't deserve that reaction. You hurt him. He can put on a mask of indifference, but his heart is so big. He feels things very deeply. Maybe someday he'll be in a better place and reach out to you."

She was right but hearing it from a dynamic woman she could never hope to impress... God, she'd been devastated. She'd no idea what to say or how to say it. So, in the end, she turned away and left.

"Do you blame them?" Dawn sat down beside her. "Look, you aren't that scared girl any longer. You're a fantastic mom. You've got a career you love, and we have a good life here, but keeping this secret even a day longer is wrong. You need to call him and tell him you have to meet. Hell, invite him here or take Gage to his mom's house! Once they see Gage, they're going to know. That boy is an exact copy of his father!" Dawn pointed to the wall where Gage's pictures were on display. She stared at her son's photos and almost cried. His mischievous laugh came from Brody. The smile, a little crooked but so damn endearing, and those beautiful eyes, were exact duplicates of his father's. Every King sibling had those vivid blue eyes with a dark navy ring on the outside and so did Gage. His hair was a little lighter than Brody's, and his coloring was fairer, but there was no mistaking Gage for anything other than a King.

"Gage asked about his dad a couple days ago. He asked why his dad wasn't with us. He asked if we were divorced." Amber dropped her head into her hands.

"Damn. What did you say about that?"

"I told him the truth. That his father and I never got married, and I moved away when I was pregnant with him. His father didn't know about him."

"Yeah, and if I know Gage, he asked if he could go meet his dad, right?"

She nodded. "He jumped up and grabbed my laptop and said, 'You can find him and tell him about me.'"

"Girl, you've got a mess on your hands." Dawn walked into the kitchen and came back with the open bottle of wine.

She stared at the wine left in her glass. "He's *never* asked such a pointed question before."

"Well at least you didn't lie to him." Dawn filled the wine glasses again, draining the bottle.

"I'm so screwed."

"Yup." Dawn agreed and took a swig of her wine.

Brody opened the door. The top floor of the warehouse he'd purchased and converted into an apartment was ablaze with lights. He'd renovated the downstairs and divided it into three smaller apartments. Two were currently rented to great tenants whose rent paid his mortgage on the entire building.

"Blay do you have to turn on every fucking light?"

His brother popped out of the kitchen. "I'm cooking for you. Stop being a dick."

"Right, I'm the dick stuck with the electric bill," he grumbled to himself, flicking off lights as he walked through the apartment.

Blay, his baby brother, was his on again, off again roommate while he was saving enough for a down payment on his own place. Blay stayed at the firehouse during his shifts but was normally here when he wasn't working, although there were plenty of nights when he went MIA. He lived the life of a young man without obligations and his whole future ahead of him. Brody rolled his shoulders and squelched the envious feelings.

The aroma of onions and garlic made his stomach rumble. "Damn, that smells good. What are you making?"

"I'm testing a new recipe for the station. I'm on rotation to cook for the next shift. This is Cajun risotto." Blay smiled at him as he poured red wine into whatever was in the massive skillet on the stovetop.

"I'll be your crash test dummy any day. Want a drink?" He reached up and grabbed a rocks glass.

"Yeah, that'd be good." Blay stirred the pot and glanced at him. His brow furrowed and he angled his head. "What's up with you?"

Brody chuckled. Blayze was the youngest son of the family, and he'd learned to gage his older brother's moods while growing up. The little prankster knew to run fast when he pushed his practical jokes a bit too far. "I'm tired, man. Thirty hours straight. Went from the wedding to the precinct and then straight into an op with the DEA."

"Did you return your tux?"

Brody blinked at him. "Ah, that would be a no." The damn thing was still hanging up in his office tucked behind the door. He sighed and poured them each a fat finger's worth of bourbon.

"You're going to pay through the nose for that."

"What else is new?" He placed Blay's drink beside him and then slid his ass onto the countertop and leaned back against the upper cabinets.

"How did it go? The DEA thing? Did you catch the bad guys?" Blay ladled what looked like beef stock into the rice and meat mixture.

His stomach rumbled at the tantalizing smells. "Yeah, the bust went down. One of the DEA dicks grandstanded, trying to pull all the credit, but Terrell wasn't backing down." *That and Amber had snipped the agent's credit snatch in the bud.*

"Good bust?"

"Yeah, coke, guns and money, and we have a bird who's singing. The interrogators were putting him on ice for the night, and we'll be back at him in the morning. The DA is willing to play, to a degree. So far, we only have him on weapons charges, but ballistics isn't back yet. There've been several drug related hits still open and the Uzis those four were carrying could very well be the weapons involved."

"You skipping the family dinner tomorrow night?"

"No, I'm taking the seven to three shift. I'll be there." Getting his ass up as six in the morning would suck, but these dinners meant so much to his parents.

"Thank goodness, with Brock on his honeymoon and me at the station, Mom would be upset if you didn't make it." Blay continued to stir the mixture.

God, it smelled divine.

Blay stared at the contents of the skillet and shook his head. "I could never do what you do. It would be too depressing. You stop one source, and three more start pouring drugs into the city."

He took a sip of his bourbon and closed his eyes, enjoying the taste before he responded to his brother. "And you run into burning buildings. That's something I could never do. It takes a special strain of insane to be a spark-head."

"Hey, at least I found my tribe." Blay reached out and grabbed his drink. "Where's the ice?"

Brody groaned and slid off the counter to retrieve a couple ice cubes. He plunked them in his brother's tumbler and resumed his position. "You ever wish you could replay your past and delete certain portions?"

Blay's eyes snapped up. He nodded slowly. "I don't think there is anyone alive who doesn't have that wish at one time or another." He added another ladle of liquid and continued to stir his creation. "What do you want to erase?"

Brody rubbed his face and groaned. "If I tell you this shit, you can't tell Mom or the girls. You've got to swear to it. Blood oath, man."

"You know it. Brothers before mothers. What's up?" He turned, dividing his attention between what he was cooking and the conversation.

"Remember Amber?"

Blay stopped stirring and shot a laser sharp stare in his direction. "Yeah. I was still in school, but I remember her."

"She's a DEA agent now."

"No shit?"

He nodded and added, "Yeah, and she's been assigned permanently to JDET."

The muscle in Blay's jaw flexed before he ground out, "Tell Terrell you want nothing to do with her. She almost killed you, man."

"She didn't cause the accident."

"The fuck she didn't! You were going after her when the drunk bastard t-boned you. Your truck was totaled, and it took the first responders over an hour to cut you from the wreckage." He splashed another ladle of stock into the pan and shook his head, cursing under his breath. "If you can't avoid her, ask for a transfer."

"I worked hard to get into JDET, and I'm not letting anyone chase me off the team. I'll talk to Terrell if it becomes a problem. She can report directly to Anderson, and we'll have a minimum of interaction." He'd work the rotation so they didn't work the same shift. They'd see each other during major operations or only when necessary for the job.

"What do you wish you could erase?"

Huh? "Sorry, what?" He took another sip of his bourbon.

"You asked if I wished I could erase something from my past, would I do it. What do you want to erase?"

He looked into the dark caramel color of his bourbon. "I'd erase the proposal."

Then maybe she'd still be in his life. He fucking missed her, missed what they had. Hell, he still dreamed of her on occasion. She'd been his everything, and when she'd left it had drained the energy from his life. Damn. He'd become a shell of who he'd been. Her reappearance slapped that fact in his face and kept him staring at it.

Blay stirred the mixture, not looking at him, but asked, "Do you think it would have mattered?"

That was a question he asked himself countless times over the years. "I guess we'll never know." He shrugged and nodded to the food. "How long until that's ready?"

"Ten minutes."

"I'm going to grab a quick shower then. Be right back." He slipped off the counter and headed to his room.

"Hey, Brody."

He turned and looked at his little brother. "Yeah?"

"Don't let her hurt you again."

"I don't plan on it. I wasn't enough for her. There's no reason to dredge up the past. We've both moved on."

He gave a tight smile and hoped like hell his brother couldn't see through the lie. It appeared Amber had moved on, but he'd fallen back into the pit of anger, hurt, and confusion he'd thought he'd climbed out of years ago.

CHAPTER 3

"**M**om! Johnny got a VR game for his birthday! It was awesome!" Gage tore into the house, the door slamming shut behind him, and dropped his backpack at the door.

She looked up from the clothes she was folding and glanced into the kitchen. "That's amazing. Where's Aunt Dawn?"

"She's going to the store." Gage flopped down on the sofa. "We played *all* night long and had pizza, like at midnight. But Johnny's dad said it was okay. He played with us. It was me, Johnny, Nick and Simon, and Johnny's dad. Finn couldn't come 'cause he's grounded."

Amber stopped folding the basket of clean

laundry and gave her son her full attention. "Grounded? Why?"

"He got into a fight at school."

Finn was a good kid; fighting didn't really fit with what she knew about him. "A fight? With who?"

"Some sixth grader. Finn was sticking up for another kid, but he hit the sixth grader, and that's what got him in trouble."

Ah... that did fit Finn. He was a protector, always watching out for his friends. "I can see how Finn would stick up for someone. Taking care of those who can't stand up for themselves is important, but violence is always a last resort."

"I know. Finn should have told the playground teacher, but the sixth grader was wrong for pushing a fourth grader down. I would've punched that guy, too." Gage picked up the remote and turned on the television.

"I sure hope not. We've talked about this before. Why was the sixth grader on the playground the same time the fourth and fifth graders were?"

He shrugged and flipped the channels. "I would've *wanted* to hit him. He was picking on someone littler than him."

"But why were they together?" The grades

didn't have recess together or in the same area for that matter.

"It was before school, after the busses dropped us all off."

"Well, that makes sense. Did you thank Johnny's mom and dad?"

"Yep." He muted the TV and sat up on the couch. "Did you catch the bad guys?"

"We sure did." She smiled and winked at him.

"Nick and Simon said being a cop is badass."

She narrowed her eyes at him. "Language."

"*I* didn't say it. *They* did."

"*You* repeated it."

"Well, yeah, but to tell *you*." He brushed his hair away from his eyes and released that mischievous smile.

"Riiight." She gave him a nod and waggled her eyebrows a couple times.

His laughter bubbled through the room. "Johnny's dad is taking him fishing at the harbor next weekend. Can I go?"

Johnny's dad was great about including Gage in activities, and today, instead of being grateful, she felt guilty. Guilty about keeping Brody and Gage apart. She folded the jeans in her hands before she answered, "Were you asked?"

"Well, yeah." He rolled his eyes at her.

"Then yes you can go, unless something comes up."

"You always say that. What's going to come up?"

She started to sing, "The sun will come up."

"Mom, that's so embarrassing." He unmuted the television, to block her tone-deaf notes.

"It's my job to embarrass you. We've been through this before."

He snorted and flipped the channels. "Yeah, but why do you have to be so good at it?"

"I practice."

"Lucky me."

"Yes, sir. Here, these are yours. Put them away at the next commercial." She stacked his clean clothes next to him.

"Okay." He dropped down onto his side and curved his legs around the clean clothes. She smiled and stood to put away her clothes and place Dawn's in her room. Gage's eyelids were already heavy with sleep. She'd learned through the years, sleepovers for young boys rarely included sleep.

With the laundry sorted, she walked into the living room and leaned against the wall. Gage's mouth was open and small snores rhythmically punctuated the low sound track from the television. He looked so young. She carefully extracted his clean clothes from behind his legs and carried them to his room. He was a wonderful young man, and Dawn was right. It was time she bit the bullet and told Brody about Gage. She slipped her hand into her pocket and grasped her phone. Before she could talk herself out of it, she called up his number, the one she'd been given when she in-processed to the team. She punched the numbers and prayed it would go through to voicemail. Chicken shit at best, but this was one hell of a bullet to eat.

"King."

Damn it, her hands were shaking. "Brody, this is Amber." And so was her voice.

"Standby." The clipped comeback didn't bode well. He obviously wasn't in a good mood, and yet she heard laughter in the background, both men and women. A quick glance at the clock confirmed she'd probably caught him at his parents for Sunday supper. It was a tradition. One she'd used to enjoy. Brody's family had always been so welcoming. Well, except for his mom. She'd never understood why Hannah had always seemed disappointed in her.

"What?" Sharpness edged the question.

"I need to talk to you. Face-to-face."

"I'm not agreeing to a meeting unless it's work related." He bit the words off, his anger a tangible thing. It pooled between them like lava flowing from a fissure.

She pushed the words forward in a rush, "I need ten minutes. Ten minutes, Brody. If you never want to talk to me again after that, I'll shut up, and you'll be rid of me. I'll even ask for a transfer from JDET." She prayed he wouldn't make her leave. The DEA's travel made the JDET's hours seem like a nine-to-five job even though it wasn't. It was more stable than what she had now, which is why she'd put in for the job.

"Where are you?"

"I'm at Dawn's. Do you remember where––"

A harsh laugh cut her off. "Not likely to forget *that* address."

Defeated, she hung her head without saying a word. His words stabbed like a knife into her chest. She'd never escape the guilt.

"Never mind. I'll be there in a half hour. You'll have ten minutes. Use them wisely." The connection was cut.

She drew a shaky breath and immediately called Dawn. "Where are you?"

"On my way home. Why, do you need me to stop and get something?"

"No, but could you come straight home and stay with Gage? I invited Brody over. I'm going to tell him the truth, and I need Gage preoccupied if he wakes up."

"Damn it. Yeah, I'll be right there. I never thought you'd do it."

"You were right. It's not fair to Gage *or* Brody."

"Well I hate when I'm right. It isn't going to be easy for any of you. Gage needs to come first. Whatever angst you and Brody are going through needs to stay away from that boy."

"Yeah, I know." She'd fight tooth and nail to make sure Gage wasn't hurt by anyone, especially Brody. Not that she thought he would do anything to jeopardize a relationship with Gage. Well, the man he was before wouldn't. This Brody? That angry, bitter man, she wasn't too sure about.

"I'm about five minutes away. I'll see you soon." Dawn hung up, leaving her staring at the wall of her bedroom.

Brody's heart beat a bit faster as he drove through the intersection a half mile from the house of Amber's sister—the intersection where his truck had been obliterated by a drunk man driving a delivery truck. Fragments of memories still haunted him. The concussion of the hit, the truck rolling, the sharp jarring and breaking of his body, the stabbing pain and the sparks as the fire department cut the metal from around him. He'd woken up in the hospital two weeks later. His mom, dad, brothers and sisters surrounded him—everyone he cared about—except Amber.

He drove down the quiet street and slowly drove up in front of the little house. Even though it was sprinkling, he didn't turn off the truck. He wasn't going in. If she wanted to talk to him, she could come to him. That's exactly what happened. She jogged to the street wearing jeans, a t-shirt, white tennis shoes, and a lightweight windbreaker. She opened the passenger side door and slipped inside. He made a point to look at his watch, turned his head to her, and raised an eyebrow.

She drew a deep breath and closed her eyes. Her hands were fisted so tightly her fingers were white. Whatever she had to say was important, at least to her. "This isn't going to be easy, and if you stop me to ask any questions, I won't be able to finish, so don't, okay?" She opened her eyes and glanced at him.

He narrowed his eyes wondering what in the hell was so critical after ten years, but he nodded, because at this point, he was intrigued.

"Okay." She took a breath. "Okay. When you proposed, you terrified me." She held up a hand at his disgusted snort.

This? Really? This is what she needed to talk to him about?

"Stop, you agreed to listen."

He cleared his throat and nodded for her to go ahead.

"We'd always talked about how my mom was trapped by marriage to my dad and then by me, by having a kid. My dad divorced her and married Dawn's mom. My mother was a miserable soul and lived with regrets her entire life. If it wasn't for Dawn's mom, I wouldn't know what a good mother was like. Well, until I met your mom. I explained how I didn't want to live that way. Ever. When you asked me to marry you, I freaked.

"I'm not proud of freaking out, but I did. I came back here, but after an hour or so, I realized what I'd done. I'd run away from the man I loved, and I was horrified. I called and called. Finally, I called your mom. She told me what happened. I went straight to the hospital. The accusing looks I got from your brothers and sisters... well, how could I blame them? I agreed. So, when your family wasn't there, I sat with you. Every night until the nurses made me leave. I came back, and you were awake and talking to Brock. I heard you tell him you never wanted to see me again. You wanted nothing to do with me. Your mom heard it, too. I left. I didn't want to cause a scene, so I called your number at least five times a day, but you never answered, and then your voice mailbox was full. Probably from me. I finally realized you really meant what you'd told Brock. You wanted nothing to do with me.

"I packed my clothes and moved in with Dawn. A couple months later, I went back to our old place. I, ah, really needed to see you. You'd moved. The landlord gave me the rest of the stuff you'd boxed up for me. I went to your parents' house. Your mom was polite, but also blunt. She asked me to give you time to heal, and assured me you'd call me if you wanted to talk. You never did." Large tears fell down her cheeks, but she didn't wipe them away. "The reason I tried so hard to find you, why I went to your parents, is because I discovered I was pregnant." Her eyes drifted from her lap to his.

He turned away from her and gripped the steering wheel. *She'd been pregnant?* Well, she wouldn't have had *his* child. She was right. They'd talked about her desire to see the world, do things and go places. A child wouldn't have fit into her plans. Hell, if a husband, who would have done anything to give her that life, didn't fit, what hope did a helpless baby have? It sickened him. *She* sickened him. Pain lanced through his soul at the thought of her terminating their baby, but there'd been no legal requirement for her to inform him of what she'd done.

A calliope of conflicting thoughts and emotions pummeled each other. Her story was plausible. His phone had been destroyed in the car accident. He didn't bother buying a new one for months and by then he'd dropped the old carrier and signed a contract with a new carrier for a new number. He'd let the apartment go because he couldn't climb the stairs to the third floor walk-up. He'd demanded his family have no contact with her, even if they could find her, not that he thought she was going to stick around Hope City. Hell, he'd lived with his parents until his body healed. He remembered the day his mother'd said she'd talked to Amber again, and he should consider talking to her, for closure if nothing else. He'd refused; he couldn't pick the bloodied scab again. *And she'd been pregnant with his child.*

He turned to look at her, not even trying to hide the disgust which rolled through him. "Why are you telling me this now?"

She swallowed hard and took a picture from her pocket. She extended the square to him. "He'd like to meet his dad."

He jerked back. His eyes pinged from her to the photo. "What?" His hand visibly shook as he extended his fingers to carefully take the photo from her. He brought it closer and sucked air when he saw... his son. He traced the boy's smiling face. Warring emotions scrambled his cognitive reasoning. His head snapped up. "You didn't abort?"

She flinched. "No! I couldn't do that, ever! What did I ever say to make you think I'd terminate a pregnancy?"

He stared at her. "So it wasn't that you didn't want to be tied down. You didn't want to be tied to *me*. Good to know."

She gasped, "That isn't true."

He didn't bother to argue the obvious. He examined the photo again. He'd realized years ago it was possible Amber had never really loved him —at least not the same way he'd felt about her. It didn't matter anymore. He stared at the photo. His son. Light brown hair, his eyes. Damn... he blinked back the emotion. "What's his name?"

"Gage. He's almost ten, going on thirty some days." She laughed a little. "He asked about you a while ago. I mean, he's asked in the past, general type questions which I could lead him away from, but this was a pointed question, one I couldn't reroute or redirect. So, I told him you didn't know I was pregnant, and we weren't married. He told me to find you and tell you about him."

He leveled his gaze on her. "If our paths hadn't collided, would you have contacted me? Told me about him?"

She shrugged. "Eventually. I guess. I was afraid."

He cocked his head and asked, "Afraid of what?"

She raised her hands and dropped her head into them. "That you'd try to take him away from me."

"Huh." He leaned back against the truck's door and gazed through the windshield to the house.

"You thought I'd keep a parent from their child? No, that seems to be your forte."

She snapped her head up and glared at him for a moment before her gaze softened. She nodded. "Okay. I deserved that." She closed her eyes and leaned back in the seat. "You have no idea how many times I've run this scenario in my mind."

"Yeah? And what was the outcome of those practice runs?" He wanted to know what role she expected him to play, because his gut was telling him to storm into the house and find his son.

"Ha, well everything from you suing me for custody to us co-parenting." She rolled her head and opened her eyes. "I've had ten years to come to terms with what I've done. I'm not going to apologize. I called. I tried to find you. I went to see your mother for help contacting you. I ran into brick walls every time, but my little boy deserves to know his father."

He rolled his shoulders. Anger and accusations were so close to the surface, but the acid that thrummed through his veins and screamed how unfair it was she didn't keep trying didn't need to find its outlet here, today. He drew a deep breath and humbled himself in a way he hadn't done since the day she'd run from his proposal. "I'd like to meet him."

"I haven't told him I contacted you. If you didn't want anything to do with him..."

That fucking stung. "What have I ever done to make you think I'd turn my back on him?"

"You turned your back on me."

"I think you have it backward. You left me."

"I told you I regretted it almost immediately. But you didn't answer your phone, didn't answer my messages!"

"I never got those messages you say you left. When my truck was totaled, my phone was destroyed. I left our apartment because I couldn't walk up three flights of stairs. You said you tried to find me? I call bullshit. All you had to do was call Brock or Brianna. They would have told you where I was." He didn't try to prevent the sneer which spread across his face.

"I thought you hated me because of the accident, and then when I found I was pregnant... I tried to call your family, but no one would talk to me. I lost my nerve, and I quit trying. You have no idea how intimidating your family is."

He closed his eyes and shook his head. It was raining hard now. The sound of the patter on the windshield had become more intense. "We aren't going to find a common ground on this point. Okay."

"Okay?"

"Yep. You tried to get ahold of me. However, I believe if you had really wanted to let me know, you'd have found a way." He shrugged. He wasn't going to rehash the past. There was nothing to gain by dredging it up.

"You weren't in my shoes." She shook her head and crossed her arms.

"No, I wasn't." He could second guess her motives and intentions for the remainder of his life, but it wouldn't serve a productive purpose. "Are you going to let me meet him, or do I need to get a court order?"

"What? No! Shit, this is not going the way I wanted it to go. Look, I haven't told him I contacted you. I wanted to talk to you before I talked to him. I'll tell him and use this week to answer the multitude of questions he'll have. Would you like to come by on Saturday? We can start easy, maybe grill some hamburgers in the backyard, and you two can visit?"

"I'll be here. May I keep this?" He held the picture.

She released a huge sigh. "Good. That's good. Oh, I have more." She reached in her pocket and removed a stack of photos. She nodded to herself and took another deep breath.

He took them reverently and examined each one. Gage. The boy looked like he did at his age. He smiled and placed the pictures securely in his inside coat pocket. He glanced at her. "We can't bring this situation into work, but I want to know more about him before I meet him."

"Yeah, I imagine you would. I can call you after he's in bed tomorrow night. I'll answer any questions you have."

"That would work."

"Okay, well, I'm going to get back in the house."

"Good night."

She flicked a look his way before she opened the door and sprinted through the rain into the house.

He put the truck in gear and drove away from the curb, heading to the one person he trusted with almost every secret he'd ever had.

Amber closed the door quietly and took off her soaking wet jacket. Dawn grabbed her arm and yanked her into the kitchen. "So?"

"He was understandably upset." She drew her shaking hands through her hair and dropped into a kitchen chair.

"And?"

"And he wants to meet Gage. I gave him some pictures. I have them digitally, so..."

"When?" Dawn hissed.

"Next Saturday. We're going to grill in the backyard, let them get acquainted." She rubbed her arms, chilled to the bone even though it wasn't cold in the house.

"What did he say about not answering your calls?"

Amber leaned back in the chair and explained.

"Okay, but what about what his mom said to you?"

"I told him I spoke to her. He didn't even blink. He said she'd told him I'd been there. He said if I'd wanted to find him, I could have."

"That's true." Dawn nodded her head.

Amber threw her sister a dirty look. "Hey, whose side are you on?"

"Yours, of course, but you can't deny you could

have gone to his mom's house with the baby, or hell, even pregnant, and Brody would have been summoned to appear."

"Yeah. But by then I'd convinced myself he didn't want anything to do with me."

"You, maybe. The baby? Wrong answer."

"I was so afraid he'd take Gage away from me," she whispered. "Damn it, Dawn, I'm looking for a little support here." She dropped her head into her hands.

Dawn sighed and dropped down on one knee beside her. "Honey, I'm nothing but support. I'll be here while you guys determine which way is up. I'll be here when you need a break. I'll support you because you're my family, and I love you, but I won't blow smoke up your skirt. Dad would roll over in his grave. He taught both of us better."

"Yeah, I know. It seems like everything I thought I knew about the situation was wrong. I thought he was avoiding me. He thought I'd left him and never looked back. Both of us were abjectly wrong."

"Yeah, that's true, and it is definitely a perfect storm type of a mess, but all the bad weather is behind you. You've got clear skies now. The question is, what are you two going to do with the days ahead?"

Amber leaned forward and placed her hand on her sister's. "Love, work, and live."

It was what her father had always said. No matter the day or the hour, if the question, *what are you going to do* came up, he always answered the same way. He would love, work, and live. He always said nothing else mattered—unlike her mother who begrudged each sunrise as another day she had to endure.

"Well, that's a good plan. The little one isn't going to wake up anytime soon. How about we have a glass of wine and watch a chick flick until it's time to put him to bed, and then I'll help you herd him to his room."

She chuckled. Gage was far too big for either one of them to carry, and he was like a zombie when he fell asleep on the couch. "Deal."

"Cool. Do you want red or white?"

"Doesn't matter." She watched her sister head to the cabinet. "Was I wrong? What I did? Keeping Gage from Brody?" she blurted.

Dawn turned with two stemless wine glasses in her hand. "Wrong? Yes. Probably. Maybe. Hell, I don't honestly know, Amber. I wouldn't have done what you did, but you made the decision you thought was best for you and Gage. You can Monday morning quarterback the situation from here to eternity and never really know. I've watched you sacrifice for that little boy. You love him with everything you have. He's a great kid. Were there mistakes made? Yep, by two young lovers. Hopefully, the mature adult versions of those two lovesick kids can overcome those errors and find a way to build a new relationship."

Amber smiled at her sister. "How did you get so smart?"

Dawn shrugged. "I watch Dr. Phil. Here's your wine. Let's snuggle into the cushions and watch something fun and happy."

Amber stood alone in the kitchen for a moment. "Fun and happy." She drew a deep breath. Damn, she needed an extra dose of each.

CHAPTER 4

"What are you doing back here? Looking for leftovers?" Hannah King smiled up at him from her chair. Her e-book reader was on her lap and a large mug of lemon tea was sitting beside her.

"No, although if you have any, I won't object to taking some off your hands." Brody leaned down and kissed his mother's cheek. "Where's Dad?"

"He's out back with his new love." Hannah waved her hand and laughed.

"It's your fault. You bought it for him."

"You're right. What was I thinking?" She chuckled and picked up her reader. "The leftovers are in the red lidded containers. There are three. Take one for you and one for Blay."

"Thanks, I'll grab them on the way out." He headed to the backyard. The familiar slam of the screen door brought back so many memories. How many times had he run through that door while he was growing up?

His father straightened from a large telescope on a tripod at the sound, and even in the darkness he could see his old man's smile. "What brings you back?"

"Needed to talk with you."

"A case?" As he got closer, he saw his father's brow draw together.

"No. Personal. What are you looking at?

"Cancer's Praesepe." Chauncey King shoved his hands in his pockets and rocked back on his heels. "Take a look."

"Seriously?"

"Yep, the brightest galactic star cluster in the sky this time of year. It's exceptionally clear after the front rolled through and having this beauty doesn't hurt either."

Brody leaned down and stared at the cluster of over one hundred stars located in the constellation of Cancer. "Wow, this scope is fantastic. How big is the cluster?"

"I read an article which stated it filled a space

three times the diameter of our moon." Chauncey's words were quiet and almost reverent. "But you didn't come here to talk about the stars tonight, did you?"

Brody stood and crossed his arms. "Got a situation."

"Well then, you get the chairs; I'll get the drinks."

Chauncey picked up his expensive telescope and carried it into the house. Brody spun and went to the small shed and removed two old Adirondack chairs. His father came back with two ginger ales and sat down beside him before he passed one of the sodas. They both opened the drinks and took a sip.

"Amber Swanson is the new DEA agent permanently assigned to JDET."

His father's head swiveled in his direction. "I heard they assigned an agent. The details haven't made it to me yet. Is this going to be a problem?"

Brody released a sigh. "Yeah. It's going to be an issue."

"Why?" His father took another drink of the soda.

"How much do you remember about our relationship?"

His father dropped his head back against the chair and stared up into the night sky. "You loved her and thought she was the one for you. She didn't agree."

"Yeah, that's how I remember it, too." Brody mimicked his father's position. They'd had many serious conversations looking at the stars.

"And?"

"It isn't how she remembers it." He hit *almost* all the high points to their conversation tonight.

"So, a miscommunication and maybe a case of too little, too late?"

"That about covers it. Except for this." He took the pictures from his pocket. It was so dark, there was no way his father could see them.

"What are they?"

"Pictures."

His dad twisted in his chair. "Of what?"

Brody drew a deep breath. "Of my son. He's ten."

His father took the stack of photos from him and reached into his pocket for his cell phone. He turned on the flashlight and handed it to Brody to hold. They stared at the pictures, not a word spoken between them. Finally, his father handed the photos back in exchange for his phone. He turned off his flashlight and leaned back against the chair, staring heavenward once again. "Looks like you."

"He does."

They sat in silence for a couple minutes. "What are your plans?"

"Going to get to know him, be a father to him, and introduce him to his grandma and grandpa, aunts and uncles." *He had a son.* The reality was stronger each time he thought the words.

His father's hand patted his arm. "It's the right thing. How are you and Amber going to do this?"

"Slowly, and hopefully without interference." Brody rolled his head and stared at his father.

"Boy, you know your momma is going to get excited about her first grandchild." Chauncey chuckled. "And interfere."

"Yeah, that's why I'm asking you not to tell her."

"Awww... damn, son. You know I can't do that."

"You keep all kinds of things from her."

"Work related." His father's voice scolded him. "Not a grandchild."

"This is work related. She's on my team."

"'s mighty weak reasoning."

"But... it's true." Brody stared up at the sky

finding several familiar constellations his father had taught him to locate over the years.

"I'll buy you some time. But if she finds out you didn't tell her first, she'll be devastated."

"I understand."

"What's his name?"

"Gage." He smiled when he said the name.

"G's huh?"

"Nah, I won't have any more kids. There's no one, not anymore." Brody took a long drink of the ginger ale. He forced the 'what could have been' thoughts out of his mind.

"Don't shut any doors. Life has a way of using a battering ram to open them back up." His dad took a sip of his soda. "When can we meet him?"

"I'm going to her house this weekend. Saturday. If things go well, and he's not too overwhelmed, I'd like to bring him by on Sunday. I guess it also depends on Amber. She wants to take it slow so he doesn't get hurt, by either of us." Brody rolled his empty soda can between both of his hands.

"Well then, I guess there is only one thing left to say." Chauncey stood up and extended his hand. "Congratulations, Dad." His old man grabbed him up and into a hug. "You have no idea what a wonderful blessing that boy will be to you."

He closed his eyes and hung on to his father for a few moments. "Thank you."

"For what?" His dad drew away.

"For always being here for me." Brody cleared his throat.

"You'll do the same for Gage."

"God, I hope so." Brody crushed his soda can. "I'll put away the chairs."

"Nah, I'll do it. Leave through the McBrides' yard so your momma doesn't see and stop you. I'll tell her you had a work-related issue you had to attend to. Keep me up to date on how this situation progresses. Saturday can't come fast enough for me."

"I'll do that." Brody pitched his soda can in the recycle bin. The weekend seemed like a lifetime away.

"All right everyone, listen up!" Brody's voice lifted above the din of the bullpen. "Swanson, Rayburn, Watson, conference room one. The rest of you, download the reports from the last bust with the DEA. Any name, gang, or location which can be inferred, tracked or suspected will be checked out.

Mozingo, you've got lead, and you'll report to Lt. Anderson."

"Roger that, Sarge. You heard the man. We are officially developing leads and working the streets. Let's get the lead out." Mozingo grabbed the reins and gave Brody a farewell salute as he followed the other three agents to conference room one.

Captain Terrell stood at the front of the table reading a file. He glanced up when they entered and nodded for Brody to shut the door. He closed the door and took his seat at the other end of the table.

Terrell tossed down the file and slid a chair back, dropping into the seat. The damn thing groaned under his captain's muscled bulk. "I've been studying the reports from the information we're getting from Masters, and I think I've tied it to some information our new canary has given us."

Brody leaned forward. "What do you have?" He'd been studying everything coming from the Masters investigation and trial.

"Taylor, our singing bird, has been dropping information he has no idea he's dropping. When he was asked about the drugs he's seen, he listed off a pharmacy. Tranks, Roofies, Xanies, Special K, Acid, Black Tar, Line, Apple Jacks, and Molly off the top of the list. What has us concerned, however, is Taylor told us the cartels were making a push to set up a stream selling Gray Death."

"That shit's nasty, Captain. If they start importing GD, it isn't only the users who will be dying. A person can OD by touching it. Our front-line, the beat cop, will be facing that shit." Brody flopped back in his chair and crossed his arms. "We have to get ahead of this before the cartels make the Desert into a ghost town."

Terrell nodded. "Swanson, your paperwork came through this morning. There shouldn't be a need for me to reinforce this, but as I don't know you, I'm going to do it anyway. Nothing from this task force goes to the DEA unless I approve it. Understand?" He glared down the table at Amber.

"You don't know me, so I won't take that as an insult. I've been permanently assigned to this task force, and I work for you. The DEA wants information, they go to you, not me."

Brody fought hard not to smile. The woman was pissed by the captain's reprimand. He could tell by the way her neck and cheeks flushed red.

"I'm glad we understand each other. Now, tell me what you know about this Gray Death." Terrell crossed the tree trunks impersonating his biceps and waited.

Amber leaned forward and glanced at him but gave Watson and Rayburn equal time. "Gray Death is a composite drug which resembles cement chunks or grey powder, which is how it got its name. According to all the data I've read, it has heroin beat in potency... exponentially. The formula for cooking the shit varies, but usually a heroin or cocaine base and then they add fentanyl, U-47700 or even carfentanil."

"What the fuck is carfentanil?" Colt Rayburn leaned forward. "What's the street name? I'm not familiar with the pharma."

"There isn't a street name, yet, thank God, but carfentanil is a large animal tranq. It is about a hundred times stronger than fentanyl, and the estimate is ten thousand times stronger than morphine. We've seen cases of this mixture in Georgia and have agents assisting the Georgia Bureau of Investigations. But, if this stuff is coming into this city, you need to warn your street officers that wearing gloves might not be enough. Even inhaling this could be deadly."

"What about Narcan?" Brody leaned forward.

"If our officers are exposed would Narcan work to stop the effects?"

"Unknown. I've read some reports which have suggested Gray Death might be resistant to Narcan, and other studies indicated it could take multiple, as in five to ten doses, for the Narcan to work. Most patrols carry one dose."

"We don't have the budget for that. Hell, as it is now, our supervisors have doses, but not all patrols do." Derek Watson shook his head. "Sucks the criminals are better funded than we are."

"Nothing we can do about that. We'll need to start thinking about an education campaign. When we break here, I'll head to Briar Hill and brief Colonel Wells. He can set up the educational briefs." Terrell reached for the file he'd dropped. "Our songbird indicated his bosses had meetings, and he heard the words 'airport' and 'small planes' repeated in connection with the drug."

"Small planes." Brody pushed away from the table and walked to a map of the city. "We have no less than ten small airports within two hours of this city. Did he indicate any particular one?" He turned back to the group when he asked.

"No, but I had an idea about that. We've been dissecting Masters and Treyson's travels in the months prior to Masters killing Treyson. Treyson's routine didn't vary, but Masters? He made several trips out of the city." Terrell got up from the chair and moved to the map. He, Amber, Colt, and Derek made their way forward also.

"We don't have precise locations, but two weeks before he was arrested, he traveled to this area." Terrell circled an area north of Hope City. "It could be coincidence, but there's an airfield here."

Everyone leaned in and stared at the map. Brody frowned. "In a neighborhood?" He saw the runway depicted, but seeing houses line the runway was weird.

"A bedroom community for those of affluence who fly their small planes into other cities to work. Hangars where they keep their puddle jumpers are situated behind the houses. It would be the perfect cover for importing drugs." Terrell rubbed the back of his neck. "Unfortunately, it is a guess. I can't justify expending resources without something solid."

"What do you need?" Amber glanced up at Terrell.

"Something that could tie that airfield into this investigation."

"Something like flight plans to cities or areas

suspected to manufacture the product?" Brody interjected.

Terrell nodded. "That might work, but how do we access the plans? Swanson, since you have the contacts, get us a best guess on the hotbeds for manufacturing this shit."

"Can do. A couple of calls and we'll have it."

"Brody, you're the fucking pilot. Where are you going to get the flight plans, and do we need a court order?"

"You're a pilot?" Amber's question pivoted everyone's head in her direction. She snapped her mouth shut and cleared her throat. "Sorry."

"I have my license, yes." Brody turned back to Terrell. "We'd need a search warrant. We couldn't get a federal judge to approve it. It would be too vague for a judge to approve. Even if we have the FAA serve it at the hotbed locations, it wouldn't tell us anything except who is regularly making the flights to and from the area. There isn't a law against flying to a certain location. If we want to build a case, we'll need to go in undercover and work it."

"You could probably rent one of the houses for sale in the area." Colt was staring at the map. "Once you're in, you could check shit out, make friends with others in the neighborhood. You'd know pretty damn quick if someone was making routine runs." He tapped the map. "That's an affluent neighborhood. Renting a house would be expensive."

Damn right it would be expensive, and they worked on a shoestring budget. Brody glanced at Amber and then at his captain. "Maybe we can get some money from our Federal agencies?"

Terrell nodded. "I've already asked the FBI and the DEA." He put his hands on his hips and stared at the map. "Getting this shit shut down before it becomes an epidemic of overdoses is a priority."

Amber held up a finger. "Excuse me, I know I'm catching up here, but I'm getting stuck on what you said about Masters. He was driving around in this neighborhood. Why? Was he picking up or delivering? Was he meeting someone? I can't see this guy, an affluent lawyer, being a mule. I mean it's happened, but what else is in the area besides this airport community? Why would he drive up here when his corporate headquarters is in the city? Does he have other business in the area which would suggest a legitimate reason for his presence?"

"Damn good questions. You and King take a

drive up there, get eyes on the community and see if there is something that would draw Masters to that location. Rayburn and Watson, you pull up all the information we have on Masters. Sift through that shit and work this through. Also, get Taylor brought in and re-interview him on this topic. Get anything he can remember, the smallest detail. Find any holes before we decide on a direction."

"What about requesting an interview with Masters?" Brody braced his hands on his hips. The bastard had granted a few interviews since he'd been convicted. Maybe they could get something from the guy.

"I've put in the paperwork. Since his conviction and sentencing, he's been playing ball. Word is the man wants a move to a facility out of state. Fucker even demanded his name be altered when he's moved. He's afraid of reprisals from the cartels. Even though the man didn't give us shit, he must know enough to be a legit target. The DA is inclined to use him and keep him in isolation to keep him alive, so we should get approval."

"Swanson, go make those calls, and get an idea of where this shit may be coming from. King, I'll need a minute. Rayburn, Watson, you two hit the documents. Find me something." Terrell dismissed everyone and waited for the conference room to clear before he shut the door.

"What's up?" Brody strolled over and sat on the conference table.

"I'm going to ask you to make a few calls, too. Grey Death is nothing to mess with. Our patrolmen, detectives, and our people are at risk."

"Guardian?" Brody arched an eyebrow. His captain had never asked him to use his family ties before.

"No. Your old man. I hate to ask you to make this call, and damn it, I swore I never would, but this shit can't take root in the city." Terrell rubbed the back of his neck. "We need a push from above to get my funding requests noticed by the Feds, and I don't think the colonel will do it. We get enough to survive and that's it."

The colonel in charge of Criminal Investigations wasn't anyone's favorite, including his father's. Colonel Fenton had aspirations. Specifically, his father's job, so any successes in JDET, which was developed based on his father's impetus when he took the position of Police Commissioner, was a thorn in Fenton's side. Even though the JDET wins fell under Fenton's division, the man gave them the bare minimum needed to operate. It would be a fucking honor to do an end run around Fenton.

"You know if we do that, he's going to be hunting for your ass."

Terrell sneered, "I say bring it on. It's about time the asshole remembered those he left in the trenches."

He appreciated the intestinal fortitude of the man. "Copy that, although I'm not going to call him during duty hours; I'll talk to him tonight."

"That works for me. Now get out there and do your job." Terrell indicated the door with a nod of his head.

Brody gave the man a two-finger salute and headed back to his office. He passed through the bullpen and noticed Amber on the phone. Her head was down, and she was writing as she listened. Watson and Rayburn's noses were buried in files. Mozinga had three teams working, sorting through documentation from the trial and the interviews of their newest songbird. The energy level in the pen was high, and the focus of his people was intense. Each of the team members had been hand-picked. They were dedicated cops. He was damn lucky to be a part of the team.

He glanced at the door to his office and rolled

his eyes. That damn tux. He really needed to make time to take that thing back to the store he rented it from before he owned the damn thing.

"Ready?" Amber walked into his office.

"I am. Did you get anything with the calls?"

"The general consensus is the cartels are the only ones dealing with this shit. Penā's organization was mentioned twice in association with Florida, in particular. The favored route from Mexico is still believed to be I-10 as the southern corridor to the east and to the west. Atlanta and Jacksonville are the hot points for supplying the eastern side of the country. Not a lot to go on." She shrugged her shoulders.

"Actually, it is. An ultra-light wouldn't be used for such a trip. Single engine planes could make the distance depending on fuel and efficiency." He nodded to the door. She fell into step with him as they made their way to his truck.

"When did you become a pilot?"

"After the accident. I was going crazy. Physical therapy and rehab were so damn slow. My body couldn't move and my brain was constantly going. It was recommended I find a hobby." He shrugged. "So I did."

"You couldn't walk, but you flew?"

He snorted a laugh. "Ah, no. I could walk, and I was on the mend, but you know me, I was bouncing off the walls. So, I started classes."

"To get your pilot license?"

"Yeah. I have a cousin who flies. I went up with him once or twice."

"That's right, I remember you telling me about him."

"Yeah, Jason flies some expensive planes, and it was amazing up there, so I started classroom instruction for ground and flight school. By the time I finished classes, I was able to pass an FAA flight physical. Then I did my practical hours, which was when I was amping up my physical conditioning so I could pass the physical qualification test for HCPD. It helped me to deal with... everything."

"Meaning me."

He glanced at her. "Meaning everything. You included."

They exited the building and headed toward his truck. "Can we hit a drive through on the way up?" She strapped her seatbelt on and glanced at him.

"Miss breakfast?" He started the truck.

"Yeah, and dinner last night. I was too worried about how you'd react to finding out about Gage."

His head snapped around. "Did you talk to him?"

"Yeah, this morning. I told him I contacted you like he suggested. He was stoked, and then he got quiet. When I asked why, he wanted to know if you were mad because he was born."

"What did you say?" His heartbeat raced at over a hundred rpm's for sure.

"I told him you were very happy he was born, and you wanted to meet him."

Thank God. He wanted to meet Gage so damn bad. "Was he okay with that?"

"He was, but he's a thinker, so he'll come up with a thousand and one questions. I'll field them as they come." She chuckled quietly. "It's going to be a long, long week."

CHAPTER 5

Amber sipped her coffee and looked around the neighborhood as they meandered down the wide avenue. A small airplane came in for a landing and then taxied down the runway to one of the hangars as they quietly walked through the neighborhood. The houses were custom built on large lots. Manicured lawns bordered by spring flowers, green shrubbery and white picket fences sat facing the street while large hangars dominated the vistas beyond the homes. Several people had waved as they drove by, one lady even shouted a 'good morning' from a flowerbed where she was kneeling.

"Doesn't strike me as a drug haven." She took another sip of her coffee.

"Granted."

"I sense a 'but' coming." She glanced at him as they strolled along.

"Not three miles from here is the Treyson Shipping and Storage facility." He glanced right and left before they crossed the street. "Speculation was that Masters and Samuel Treyson were instrumental in setting up a distribution system for the Peña Cartel."

"Through a legitimate shipping company? That would take some balls." She swirled her cold coffee in the paper cup.

"Good morning!" A middle aged woman driving a van full of kids shouted and waved as she drove by.

She waved and smiled as did Brody.

"The thought process was they would receive from the global parent company, Treyson Logistics, and funnel the drugs via the parcel service." They stopped to watch another small plane land.

She watched the thing taxi, turn on a dime and pivot into a hangar behind a three-story brick colonial. "What if it wasn't coming in, but going out?"

Brody turned and frowned at her. "Say what?"

"Think about it. Peña has been building a distribution network. He's a businessman. What if he's bringing in the components, making it here, then shipping it out through Treyson's system?"

Brody stared at the airfield. "Too many possibilities and not enough information."

"I guess it's down to Masters, then." She started walking when Brody did. "Do you still fly?"

A woman exited her home with a broom. She waved and said good morning as they passed. They returned the greeting and kept on walking. "I do occasionally, to maintain my proficiency and certification." He glanced at her and grinned. "Maybe someday I can take you and Gage for a ride?"

She shook her head vehemently. "No. Nope, no way."

His smile faded, and he looked away.

"Damn, I meant *I* won't go up in a plane with you, but I'm sure Gage would *love* to go. I get so airsick in small planes you'd end up buying a new interior. I swear the last time I was up in a Cessna I puked for days. The agent and pilot I was with… well, they had to shower." She shivered at the memory.

The corners of his mouth twitched in what could have been the start of a smile, and he stooped to pick up a rock on the sidewalk before they wandered on again. "I forgot about you getting sick on the Ferris wheel."

"And on the merry-go-round. Don't even get me started on roller coasters... gah!" She made a gagging sound. "I'm doing you a favor. Saving the interior of your plane."

"I don't actually own a plane, but I'm guessing a cleaning or replacement bill would be over my budget." He screwed his face up. "Barf gets everywhere."

"You have *no* idea! Hey, how do you fly if you don't have a plane?" They started the stroll back to where they'd parked his truck.

"I rent a plane from my instructor. Todd has three of them he lets students use to keep their certifications up to date."

"Do you enjoy it? Flying?"

"Yeah, I do. But it's expensive."

"What else do you have to spend all that sergeant's pay on?" She pointed to the truck. "You don't have the same old truck, but this one isn't a spring chicken either. It has to be paid off by now."

"Her name is Wilma and don't pick on Gertie. She was a good ride."

"Wilma? Yeah, I can see it, and I have some very fond memories of Gertie. I'd never disrespect her."

She snapped her mouth shut when she noticed the way Brody tensed beside her. Damn it. "Look, we have a past. If you want me to stop mentioning it, I'll do my damnedest."

He stopped and leaned against the bed of his truck. His gaze traveled the neighborhood. "Our past is something I tried hard not to think about. When you ran out, I was..." He shrugged a shoulder. "But that's my baggage. I get you had your own response to the proposal. You need to respect mine, too." He drew a deep breath and stared at her. "I loved you. I was willing to spend my life with you, to take you on those adventures you wanted to experience, but you didn't give me a chance to say anything. I dropped to one knee, opened the box and barely asked the question before you bolted."

She moved and leaned on the truck bed, too. "I've already apologized for my actions and I explained why I did what I did. I tried to contact you."

"Until you didn't."

"Until I didn't." She bit her bottom lip and raked her teeth over the flesh. "I'll admit my actions were driven by fear. Fear you wouldn't forgive me. Fear you'd turn me away and want nothing to do with your child, or worse, take him away. When your mom said you'd contact me, to give you time, I did that. You knew I was looking for you. You didn't reach out."

"I also had no idea you were pregnant." He cut his eyes to her and then arched an eyebrow.

"Point, but you didn't contact me... I figured you were done with me. I wasn't going to use a pregnancy to make you see me. Hell, yes, it was flawed logic, but..." She shook her head. "Look, I can't change the past. I can only do better going forward. Gage is excited to meet you. He's nervous and doesn't understand why you didn't know about him. That's on me. I'll be truthful and explain it to him as many times as he needs to hear it, but what happened between us can't be used to poison how Gage feels about either of us. I'd never allow it."

He nodded. "I agree. I'd like to introduce him to my parents on Sunday if Saturday goes well."

She jerked away from the truck. "Sunday?" She flicked her ponytail over her shoulder and combed through it. The repetitive motion helped her calm her nerves and think. God, Gage may be ready to meet his grandparents, but whoa, *she* sure as hell wasn't ready.

Brody's forehead creased. "You're nervous about him meeting my parents."

She paused her hands in mid stroke. "No, not about him, about me. I mean, your mom never did like me, and now she's going to hate me. I mean what's she going to say to Gage *about me*?"

Brody moved away from the truck and walked up into her personal space, forcing her to look up at him. She trembled when he put a hand on her shoulder. God, the smell of his cologne, so familiar and comforting, enveloped her. "Come with us on Sunday. My mother isn't an ogre. She isn't hateful. She would never malign you to anyone, especially Gage. She liked you. She wouldn't say a cross word, ever."

"Yeah, maybe not in front of you, but she's always looked down her nose at me. I never was good enough in her eyes. What makes you think she's going to change her mind when she learns about Gage?"

Hannah King was the most in-your-face woman she'd ever met. She'd never been comfortable enough to be *herself* around Brody's mom. God, she could imagine the condescending looks and sugar-coated words which probably meant the opposite of what the woman said.

"I'm sure you're imagining it." His hand cupped her cheek and his thumb traced her cheekbone. The tender gesture, so familiar and yet such a distant memory. She looked up and gasped at the sadness and longing in his eyes. He blinked, cutting the connection. He dropped his hand and stepped back. "We should call in and see if Masters is willing to cooperate."

She cleared her throat. "Yeah. That would be... good."

She clambered up into his new 'old' truck and put her seatbelt on. The case. They should talk about the case now; except the only thing she could remember at the moment was the feel of his touch. God, she'd missed him so damn much. The smallest gesture from him fed her starvation like manna from heaven.

"So, I never did ask you. Are you dating or married?" Brody glanced at her as he drove away from the curb.

"Me? No. No time for a social life." As a matter of fact, there had only been Brody, and then because of Gage, she'd decided not to date unless she could see the relationship going somewhere. Most men didn't want a ready-made family. Her dating life had been as dead as a Dodo bird.

Extinct was an adequate summation. She glanced at him. "What about you?"

"Date occasionally." He shrugged a shoulder. "Guess you could say I wasn't willing to let anyone get close after... us."

"What about the tux?"

He cut his gaze from traffic to her. A deep crease cut through his brow. "I'd just come back from Brock's wedding."

"Brock's married?"

He nodded. "His wife, Kallie, is a cop. Damn good one. Homicide."

"Really? He's homicide? He'd only just come home from the Marines when..." She let the sentence fade because why make it any more awkward than it already was.

"Yeah. He's a damn good cop. He and Kallie were the ones responsible for nailing Masters."

"I heard his name thrown around by the press, but it was in connection with a shooting outside the precinct."

"Yeah, Kallie's ex-husband. He'd been stalking her, and he tried to kill her, but Brock and Sean McBride were right there along with her partner, Grant."

"And you? How long have you been on the JDET team?"

"Almost two years now. I was recruited from patrol to work undercover on a drug case. I volunteered for everything I could until I could pass my sergeant's exam and put in for the transfer."

"How long do you need to be on the force before you can test for sergeant?"

"Policy is three years, but no one makes it that early. I made it at six years and that was quick. Of course, there were the bullshit comments about nepotism, but I studied my ass off for the exam and then aced the oral portion two months later. How about you? The DEA?"

"When Gage was one, I had to do something. Dawn was still in school, and we lived off her student loans. I sent applications to every opening I could find, but no accounting firm would take me on without experience, at least not at a survivable pay. I broadened my net and applied to the DEA, ICE, FBI—any federal job which would allow me to have stability. I was accepted by ICE and the DEA about the same time. I felt the DEA would be a better fit." She snorted. "Wow, well, let me tell you *that* was a process. I attended orientation, took the written

KRIS MICHAELS

test, passed it. Went through a panel interview. That was something I never want to do again. Did the normal drug test and medical, then the polygraph and psychological assessment. When I finished with all the tests, they did a background investigation. And then shit got real. Eighteen weeks at the DEA Training Academy at Quantico which included physical and firearm training. Thank God I was getting paid. The money was deposited in the bank, and Dawn had access to it. I hated being away from Gage for that long, but it was our future, you know?"

Brody nodded. "You made sacrifices to raise him."

"It wasn't really a sacrifice. Dawn loves him and is so good with him. I knew he'd be all right. I did what I needed to do to make sure we could survive. Then Dawn got the job with her company. She's done well there, moved up from administrative assistant to office manager."

"Why the transfer to JDET? Did you request it?" Brody accelerated onto the interstate.

"Yeah. The more experience you get in the DEA, the more you are subject to being gone on cases which could last for months on end. I know JDET has some messed up hours, but I'd be home for the most part. My sleep schedule might be

88

messed up, but I'd be home. My son needs it, so do I."

She glanced at him and caught him giving her an assessing look. *Hope I'm measuring up.* She'd disappointed enough people lately.

"Would you have requested the transfer if you'd known I was there?"

She sighed and dropped her head back on the headrest. "You know, I don't know the answer to your question. I'd like to think I would have, but as shocked as I was when I saw you the first day, I don't know."

"You didn't even flinch when you saw me."

"Really? It felt like I stared at you forever. I thought you were a figment of my imagination. You in the briefing room, in a tux. Never in a million years would I have thought up that scenario for running into you."

"I'm surprised we haven't run into each other before." He hit the turn indicator to merge into the left-hand lane. "We work the same area."

"Especially the last two years." She nodded in agreement. "For the majority of the time, I've been traveling. Like I said, I needed some stability."

"Dawn watches him when you're not in town?"

"Yep. She's put her life on hold for us. She's

never complained, but we live with her, and she can't even bring a man home for the night, if you know what I mean."

"Does she resent it?"

"Nah, she's been great, but now I'll be able to be in town and for the most part home, so I'm going to start looking for a place for Gage and me. If we have an op, I can count on her to watch him."

Brody nodded. "Your options have grown even further than that. My family would be able to help."

Her gut rolled at the thought of Hannah's disapproval. She had absolutely no confidence Hannah would volunteer, but she plastered a smile on her face. "Yes, it will be a nice change. How is your family?"

"Well, Brock is due back with Kallie tomorrow. Blay is staying with me when he's not at work. He's a firefighter. Brianna has opened her own restaurant. She had help, our cousin Justin gave her the seed money after she interned in his organization for a year. She's done wonderfully."

"Really? What's the name of her place?"

"Horizon."

"The one on East Jefferson?"

"Yep."

"I've always wanted to try Horizon, but we never have the time to drive across town. When Gage is hungry, the entire world knows it. Growing boy. You'll see. I know Bekki is on Channel Two. I've seen several of her reports. She's good."

"She's a brat, and a rock star in her own mind." Brody's full bodied laugh was music to her ears. This was the man she remembered.

They exited the interstate and she regretted their time together was coming to an end. He merged into traffic and stopped at a red light. "If you don't mind, I'll call you tonight. We should probably talk about what is going to happen on Saturday."

"I already told you I'd like it to happen. I think us communicating is a good thing. Good for us and good for Gage. If he sees us tense or uneasy around each other, he'll pick it up immediately."

"I can't act like it didn't happen, but I promise I'll take your lead on how to deal with his questions."

"Tell the truth. Anything else is a waste of time. If he asks why you didn't come to see him, tell him the truth. You didn't know about him." She'd take the blame for keeping Brody in the dark, since it was her fault.

They drove into the parking lot, and he turned off the ignition. "I'll do that. Let's go find out if Masters is going to play ball." He nodded to the small building beside the precinct where JDET resided. It was time to put her game face on. Gage and Dawn needed her to do well in this job. Gage needed her home.

CHAPTER 6

The heavy, iron-barred doors slammed, and the noise echoed down the vacant corridor. The desolate sound still made him flinch, even though he had heard it a thousand times. Amber's eyes flicked back toward the now locked barrier. Yeah, it was a sound you wouldn't get used to unless you worked in the prison. Or, God forbid, became a resident. They followed the sheriff's deputy down the long hallway. Muffled voices from inside the interview rooms could be heard as they passed by the occupied spaces.

Perhaps it was the unmistakable odor of the facility which added to the overall feeling of hope-lessness. No matter what time of year a person entered the facility, the smell of too many people in too small of an area, plus the undeniable dank muskiness of a ventilation system which didn't work as well as it should, imprinted the odor on a person's olfactory senses.

The deputy stopped in front of one of the interrogation rooms. "Masters will be here soon. We have to pull him up from isolation. The ADA is in the facility, and he knows you're here." He opened the door to the interview room and nodded his head.

He and Amber shuffled through the open door and took a seat at the six-foot-long metal table. "I thank God I'm not claustrophobic."

Amber grimaced and glanced around the room. He scanned the interview room. Barren, bleak, and starkly furnished, with four chairs and two posters —visitation rules and prisoner rights.

Cliff Sands, the ADA, walked into the room. He and Amber stood to greet the man.

"Cliff, it's good to see you again." Brody extended his hand.

"And you. What are we looking for in partic-ular with this interview?" He placed his briefcase on the gray metal table and removed a three-inch-thick folder, dropping it to the surface with a thud.

"We have numerous pieces of information

which lead us to believe the Peña cartel is in the process of, or has already started, importing or exporting Gray Death into Hope City. We need Masters to explain his role in the process. Barring that, we need him to explain why he was in the Fairhope neighborhood on numerous occasions prior to his arrest." He spun his chair around and straddled it as the others sat down.

Cliff nodded and opened his folder. He looked up and smiled. "I'm sorry, I forgot my manners. I'm Cliff Sands, Assistant District Attorney. And you are?"

He hurried to make the introductions. "Damn it, I'm sorry. Cliff, this is my new teammate, Amber Swanson. She's been assigned to the JDET team permanently as a DEA liaison. Amber, this is Cliff Sands, and he's more than an ADA. He's one of Brock's best friends. They served together overseas."

"It's nice to meet you, Cliff. Is that file all on Masters?" She nodded to the dark brown pressed cardboard holder.

"Indeed. As he is representing himself legally, it streamlines the paperwork, believe it or not. I'm not sure how much information you're going to get from him. He seems to be playing games. I believe his sense of self-worth may outweigh the information he actually can provide, although at this point the DA is willing to see what we can get from him. We were informed the FBI has utilized some of the information they received from him to take down a payment system Peña's cartel had been utilizing for several years. But as you well know, you plug one hole, and another leak appears." Cliff leaned back in his chair. "What specifically are you looking for from him?"

"Based on the suspect's access to his company's worldwide and national distribution system, we feel Treyson or Masters are either bringing drugs into the country, or as Amber suggested this morning, shipping them out."

"From where? Do you have a manufacturing site under surveillance?" Cliff angled his head at them.

"Actually, our sources have mentioned small airports. Masters' phone triangulation prior to his arrest puts him in the Fairhope neighborhood repeatedly." He leaned forward. "There is a flight line community up there. Small airplanes in hangars behind houses which line a private airstrip. It would be the easiest way to transport drugs out of the city, under the scope."

"But you have nothing to base it on except a hunch?"

"Right. That's why we need Masters to tell us why he was up there."

Cliff frowned. "And if he has nothing?"

Amber lifted her hands and spread them wide. "Then we start over. Half our job amounts to nothing more than chasing hunches and running down possibilities."

"You're going to have to ask specific questions. The man doesn't postulate. He likes to think he's smarter than us." Cliff shifted in his chair as the door opened.

Brody shifted his attention to the inmate who was being delivered. A middle aged man shuffled into the room. A paunch bulged his orange jumpsuit around the middle. Shackles made the man shuffle, but the pompous look in the man's eyes was definitely that of the lawyer he'd seen on television.

They waited for the man to take a seat and the guard to fasten the handcuffs to the bar in the middle of the table.

"Really?" Masters held up his hands and glanced at Cliff.

"Really. Now these detectives have several questions for you."

"What do I receive if I cooperate?" Masters arched an eyebrow.

"Continued isolation and protection from the Peña cartel. Unless you've decided you're no longer in jeopardy." Cliff stared at the man in a silent face-off.

Masters blinked first and turned toward them. "Who are you?"

"Not necessary for you to know," Cliff interrupted when he would have answered. "Detective, your questions."

"What do you know about Gray Death?" Brody still straddled the chair, his arms crossed over the back of it.

"Getting old and dying? Not much." Masters chuckled to himself. He was the only one who found the joke funny.

"I think we're done here. You'll be remanded back to general pop." Cliff stood and they followed suit.

"Wait! Just, wait." Masters drew a deep breath, but no one sat down. "Peña's people are looking for a way to get drugs into the city. The drug interdiction teams are seizing about one in four shipments. He's tired of losing money."

Cliff sat down but didn't take the file from his briefcase. "That wasn't the question."

"The drug is dangerous. It kills anyone who breathes it in or touches it. Unless it is hermetically sealed, it can't be shipped through normal channels. The way packages are shipped and processed, normally, damage can occur, and the shipment would be lost, but more important, the routes would be compromised. Gray death *can't* be shipped by conventional means."

Amber glanced at him. Masters had just admitted that Peña's crew were shipping the drugs. They'd report the information back to Terrell.

Brody stared at the man before he asked, "What is Peña's interest in the Fairhope flightline community?"

Masters chuckled. "What do you think?"

Amber leaned forward. "Have you ever picked up any of Peña's shipments, Mr. Masters?"

The man jerked back. "Of course not! I am a lawyer, not a transporter." His offense was almost comical.

"You are also serving life for attempted murder of a law enforcement officer," Cliff growled.

Masters' jaw ground together before he answered. "I do not transport drugs."

"Do you know if Peña has people in place or perhaps recruited people to fly from that vicinity?" Brody wanted to know if those drugs were coming into, or hell, being routed out of the city. Either way, it didn't matter.

"For a fact? No. Assumed? Perhaps." Masters shrugged.

Amber took her turn, "Was that why you were in Fairhope numerous times immediately before you were arrested?"

Masters flicked her a glance before dismissing her with, "I had other business in the area."

Brody fired back, "What kind of business?"

"I was representing a client in purchasing property." Masters turned to Cliff. "I'm not saying anything further about my client. That is covered under attorney-client privilege."

He could smell blood, and he was on the trail like a hound dog. "Is this client involved in the transportation of drugs?"

Masters slowly turned his head toward him. "I have no knowledge of that. Have we met?"

He shook his head. "No, we've never met."

"You look familiar."

"I get that a lot. What do you know about Peña's use of aircraft to transport drugs?"

"Only that he'd mentioned it." Masters shrugged. "My involvement was limited."

"Yet, he mentioned possible avenues of transportation while you were present?" Amber cocked her head. "Why was that, Mr. Masters?"

"I'm sure I wouldn't know, Detective...?"

Amber smiled at him but didn't give him her name. Masters narrowed his eyes and turned his attention back toward him. "You look very familiar."

"Detective, do you have any further questions?" Cliff asked with a pointed look in his direction.

"Mr. Masters, did you coordinate shipments of drugs through any entity of Treyson Enterprises for the Peña cartel?"

A smile spread across Masters' face. "On more than one occasion, and I assume the methods are still being utilized, but I will only tell you about those processes when the DA agrees to transfer me from this facility to an out-of-state, minimum-security prison, with an untraceable name change. I want a guarantee in writing." He turned and yelled, "Guard!" Then looked at Cliff. "That's my trump card, Mr. Sands. How badly does your DA want to stop the drugs?"

They sat in silence until Masters was taken out of the small room. As soon as the door shut, Brody said, "I'll brief Captain Terrell on this interview. I'm sure he'll want a sit down with you and the DA to hammer a way forward regarding the shipments through Treyson's empire. In the meantime, how do we get a look at the property sales in the area?"

"Easy. Property sales, terms, or conditions of mortgages, and such, are recorded in the jurisdiction where the property is located. It's public information. If it's not online, you can go to the Office of the Recorder Of Deeds."

"Why didn't you want to give him our names?" Amber asked as Cliff stood.

"Ah, well I suspect the name Detective King would put Masters in a foul mood. Brody's brother Brock was the cop he tried to kill, and Brock and his partner are the reason the man is here. I'm surprised he didn't see the family resemblance sooner. I had the sense he was starting to put two and two together, hence my hurrying the topic along. Did you get what you need?"

"I think we have enough information to look into it further, but it will be up to Captain Terrell."

They shook hands, and Cliff went one direction, deeper into the bowels of the prison, and they went the other.

Amber took a deep breath as soon as they'd collected their weapons and exited the prison. "The smell of a prison. There's nothing like it."

"I was thinking that on the way in. Too many bodies, not enough fresh air." He held the outer gate open for her when the deputy buzzed them out.

"Unless someone has been inside a jail, they have no idea. I'm damn glad we're on the right side of the bars."

He did a double take at the smile she flashed. For a moment she looked like the young woman he'd fallen in love with. He lowered his head and walked to his truck with her matching his step.

"Did I say or do something wrong?" Her question floated to him, low and filled with concern.

"What? No, not at all. I was lost in thought." Which was true. Thinking how damn much he missed the woman he'd given his heart to. How much he wanted to meet his son and how much he detested the fact she hadn't told him about Gage until now. His emotions warred with each other in a never-ending argument. The past couldn't be changed, nor could his emotional responses, yet he'd grown enough to know he'd deal with the turmoil meeting his son would spawn.

"What are the chances the captain will let us pursue this?" Amber asked after she'd buckled her seatbelt.

He started the engine and considered her question. "Short answer? It depends."

She chuckled as she checked her phone. She dropped it back to the seat beside her. "And the long answer?"

He shrugged. "Terrell will make a call based on available funding and the leads the guys are developing from the latest bust. If there are more concrete leads developed, we'll table the weaker ones and act on the information which will take the players, money, and drugs off the streets, and then pull any leads we can from those busts. It is a never-ending cycle. The cases we have to develop and expend man-hours and money on will slide from front and center of our workload to the rear of the pack depending on what's happening. So, like I said, it depends."

"How is surveillance handled in this unit?" She adjusted the vents in the truck and turned up the fan. "Getting warm."

"About time, it was a long damn winter." He hit the button starting the air conditioning, and she groaned a thank you. He chuckled and leaned his arm against the closed driver's side window. "We usually take shifts. The most senior are entitled days, which is everyone except you. I can talk to Anderson if you need me to do that."

"Why?" Her head snapped his direction.

"So you can be with Gage."

"Ah, no, I don't want you to do that. I don't want special favors. It would piss everyone off, wouldn't it? I know what comes with doing the job. Dawn and I can work it out." She crossed her arms and looked straight forward.

"You mean, Dawn, you and *me*, right?"

She turned her head toward him and blinked several times. A small smile made a brief appearance. "Yeah, I guess. I think we have quite a few steps before that happens, but having your help would be... nice."

He focused on the traffic. Nice? No, spending time with his son would be his definition of perfect.

CHAPTER 7

Amber drove into the driveway and parked. As she walked through the garage, she secured her weapon in the lockbox and headed inside.

Dawn met her at the door. "He's been asking me questions all day. You're up to bat. I'm going for a run." Her sister brushed past her.

"Wait, what did you tell him?"

"That you would explain everything." Dawn shrugged and grabbed her foot, pulling it back in a quad stretch. "I'm running while you do the explaining. I'll come home and cook so you can work out. Sorry, but I'm bailing on you." She dropped her foot and stretched the other quad.

"God, has it been that bad?" She put her lockbox

on the high shelf out of sight and dropped her purse on the table with her keys.

"Bad? No. Hard for me not to sit him down and explain everything from my point of view? Yes. I'm not going there. This is on you." She dropped her foot. "I'll be back."

She watched Dawn jog from the garage and take a left at the street.

"Mom?" Gage called from behind her.

She spun and smiled. "Hey, buddy."

"Did you talk to him today?"

"I did. I spent the day with your father, actually." She slipped off her shoes and put her hand on his shoulder.

"At work?"

"Yeah, your dad and I are going to be working together. Come on, let me in. I need a bottle of water. Auntie Dawn said you had a lot of questions."

"Yeah, but she wouldn't answer them. She said I needed to hear the answers from you."

"Well that's true." She opened the fridge and grabbed a water. "Want one?"

He shook his head. "Why didn't you tell him about me?"

"Oh, gosh, the big questions right off the bat, huh?"

"Sorry?" His face tightened. Confused and maybe upset.

"No, come on. Let's crash on the couch." They moved into the living room. Gage plopped down right beside her, and she dropped an arm on his shoulders. "Okay, how do I explain this?" She held her water bottle in front of him, and he opened the top for her, keeping the cap. She took a drink. God, this was harder than she'd imagined. "I dated your dad for a long time. We met in high school. We didn't date then, but we knew each other. Then when my momma got really sick, I moved here with Auntie Dawn and my dad and stepmom."

"Yeah, I know. I remember pictures of Granny Dot and Grandpa Wallace."

"Right, so I didn't see your dad for a couple years. Then after I graduated high school I went to the junior college and then to the university. Your father was in most of my classes at the university. We were both majoring in Criminal Justice."

"You did two, right? Criminal Justice and Accounting." He smiled up at her.

"Right."

"You still suck at math. Why is that?"

"Well I don't suck at all math, only the stuff you do in the fifth grade." God knows the way they taught her son to add, subtract, multiply and divide was baffling. He got the right answers, but damn, how he got there was beyond her.

"I'm not buying it, missy." He narrowed his eyes at her and made his voice deeper, only to giggle when she tickled his ribs.

"Don't you get too big for your britches, mister."

He squirmed away from her and twisted on the cushion to look at her. "Finish telling me, Mom."

"Okay, well, we dated in college and in our senior year we moved into an apartment together."

"Were you married?"

"No."

He lowered his eyes to the water bottle cap he was spinning in his fingers. "Did you love him?"

"Very much. With all my heart." She blinked back the emotion the answer released.

"Did he love you?" He looked up at her. His big eyes, those beautiful blue eyes with darker rims of navy blue stared up at her.

"Yes, he did."

"Then what happened?" His innocent question almost broke her, but she owed him the answers.

"Well, have you ever been really afraid of something and run away from it?"

"Like the mean kid at the skate park that one time?"

"Kind of like that. See, when I was growing up and I was your age, my mom wasn't well, up here." She tapped her temple. "I didn't know that. She was my mom. She told me every day how marriage had trapped her, had killed all her dreams and prevented her from living the life she wanted. That if she hadn't married Dad, she'd have had a wonderful life. She told me the day I got married was the day my life was over. I heard it so many times. Every day, so many times a day, for the entire time I grew up. When your dad asked me to marry him, I got scared because what my mom told me was stuck in my head. I ran away."

"You did?"

She nodded. "I did. But when I got here to Aunt Dawn's, I sat down, and I looked at my fears. I realized what I'd done, running away, was wrong. I loved your dad and a life with him was what I wanted."

"What did you do?" His eyes were wide, and he stared at her intently.

She leaned forward, put the water bottle on the table, and grabbed a tissue to dab at her eyes. "Ten years ago, after he asked me to marry him and I ran away, he got in Gertie--"

"Gertie?" His voice cracked, changing pitch.

"That's what he called his truck"

Gage made a face. "That's a weird name."

"It is. But anyway, he got in Gertie and was driving here because he knew this is where I'd go. There was an accident. A delivery truck ran into Gertie. Your dad was hurt. Bad."

"Is he okay?"

"He is now, but it took a long, long time for him to get better. At first he was in the hospital. When he got out he stayed with his parents.""

"But he didn't call you?"

"No, when I ran away, I hurt his heart. I made him feel like I didn't love him."

"But you did?"

"I did. When he got better, he didn't want to talk to me. Finally, I went to see his mom to ask her if she'd let me talk to him because by then I knew I was pregnant with you."

Those big eyes stared up at her. "Waddid she say when you told her about me?"

She took a deep breath and blew it out. "I didn't tell her. I don't know why." *Bullshit, she was afraid of Hannah King. The woman intimidated the hell out of her.* "She told me she'd let your dad know I came by, and he'd contact me if he felt like it." Which was the truth.

"But he didn't?"

"No. He didn't."

"Do you still love him?"

She smiled at her son. "I will always love your father because he gave me you." Unfortunately, any hopes of rekindling in Brody's heart the love she still carried for him was long gone. The anger that had radiated from the man when she'd first tried to talk to him had solidified that as fact. She'd burned that bridge ten years ago, and now, each passing day erected a barrier neither of them could scale.

"What's his name?"

"Brody King."

"He's a police officer, right? You said that this morning at breakfast. You're going to work with him now?"

"Right. He's a detective sergeant on the team I joined."

"Does he still want to see me?"

"Yes, he does. Family is very important to your dad. If you want to, we can go meet your Grandma and Grandpa King on Sunday."

"Do you think he'll like me? Do you think they'll like me?"

"No, I think they'll love you. Can I let you in on a secret?"

"What?"

"I think your dad is as nervous about meeting you as you are about meeting him."

"Really?" He sat up and twisted to look at her.

"Yep."

"That's kinda cool. It's gunna be weird, you know."

"I figured."

"I mean, like what do I do?"

"You be yourself. He wants to know you. That's it."

"Does he like to fish? Play lacrosse? What about football?"

"Those are great questions. Maybe you should ask him those on Saturday. What do you think?"

"Yeah, okay." He stood up and then turned to her quickly. "I don't have to go live with him, right? I can stay with you?"

"What? Of course, you're staying with me! Why would you ask something like that?"

"A judge made Tabitha spend time with her dad. He's got another family, and they aren't exactly nice to her."

"Ah, well see that's not going to happen here. Your father and I will work really hard to make sure nothing happens in your life that you aren't one hundred percent comfortable with. You know you can always talk to me, no matter what, right?"

He nodded. "I know. I just..."

"You get scared?"

"Yeah."

"Well, I promise, pinkie swear even, nothing like that is going to happen between your father and me. Okay?" She held her pinkie up, and Gage wrapped his around hers. God, she really hoped what she believed in her heart and had just promised her son was the truth.

"Okay."

"Cool. Are you done with schoolwork?"

"Yeah, it was math and spelling. Aunt Dawn quizzed me already on my spelling words."

"Perfect. Let me change and we'll go for a jog." Which meant he'd ride his bike as she jogged. The constant conversation kept her mind off the miles they logged.

"All right. Can we have fish sticks for dinner?"

"Gross!" She called over her shoulder as she headed to her room. She didn't mind fish sticks, but the boy would eat them every night if she'd allow it.

"Is not!" he called back.

"Ask Aunt Dawn, when we pass her, she's cooking dinner."

"Score!" His laugh followed his shout. Dawn was a sucker for an easy way out when it came to dinner.

Brody's phone rang as the talking head for the nightly news droned on. He muted the television and glanced at the caller ID. Amber. He drew a deep breath and answered with a question, "How did it go tonight?"

"Your son is really inquisitive." She chuckled and then sighed. "He wanted to know if we loved each other when we were together and why I left."

"What did you tell him?" Brody turned off the TV and leaned his recliner back.

"Honestly?"

"No, Amber, after all this time, I want you to lie to me." He rolled his eyes.

"Smart ass. Fine, I told him I loved you with all my heart, and I screwed up bad by running away."

Brody let her words settle around him. Her admission she'd overreacted in the truck last night wasn't much of a salve to the wounds he bore. But her words just now and telling their son she loved him? That numbed some of the lingering pain. He had to know. "Did you? Love me? I've asked myself that question a million times since that day."

She was quiet for several moments. "With all my heart. I will always regret the way I responded. I was so afraid I'd broken us, especially when I found out about your accident. I was standing outside your room at the hospital when I heard you tell Brock you never wanted to see me again. Then after I found out I was pregnant, I contacted your mom... You didn't call."

"I was wounded, physically and emotionally. I put myself out there. I confessed how much I loved you and asked you to spend your life with me. I wanted to take you on those adventures you dreamed of having. I wanted to be a part of your life. When you shook your head and said no, then literally ran away, you killed a part of me."

The young man he used to be had indeed died that day. His outlook on life had changed. He'd closed off, and yes, he'd become bitter. He trusted very few people now. His family and his team comprised the extent of those few. Learning about Gage and even about Amber's rationale for her actions wouldn't change the circumstances. Gage was family, enough said. As parents, he hoped they would be able to communicate, but on a personal level, she was his kryptonite.

"I know. How do I make amends for a bad choice I made ten years ago?" She whispered the emotion-filled words.

He had a very thin layer of scar tissue over that particular wound. He wasn't willing to open it again. He'd bleed out. "I don't think you can. Instead, tell me about Gage."

"He's amazing. Where do I start? He's pretty tight with his best friends, Johnny, Nick, Simon and Finn. They do a lot of weekend sleepovers, and we parents rotate the duty. Johnny's father is a stay at home dad, and he holds two sleepovers a month. The rest of us divy out the remainder."

"Good people?"

"Yes, and before you ask, I did check them out, very carefully. All the salt-of-the-earth-type folks. Let's see, what else... Oh, Gage loves to play base-ball, lacrosse and soccer. Football, not so much, but that's because the pee-wee coach saw how much bigger he is than the other kids his age and made him do the tackle thing. He wants to run and catch the ball, but I can't throw a football to save my soul, so he doesn't get much practice at that."

"I can help with that. I was quarterback in high school."

"I remember. You were a popular jock who was nice to everyone. I'm still surprised you didn't play in college."

Her voice had mellowed out. It reminded him of all the late night talks they used to have. He sighed and pushed those thoughts from his mind.

"If you remember, I'm not the greatest student, and had I played in college, my grades would have suffered. Is Gage a good student?" He rerouted the conversation back to his son.

"Oh, yes. He's so smart. I had him tested for advance placement in English and math. He reads on an eighth-grade level, and he runs circles around me when it comes to math."

"Say what? You were always good in math."

"New math. I swear to the heavens, the way the kids do math now is some kind of hocus-pocus magic thing. I can't wrap my head around it."

He had no experience with that, so he changed the subject. "Is he allergic to anything?" He had seasonal allergies. They sucked but weren't extreme.

"Not that we've found. He's had the chicken pox and has a small scar above his right eyebrow from that. He's had all his childhood vaccinations and broken his arm from falling out of a tree we'd told him repeatedly not to climb. He loves to fish, ride his bike, and play video games. He'd run barefoot all summer if I let him. I've had to re-home frogs, small garden snakes, and snails, which have made it into his room when we weren't looking."

Brody chuckled at the mental image of Amber carrying a small garden snake back outside—the woman who freaked about a little spider in the shower. "Does he have a pet?"

"No, I work too many hours. Dawn has a full-time job, and with Gage in school all day and at the after-school program until either Dawn or I pick him up, it wouldn't be fair to an animal. He wants one. He's even got a name picked out."

"Yeah, what's that?"

"Bullet. He wants a German Shepherd named Bullet. I talked to a breeder, and he recommended we wait to get one. They need a lot of exercise and leaving them alone for long periods of time while they are growing up, well... the trainer said he wouldn't want anyone to do that to such an active animal."

"You told me he asked if you loved me. What else did he ask?"

"Well he wanted to know what you liked to do, and then he asked if I thought you'd like him. He seemed a little worried about possibly meeting your parents. Then... well, he asked if he had to go live with you." Her voice trailed away.

"Why would he ask that?"

"He has a classmate who was forced to spend time with her father. I'm assuming it was a divorce. I guess it wasn't amicable."

"He's afraid I'll take him away from you."

"He's not the only one." Her words were a mere whisper on her breath, but he heard them.

He sat forward, lowering his recliner gently. "I've no intention of taking him from you, but I will be a part of his life. I know I'll have to go slow, but I want to be involved with him."

"I'd like that, too." She sighed. "I'm dealing with

a lot of guilt over this, even though I believe I made the best decision I could at the time."

He could hear the emotion in her voice. Was he still angry she'd robbed him and his son of ten years' worth of memories? Of seeing him born, first words and first steps? Hell, yeah. Was he going to let the hurt go anytime soon? Probably not. *Definitely not.* But those were his emotions to deal with, as the guilt she was feeling was hers. He couldn't offer her solace for them anymore than he could negate what he was feeling.

Before the silence drew on too long, he asked, "Do you need me to bring anything on Saturday?"

"Dessert?" She cleared her throat. "Gage loves anything chocolate, so..."

"Got it. I'll see you at work tomorrow. We've got a briefing with the captain first thing in the morning."

They'd gotten back from interviewing Masters late. Terrell and Anderson had both clocked out. Nothing that Masters had given them was life or death urgent, so they agreed to brief the team leads in the morning.

She yawned. "I'll be there at eight."

"Good night, Amber." He hung up the phone without waiting for her to reply.

Visions of her tired and sated next to him in bed flashed through his memory. He groaned and dropped his head into his hands. How the hell was he going to manage? Everything about the woman was seared into his brain, branded there for eternity. He dropped back in his chair and looked up at the painted ceiling. Sleep would be a long time coming tonight.

CHAPTER 8

Amber sat beside Lieutenant Anderson and leaned in to look at the map. He'd asked her to bring him up to speed on what she and Brody had learned about the area yesterday. "The third house down is vacant with a for sale sign in the yard. Here." She took a pencil and circled the house. "But the house is at the back of the development. There is a house here and one here toward the front which have potential. This one can see the entrance to the housing development. I'd recommend it. The sales company was Ellis-Barker Reality. I took a picture of the sign, and I can send you the contact information."

"Thanks. Text it to me?" He smiled and held her

gaze for a moment too long, making the contact personal and completely uncomfortable. Nipping any ideas he had in the bud needed to happen sooner rather than later. She dropped her eyes and grabbed for her phone, giving herself a reason to put some distance between them.

She strolled away as she sent the picture, praying the rest of the team looking into the Gray Death issue would arrive soon. She spun and took a step back. "Whoa, I did not hear you." She stiff armed Anderson and stopped his advance. "Listen, we need to get something straight here. I don't date people on my team." The lieutenant was good looking with broad shoulders, muscles, sandy brown hair, and hazel eyes. He was tall and yeah, he was sexy, but he wasn't... Brody.

"Really? Why not." He leaned in and planted his hand on the wall, pinning her to the plaster.

She narrowed her eyes and glared at the man. "I'm going to tell you this once. Move. Back up, or I will rack you so hard your balls will crawl so far up your insides they'll never drop down. Get it?"

"Damn, aggressive. That's the type of woman I like." The man chuckled, but he did step back.

"Never going to happen. I am not in the market

for anything you're selling. Go cast your net somewhere else." She crossed her arms and dared the
man to make a move toward her again. She could
hear heavy footsteps coming down the hallway.
Finally, the rest of the team.

"Well, make sure you let me know if the status
changes."

"What status are you talking about?" Captain
Terrell asked as he entered. "What's up, Logan? I
thought you were working with Mozinga?" He
glanced from Anderson to her and back again.

Brody walked in, and she saw the instant he
registered the tension in the room. "Problems?"

Anderson chuckled and shrugged. "Nothing but
communication between coworkers." He smiled
salaciously at her and winked, but the men behind
him couldn't see his expression.

Floored, her mouth dropped open. "No, oh hell,
no. There was no communication. It was a one-
way flow of information, and the message is, I am
not interested. Period." She'd be damned if she was
going to put up with his shit. "Captain Terrell, I
don't appreciate being hit on at work."

"Hit on?" Terrell slowly turned his head toward
Anderson. "Logan?"

"She's full of it, Ryker. Like I'd need to shit where I eat?" He shook his head and looked disgusted. "Looks like we have a drama queen in our midst. Isn't this going to be fun." Anderson turned and jacked a thumb in her direction. "She called me in here to show me something about a case I'm not even involved in."

"That isn't true." Amber ground her teeth together. Anderson had approached her in the break room but there was no one there who could corroborate her side of the story.

Brody spoke clearly, "As you're aware, I've known Agent Swanson for a long time, Lt. Anderson. I've never known her to cry wolf. I'm curious, do you do this to all the new female team members?" He glanced at Terrell. "Hardin and Clausen left the team shortly after arriving." Brody turned back to Anderson. "You insinuated both of them were drama queens, too."

"Oh, I see. You want her even after she ditched you. I'm not getting in the middle of this shit. The woman is fabricating drama." Lt. Anderson shrugged. "Either way, not my problem, and I don't appreciate being caught up in this shit. Ryker, you and I need to talk about this situation."

Amber couldn't believe the man—of all the

bullshit moves. Captain Terrell's eyes narrowed. "You're right, we do. Anderson, my office. Swanson, I want a sworn statement on my desk in the next ten minutes. King, you've got this meeting until I deal with this mess. Tell Rayburn and Watson to brief you on what they got from our informant." Captain Terrell spun on his heel and bellowed Anderson's name as he strode down the hall.

Anderson narrowed his eyes and mouthed the words, 'Fucking bitch,' as he shoved past her.

"Oh my God, what the hell was that?" Amber looked at Brody and plopped her ass down quickly on the first available chair. "I've never had someone approach me like that."

"Get to your computer and write up the statement."

Brody's anger-laced growl snapped her head up.

"You're mad at *me*? You can't think *I* started that!"

He jerked back and narrowed his eyes. "I'm not mad at you. I'm pissed someone on my team could be creating a hostile work environment. As if dealing with criminals isn't hard enough."

"Oh." She took a breath and closed her eyes.

Thank goodness he believed her. "How did he know about us?"

"He knew I asked you to marry me, and you said no. I let it slip the first time I saw you. That's all he knows. Everything else is an assumption. Go write your statement. Terrell is an excellent leader; he'll make this right." Brody dropped the file he was reading and produced his phone. "Rayburn and Watson will be here in a couple of minutes. Go do your statement and send it to Terrell."

She nodded and drew a deep breath. "I won't be long." She got up and headed to the bullpen. She didn't need this shit. With each step she took, the more she regretted saying anything. She was the new team member, and she wanted to make a good impression, but what Anderson had tried to do... that was reprehensible. She squared her shoulders and steeled her resolve. No. Hell no. Had he acted like that at a bar; she'd have been prepared. She *would* have racked him if he'd persisted.

The threat wasn't idle, but assaulting a teammate, even one using his position as one of her superiors to coerce her for sex? Something like this could get her ass shipped back to the DEA with a black mark scratched across her folder. She'd be lucky to pull anything but shit assignments for the rest of her career. She called up a new document on her computer and let her fingers fly, putting the facts and only the facts in the sequence of events. She attached it to an email and fired it off to her new captain. She locked her computer and headed back to the conference room.

Watson looked up and smiled. "Hey, morning. We brought breakfast." He nodded to a brown paper bag with grease stains.

"Fabulous." She headed straight to the bag and drew a deep breath. "Oh man, are these breakfast biscuits?"

"Grease included, free of charge." Rayburn reached past her and dove into the bag. He grabbed two from the bag and tossed one to Watson. "Sarge?"

"God, yes." Brody leaned back and caught the paper-wrapped sandwich. She chuckled and removed the last one from the bag.

"Okay, what did you guys get?"

Rayburn chewed quickly, lifting a finger until he swallowed. "We corroborated what our shooter was telling us. Bonzo said Peña's crew is starting to bring the shit in, but there isn't much out there yet. The product is already broken down and packaged, and word has spread on the street for the dealers not to touch the opened product. Bonzo was sweating it, man. He knows he has to push it, but he ain't liking it."

"Where is he getting it from?" Brody took a bite of his sandwich. "Won't give up his supplier." Watson answered for Rayburn. "He's willing to give us general intel, but he ain't filling in the upper supply chain for us."

Amber swallowed a bite of the greasy, cheesy, eggy heaven. "Can you pressure him?"

"If we do, we lose a good source of street level info. He deals, but he isn't a snitch when it comes to the supply channels. We've decided the information we get from him is more important. We went another route." After he finished speaking, Watson took the last gigantic bite of his sandwich.

Rayburn continued, "We hauled in Little K."

Brody leaned forward. "Did you link him to the drive-by you've been working?"

"The guys in the bullpen corroborated with street cameras."

Brody wadded up his paper wrapper and shot it into the trash can. "The ADA willing to work with him?"

"Yeah." Watson grunted.

She liked these guys. They got it. Sometimes bad people got deals in order to take down worse criminals. It sucked, but it worked.

Watson leaned in and looked at her. "Little K gave the guys in the pen a fuckton of information, and not only on this case. Once word hits the streets, the man will be a target, but Little K has protectors inside. He's probably safer in jail than he is on the streets at this point. K said they're bringing the GD in from Florida. Flying it in."

"We still haven't tied the import of this product to any specific neighborhood." She sighed and shook her head. There were a hundred different ways the cartel could be flying the drugs into the city.

"K said they were flying the shit into suburbia. He didn't know anything else." Rayburn tossed his paper wrapper into the trash.

Brody stood and went to the map spread flat on the far side of the long table. "It's enough. We can work a cursory surveillance." He pointed to the house she'd told Anderson about earlier. "This is the best observation point available. We'd need a minimum of two cameras at each point, long range and wide angle, covering the closer area. We could install them outside. About every house had some type of alarm system."

"I've been thinking about it. The neighborhood seemed pretty friendly."

"You mean nosey." He chuckled.

"Yeah, they are going to know if we are doing a rotating surveillance. The team will probably have to have someone move in, and since you're the pilot..."

"I guess I'll be sleeping on an air mattress for a couple weeks if the captain and the lieutenant determine this is a workable situation. It comes down to money right now."

"We have two fingers pointing this direction. Masters, and now Little K. Is the bullseye directly on this location? No, but we have Masters' movement in the area; and the purchase of a house for a client he wouldn't disclose. Add to that, Little K's indication it is coming in via suburbia, and Bonzo's assertion it is coming in by air, and we have enough. We need to find which houses have been purchased in the area lately and make sure we have good observation on those houses. This house might not be the best place to set up if the one his client purchased is further inside the neighborhood."

"I can get the information." Rayburn rubbed his hands together and stood up.

"Good. We'll need the statements from Little K, and make sure you write up your conversation with Bonzo. Keep him covered as a confidential informant. We don't need him disappearing on us."

"Halfway done with the report already. We presenting this to the captain?"

"We are. Rayburn, when you get the information, bring it to me, and we'll grab the captain."

"Done deal." Watson and Rayburn headed back toward the bull pen and the rest of the team.

"Grey Death is extremely dangerous. What kind of upper middle-class resident would risk dealing with it?"

"Someone who needed the money." He shrugged. "Or someone Peña has dirt on, perhaps."

She rolled her wrapper into a ball. "Yeah, I can see both of those scenarios. I can't work out the logistics of Peña's route though. They fly the drugs up from Florida, probably Jacksonville if my sources are right, and then what? Soccer mom drives the shit to a waiting drug dealer?"

"That's what we need to find out, and that's why we're pinpointing this area and these recently purchased houses. Nothing else has sold in that development for years. We'll set it up so we can monitor the other residences without being noticed." Brody's voice stopped her when she moved to stand up. "I need to check with the captain about this, but what if we ask some of your counterparts in Jacksonville to watch for planes we know are hangared in the neighborhood?"

"Resources and money would be the issue. I do have a few agents in the Jacksonville area who owe me a favor or two. If we could narrow down the times they'd need to be at the airports..."

Brody nodded. "This is workable. It could narrow our list of suspects. Hell, for that matter, it could give us the person bringing the stuff in."

"True. Lots of moving parts though." There was a trail, a ghost of a trail, but it was a place to start.

"All right. We move along this path. I'll need the contact information for the realtors in the area. Call them and see if any of these houses would be available for rent. If they've been on the market for a while, maybe the sellers will consider renting the houses."

"On it." She stood and headed to the door. "Oh, and thanks, for earlier. For having my back."

"I'm sure we haven't heard the last of this issue.

Lieutenant Anderson has a lot to lose. He won't go down without a fight."

"I'm not looking to take him down. I want him to stop using his position of authority to make sexual advancements." She shrugged. Maybe she did want to take him down after all.

CHAPTER 9

C aptain Terrell stood in front of the map and listened as Brody outlined the information he'd just forwarded his team leader. "Do we have options as to housing?"

"Here." Brody pointed to the house at the end of the neighborhood. According to Rayburn's digging, two houses had sold recently. They'd be able to get damn good coverage of both with cameras installed on that house.

"We need a warrant."

"Yeah. I've compiled the information in the zip file I just sent you. I don't know if we can get approval, but I put everything I could into the narrative."

Terrell nodded. "I'll print it up and get it to

Judge Freemont. Hell of a good job. I think this will float," he said as he moved to the massive chair behind his desk. "Now about Anderson."

"Sir?"

"He denies everything. I've worked with Logan Anderson a lot of years. He's a womanizer, but I've never seen him push himself on anyone." He held up a hand before Brody could jump in. "But I trust your judgement where Swanson is concerned. So, we're doing it this way until I can find Hardin and Clausen and ask some direct questions. Swanson reports directly to me. Your past eliminates you as a supervisor. I don't want Anderson having anything to do with her. I've told him point blank not to be around her unless there are others present. I'm telling the same thing to Swanson when I inform her I'm her supervisor. I've looked at Swanson's jacket from the DEA. Only commendations and no indication of any improprieties. I also examined Anderson's and evaluated it the same way. Again, commendations and no mention of any difficulties. So, I'm at a standstill for the time being. I'll be talking to Lawrence, Patel and Driggers, and I'll be digging. This isn't over, but it is stalled for the moment."

Lawrence, Patel, and Driggers were the three

other women on the team. They were street-toughened cops, and Brody had complete faith they'd be honest with the captain. "I understand. Thank you." He rubbed the back of his neck and glanced to the bullpen where Amber and Rayburn were working. Before he made changes to his life insurance and pushed the paper across his boss' desk, he needed to fill the captain in about Gage, but he wasn't going to tell his supervisor before he told his family. It could wait until Monday.

"You need something else?" Ryker arched an eyebrow.

"Yeah, but it will wait. I have to do some legwork before I bring it to you."

"Perfect. I'm contacting a person I know. He owns a large real estate brokerage firm and construction company. If he doesn't control those agencies, he'll know who does. We need to be rent free. Money is tight, especially with the overtime we've been logging."

Brody peered at his boss. "Ops and payroll from the same pot?"

"No, but when it comes down to paying our team or using the money for operations and equipment, our team comes first. I haven't had to go there, yet." Ryker's forehead furrowed. "The budget this year was a little more than half of last year's and our workload has doubled."

Brody stared at his shoes. "What would you think about introducing asset forfeiture as a way of funding the unit?"

"What?" Ryker shot him a look.

"That phone call you asked me to make after duty hours. I did. I learned Hope City PD utilizes asset forfeiture. We can request a percentage of the funds and assets we seize as a means to update equipment and fund training. The lab requested funding from forfeitures. That's what got them all new equipment and the remodel. If we requested a percentage to upgrade the infrastructure, equipment and comms, would it alleviate the pull on the operational side of the house?"

"Hell yeah, but I wouldn't have a clue where to start with something like that, and I don't imagine I could push it through Colonel Fenton."

"Ah, well, the good thing about it is it doesn't come from this unit, so you don't need to worry about Atilla." The nickname they'd given the colonel fit. He fought everything the team tried to accomplish yet took all the glory for their successes. The asshole who wanted his dad's job was a total prick.

"Who requests it?"

"That would come from the Commissioner over the Finance Department, and since the Chief Financial Officer's position is vacant, the Financial Services Director is responsible for up channeling all forfeiture spending requests." Brody crossed his arms and waited for shit to sink in.

The man leaned back and leveled a laser sharp glare his way. "Debbie McGuire. You used to date her. For a couple years, right?"

"I did."

"Did it end amicably?"

"I believe so. It ran its course." Busy people with busy lives. The sex had been good, and they got along well together, but they'd both realized they wanted different things. She wanted career advancement and really got off on the status of dating the commissioner's son. He wanted... hell, he didn't want anything except the status quo. A routine partner who was there when it was convenient for both of them. Debbie was a wonderful woman, but not once had he envisioned a lifetime with her. They drifted apart a long time before they officially called it quits. He didn't lose any sleep over the breakup, nor did she.

"I guess it doesn't hurt to ask, but I don't want

you to get your ass in a crack between Debbie in finance and the woman out there." He nodded toward the window.

Brody's eyes followed the nod. Amber chose that second to throw back her head and laugh at something Rayburn had said. She was absolutely beautiful. "There isn't any concern there. We share a past, among other things, but there can never be anything between us again."

"Never, huh?"

"Yeah."

"Fucking long time, never."

Brody glanced through the window again and sighed, "Yeah."

Out of the corner of her eye, Amber caught Brody going to his office, just as Terrell's voice shattered the low thrum of conversation in the bullpen. "Swanson, when you're free."

Rayburn leaned over. "That's code for getcha ass in here."

She gave him the stink eye. "I deduced that all by myself."

"See, I told you she was smart." Watson shot a

rubber band at Rayburn, who ducked quickly. The band flew behind him and hit one of the other team members in the back. The guy saluted them with his middle finger but didn't stop the conversation he was having on the phone. Both Watson and Rayburn laughed like loons.

"You two have the combined mental capacity of a Shih Tzu." She grabbed her phone and pocketed it as she headed to the captain's office.

"Hey, I heard those were really smart animals!" Rayburn yelled after her.

She shook her head, a smile spreading across her face as she knocked on the door bearing his name, Captain Ryker J. Terrell. She ignored the man inside the office next door. Lieutenant Anderson was a non-person as far as she was concerned.

Terrell looked up and motioned to the chair in front of his desk. "Swanson. Shut the door and take a seat."

She did what he asked and laced her fingers together over her knee, waiting for the reason she was summoned.

"Thank you for the statement. The situation is being looked into, and I want to assure you it will be impartial."

"Ah, he's still denying it." Captain Terrell didn't respond, but it was all right. She was certain Lieutenant Anderson was professing his innocence.

"I'm continuing with my investigation. From this point forward you will report directly to me."

"Yes, sir." She was good with it.

"Do you have any problem working with Sergeant King?"

She snapped backward. "No. Why?"

"I need to make sure there is nothing from the past which can interfere with an ongoing investigation. Should I need the two of you to work in close proximity, there wouldn't be any reason for concern?"

Her head moved side to side. "No sir. None that I'm aware of."

"All right. Your current assignment is with Sergeant King and Detectives Rayburn and Watson. Please do not contact Lieutenant Anderson unless absolutely necessary and then only if witnesses are available."

She snorted. "I'll have no problem following that order."

"Good. I look forward to working with you, Agent Swanson."

"And I you, sir." She stood and headed from the office.

"Swanson, leave the door open."

She nodded and did as he asked before she headed to the break room. She grabbed a soda and a bag of chips and returned to her desk. She was waiting for calls from several agents in the Jacksonville area. She needed to make contact, determine what they knew about Gray Death production in Jacksonville, and ascertain if they knew how the product was being transported. From what she'd read online, there had been numerous deaths from the drug. One of the fatalities was a police officer. The patrolman had worn gloves but inhaled the fine powder which had escaped when the wrapping was opened. The shit was worse than pure heroin. It was so deadly, she wondered why the suppliers were pushing it. The product could kill a large portion of their clientele.

Her phone vibrated. She palmed it. "Agent Swanson."

"Hey Amber, got a message you called?" Terry Goldsmith's voice made her smile.

"Hey Terry, how are you doing?"

"Busy. You?"

"Same, but I've been permanently assigned to a Joint Task Force up here in Hope City."

"Demotion?" The man's concern was immediate.

"No actually, I asked for it. I needed to be home more."

"Ah, yeah I get it. I missed so damn much of my kids growing up, but you gotta pay bills, you know what I mean?"

"I do. Speaking of which, what do you know about Grey Death production in the Jacksonville area?"

He sighed in her ear. "That shit is insane. Whatever you do, get your first responders gloves and access to masks. They're using elephant tranquilizers in the shit."

"I heard that, too. Where the hell are they getting the tranqs?" She glanced up as Brody strode to the break room while talking with two of the other detectives.

"Rumor has it a big shipment for an elephant refuge in Tennessee was nipped."

"Excuse me, where?"

"You heard me. A huge preserve for the African and Asian elephants that are rescued in North America."

"Dang. Didn't know anything like that existed."

"Well, neither did I until we started tracking this shit. Anyway, this is all rumor, of course..."

Amber chuckled. "I got you. Not a soul will know where I'm pulling my info."

"Smart girl. Anyway, we've been watching. We know it's being cooked here, but no idea where it's made or how it's transported."

"How do you know it's being made down there?"

"Ah, three dead bodies, two executed and one OD'd after Jax PD arrived. There was a small amount of the shit found underneath a ransacked workbench. It was unwrapped and uncut. The equipment was missing, but you could tell where it had been located. Unfortunately, we haven't been able to get any information from our CIs on who's running the kitchen or where it went. We've got no idea where it's going or how it's getting there, so yeah, a whole lot of nada."

"I might have that end of the problem figured out. Would you be averse to sharing a bust? We can give you partial credit."

"At what point do you think I'd say no to that?" Terry chuckled.

"Well then, may I interest you in taking down

the Florida based portion of a potential interstate trafficking ring?"

"I think I could handle it. Is the Agency involved?"

"No more than you and I."

"I'd have to bring them in."

Amber cautioned, "When we get ready to move and not before. You know the glory mongers will swoop in if you give them a whisper of this information."

"Deal. How much off the books work am I going to be doing?"

"Right now, not much. I need you to examine smaller airports in the area. Probably with easy access to the city."

"They're flying the shit out."

"We believe so, but we are a long way from knowing for sure. You'll get a couple hours notification, and then it will be up to you to try to find where the planes are landing."

"Why don't you get a warrant and have the FAA get you the flight plans?"

"You need this thing called probable cause. When we get to that point, I'm sure the team will execute one, but this is in the roughest of planning stages."

"Okay, I get it, and I'm glad I'll have some time. I have a rookie who I need to kick out on his ass. It's sink or swim time for him."

"Not doing well?"

"Oh, according to him he is. He's one of these know-it-alls who doesn't need any help from a trainer." Terry snorted.

"You are the best training agent in the DEA. He's a schmuck if he doesn't realize it." Amber loved Terry and his wife. Since she'd joined the agency, they had taken her under their wing and treated her like family.

"Compliments will get you everywhere. How's my boy?"

"Gage is fine. What about your grandkids?"

"I have six now! I'm overrun in ankle biters." Terry laughed indulgently. "But damn it's nice to get them all hyped up on sugar and send them home with their parents. Truly a perk of being a grandparent."

"You are evil!" She laughed as he scoffed.

Terry's laughter settled down. "Give me as much heads up as you can. I'll do my best down here."

"I will. Hug Marla for me?"

"You got it. Take care of yourself."

"You, too." She disconnected the phone and shoved her fist into the air. *Wow, what a coup!* Terry was one of the sharpest agents she'd ever met. Before he transferred to Florida to be closer to his daughters, he'd taught her the ropes and so much more. She owed the man a bust like this, and he'd work his ass off in Florida. She could take it to the bank.

"Good call?"

"Real good." She glanced at Watson who was typing as he looked at her. "How do you do that?"

"Years of practice." He smiled and kept typing.

"What he isn't telling you is he is making a million mistakes." Rayburn flipped through a document he was reading.

"Bite me." Watson shot back

Rayburn pointed to the computer. "Bet you just typed that."

"Shit." Watson hit the delete key and Rayburn snickered.

"You two, I swear. I'm going to go brief Brody. We have trustworthy assistance in Florida."

"Fucking-A. About time we got a break. I'm reading up on Gray Death. This shit can be compressed into pills, too."

"I thought it was sold in rocks?" Watson stopped typing and glanced at Rayburn.

"Powder, rocks *and* pills." Rayburn reiterated.

"Pills would mean not only a cooking site but a processing point. A big operation." Watson started typing again.

"Don't think Peña knows the meaning of the word small." Rayburn's nose stayed buried in the information he was reading.

"I agree. I'll be back in a minute, going to tell Brody about our help in Florida." She headed across the bullpen and veered away from the line of sight of Anderson's office. Avoidance was her new mantra where that man was concerned. She lifted her hand to knock on Brody's door when she heard him chuckle, low and soft. "Yeah, okay. Dinner tonight. No, you're right it's been too long. Yeah, I've missed you, too." He turned around and shock sent his eyebrows north as he finished. "See you soon."

Her gut dropped. He was going on a date. Tonight. She blinked and then swallowed hard. The knowledge... hurt. But why should it? They weren't involved. She didn't have a claim on him, even though they had a child together. But a kernel of hope had already blossomed hadn't it?

Brody placed his phone on the desk, and he leaned forward. "What's up?"

"Ah..." *God, get a grip.* "I've recruited an agent in Florida to help us, off the books for now. He's damn good, and he'll keep this under wraps until the last moment."

"Good. I'm glad we have your resources available." He glanced at the clock and then back at her. "Let's call it for the day. We should have some answers on the house by tomorrow, and then we'll be able to work the particulars of the surveillance with the captain and get this case rolling."

She nodded and stepped back. "Okay. Night."

"Amber?" Brody's voice called her back to the office.

"She's a friend. Nothing more." His voice was low and quiet, and he didn't glance up from his computer.

She leaned against the door. "Okay." She glanced over her shoulder. Anderson's door was open. "May I come in and close the door?"

He glanced up at her from his desk and nodded. She pushed the door shut behind her and leaned against it. The shades on the windows were open so everyone in the pen could see them. "I'm sorry I overheard your conversation. It kind of threw me for a loop." She crossed her arms over her chest and looked at her shoes for a moment to collect her thoughts before she continued, "I know I don't have any claim on you. I want to assure you I'm not going to pull the jealousy card. The only thing I ask is if you do get involved with someone, please make sure it is serious before you introduce her to Gage."

"Noted and understood. I assume the same would apply to you?" He swiveled in his chair to face her.

"What?"

"You only introduce the men you're serious with to Gage, correct?"

With a very unladylike snort she replied, "I've never introduced anyone I've dated to Gage." There was a hope for a while, but the thought of a kid didn't thrill Darnell, and the relationship died quickly.

"Never?"

She shook her head. "Why?"

"I'm curious." He glanced past her and groaned. "Damn it."

"What?" She moved away from the door and turned.

"That damn tux. God, I'm going to owe more

than the damn thing's worth if I don't return it soon."

She chuckled and opened the door. "Maybe you should wear it to dinner. Get your money's worth from it."

Brody threw back his head and laughed. "Brianna's restaurant is nice, but not that nice."

"Then take it back before dinner."

"The store is on the other side of town." He glanced at the clock. "I'd never make it in time. Hey, you live over––"

"Oh, hell no, Sergeant King, I'm not your minion. Take it back on your own time." She laughed as she spun away, damn near colliding with Lieutenant Anderson as he exited his office. She stopped and stepped away immediately. Anderson glared at her and strode past. She glanced back at Brody. His eyes followed Anderson. She drew a fortifying breath and headed back to her six square feet of office space to retrieve her purse, phone and say good night to Watson and Rayburn. It had been one hell of a crazy day.

CHAPTER 10

Brody leaned back in the chair, replete from a fantastic meal and easy conversation.

"This restaurant gets better and better." Debbie took a small sip of wine.

"Brie has worked hard."

The decor, the food, the waitstaff, everything had improved since she bought it four years ago.

"I haven't seen her in ages. Is she here tonight?"

"She said if we lingered over drinks, she might get back in time. For some reason she's going to the City Council meeting tonight."

"Really? I wonder why?" Debbie took another bite of her dinner.

"I have no idea. Knowing Brie, she's championing some cause or another."

Debbie put down her fork and eyed the half-eaten portions on her plate. "I tried, but it's too much food. It beat me. So, let's talk about what brought us here." She lifted her wine glass and leaned back in her chair. "I can get you the paperwork to fill out. There are several units that need the money, but your unit is the single largest contributor to the forfeiture program. I can spin it and submit it. I'm pretty damn sure it will fly through the next department head meeting."

"Without Fenton's knowledge?"

"He's not a department head. He won't be notified until it is approved and your coffers start to get the trickle-down effect."

"Can he subvert the money, give it to other units under his control?"

She smiled and shook her head. "Nope. I'm in control of the allocations. If he attempts to move money, he has to go through me."

Brody leaned forward. "Deb, I don't want you to get into any trouble from this. Fenton is a vindictive asshole."

"Ha! As if. I have four Deputy Commissioners, a Chief of Staff and Legal Affairs Director on my side. Hell, I used to date the Commissioner's son. If he tries to stir up shit, he's going to find I have a lot more friends than he does. Doesn't he realize he'll never be more than what he is now? Everyone sees what he's doing. He's a worm."

And that is why he and Deb got along so well. They both called it like they saw it. "Thank you, then, for taking on our cause. We aren't asking for the moon, but perhaps the ability to upgrade equipment and pay for the hours we have to put in."

"Understandable." She leaned forward, put her wine glass down, and covered his hand with hers. "The night is still early. If we don't linger over drinks, we could have dessert back at my place." Her low sexy purr stretched across the short distance between them.

The proposition was expected. They'd hooked up from time to time after they went their separate ways. His smile slid from his face. "Normally I'd say yes, but there have been some developments in my life I need to work through."

Her hand slid from his. "Oh." Deb sat back and cleared her throat. "Is it serious, this development you need to work through?"

He shrugged. "I don't know, and I don't know if I'm being stupid for turning you down..."

"Oh, believe me, you're being stupid for turning me down." Deb smiled impishly at him.

"Okay, true, I am, but I need to make sure I'm not hurting anyone."

"Especially yourself. Regardless if we have sex or not, you're my friend. If you find someone to take the sadness inside of you away, go for it. Even if it means leaving our friendship in the dust." Deb slid her hand back on top of his. "Nice guys are hard to find. Good looking nice guys, who are demi-gods in bed? They're almost non-existent. Everyone has heard about them, but no one has ever caught one. I was fortunate enough to have one on the line for a short time, but you never belonged to me."

Why in the hell couldn't they have fallen in love? An image of Amber flashed through his thoughts. Yeah, that was why. He was a complete idiot for denying Deb, but damn it, he wanted Amber. Even with all the unresolved issues between them, their past, her decisions, Gage, his anger, her fear, he still wanted to know if she'd ever truly loved him. She said she had. He wanted to know if perhaps she still did. Her reaction at work when he was talking to Deb seemed to indicate she had some type of lingering attachment.

Was he being vain by hoping it was jealousy? Probably. Vain and unrealistic.

"Hey, where did you go just now?" Deb squeezed his hand.

"Sorry, thinking."

"Got it. I'm going to go powder my nose and then head home. It's been a wonderful night, Brody. Thank you for dinner."

"Let me see you out..."

"No need, the car is with the valet. Nurse your drink, and then visit with your sister. I know you don't get to see her often. I'll give you a call when the paperwork goes to the staff—and whoever she is, I hope she knows how lucky she is."

He stood as she left the table and gestured for the waiter. "Coffee."

The waiter took the dinner plates. "May I show you the dessert cart, sir?"

"No, thanks. Coffee for now." The waiter returned moments later and poured him a cup, leaving a small decorative silver pot with a delicate spout. He chuckled at the picture he must have made. Even 'dressed up' in good jeans and a button down, he got stares. He'd perfected his bad boy image. He was big, naturally so. With his frame and genetics bulking up was relatively easy, if you considered hitting the gym almost every night after work easy. He sipped the beverage and enjoyed the bitterness. He gave a chuff of laughter when he reached for the small silver pot. It looked like a child's toy in his hand.

Child's toy. Wow. He was a dad, and he was going to meet his son soon. He removed the picture of Gage from his shirt pocket. He didn't go anywhere without the picture. The first picture Amber had given him. His son. He traced a finger around the image on the glossy paper. He looked happy. The smile on his face was something else.

"Hey."

Brody jerked his head up. "Brie, sorry, I didn't hear you." He pocketed the photograph as his sister sat down.

"I could tell. You were studying that photo intently. Is it work related?" A waiter showed up with a glass of wine for her. "Thank you, Mark. How have things gone tonight?"

"Splendidly, ma'am. Chef is pleased, and the front of the house is running smoothly."

"Excellent. This table is my guest tonight."

"Indeed. I'll inform the wait staff."

"Thank you, but I can afford to buy dinner for myself and my date."

"Where is your date?" Brianna swung around; her long dark brown hair fell across her shoulder as she looked. "Who's your date?"

"I had dinner with Deb. It was business." He took another sip of his coffee. "What were you doing at a council meeting?"

She shook her head and took a sip of her wine before she said, "The city has an ordinance on the books which prohibits restaurants from giving perfectly good food to homeless shelters. It's an archaic law and forces us to throw good food away when it could go to feed people who don't have anything. If I have a surplus at the end of the night which can't be repurposed, it is ridiculous to throw it away." Brianna huffed and tapped her nails against her glass. "I've looked into it. Between the ten restaurants in a two-block radius we could supply enough pre-cooked dinners to feed the occupants of the shelter Tara runs. Every night, Brody. A warm meal for every man, woman, and child."

Brody loved the energy Brianna radiated. She was a passionate woman, but quiet where his other sister, Bekki, was loud. Brie and Bekki couldn't be more different. Brie was tall and curvy. She had long, dark brown hair and the King eyes. She was driven and successful, as was Bekki, but Bekki was model thin, had a short, trendy haircut and dominated any conversation she'd ever been in. The woman was tenacious, and her investigative reporting was getting better and better. Even though she still called when she wanted to know where to find information, her calls were growing less and less. Two very successful sisters, both passionate, both good looking, and both single. Thank God Brock had gotten married. The rest of them should get some kind of reprieve after that.

"Let me guess, you already have the logistics worked out on how to get the meals to the shelter."

"I do. Takeout containers for this purpose are tax deductible. There is a restaurant up the street, La Casita. They have a catering truck, and they will deliver the meals as long as Tara has someone to receive them. Of course, they'd be delivered at one or two in the morning, but she has staff in the shelter round the clock. They could open the kitchen. We stuff them into the walk-in coolers, and the next night, presto, a full meal. There is no downside to this."

Brody cocked his head. "Except, it is illegal."

"Yeah, except that. They said they'd take it into consideration and get a legal review." Her shoulders lowered as if the fight had left her. "I know what that means. They aren't going to change the ordinance."

Brody tapped the tabletop with his fingers. "You could ask Bekki to run an exposé on the amount of food wasted and the plight of the homeless in Hope City. Get her to ramp up the pressure by showcasing your innovative idea, and let everyone know the city council is the stopping point at this time. I mean, it doesn't cost anyone anything for this support, and Hope City has enough budget woes."

Brianna's eyes got big, and she blinked before a knowing smile spread across her face. "You are my favorite brother."

Brody laughed. "You told Brock the exact same thing last weekend at his wedding."

Brianna straightened her shoulders and flicked her wrist in an indignant flop. "That was then. This is now."

"Fickle."

"True." They both laughed at the running joke. "So, seriously, how are things going? It's good to see you out and about, even if it's a friendly date." She made air quotes around friendly and rolled her eyes.

"Deb is helping me with some paperwork for the section, and we hadn't talked in... wow, six months, I think. She agreed to help but wanted to get together to talk. We drove in separate cars, and she left after we ate. Nothing but friends."

"Can I be snoopy?" Brianna cupped her chin in her hand and stared across the table at him.

"When have you ever asked?" Brody laughed at her when she scrunched her nose up and rolled her eyes.

"Seriously, why didn't it work between you and Deb. You really seemed to like each other."

He shook his head. "Liking isn't loving."

"She still haunts you, doesn't she?"

He didn't need to ask who 'she' was. "If you only knew." He drew a deep breath. "She's working with me. She's been assigned to my team. She's the new DEA agent we were waiting for."

Brianna blinked. She picked up her wine glass and drank the remainder of the chardonnay before motioning Mark over. "Another please."

"Right away, ma'am." The waiter placed the wine glass on his tray and hurried away.

Brianna slowly turned back to him. "Tell me it's a lie. I'm going to punch you if it is, but damn it, tell me it's not true."

"She started the day Brock got married."

"Holy Hell. What are you going to do?"

"Well, we talked—"

"No, no, no, no, no." Brianna held up a finger. "Do not let the woman back into your life. She almost killed you last time."

"She didn't cause the accident."

"Who's talking about the accident?" She hissed and turned to smile tightly at Mark as he handed her another glass of wine. The man had the good sense to beat feet and get the hell away from the table. Brie was seething under her thin veneer of professionalism.

"She wasn't responsible, Brie."

"She tore out your heart. It changed you."

He couldn't argue the point. "Life changes everyone."

"She didn't come see you at the hospital, or after for that matter!"

"She did come to see me."

"When?"

"When I was in a coma, and then she tried again about two months after the accident. She went to Mom and Dad's looking for me. She asked if she could talk to me."

Brianna's mouth dropped open. "What did she

say?"

"I wouldn't talk to her back then. I should have."

"Why?"

"Maybe it would have answered questions I've been living for ten years." Hindsight was a ruthless motherfucker. Ten years wasted. He shrugged and changed the direction of his thoughts. "Are you going to be at dinner on Sunday?"

"Don't think I didn't see that change of topic, but yeah, I should be. Seriously Brody, when Mom learns Amber is back, and you're working with her, she's going to implode. A black hole of motherly concern. She'll have the hover-copter out, and you'll get four or five calls a day."

"Meh, Mom and I have come to an agreement. She can call, but if I'm busy, I'll call her back."

Brianna's eyes opened wide. "How in the world did you get her to agree to *that?*"

He laughed at his sister's bug-eyed stare. "I sat her down and explained I loved her, and I wasn't ignoring her, but sometimes I can't talk to her. When I was clear of whatever I was doing, I'd call her back, and I always do, unlike the rest of you."

Brie rolled her eyes again. "She's trying to set me up on a date."

"Not again!" Brody laughed but he couldn't help

but feel sorry for his sister. She'd been enduring her mom's matchmaking attempts, but some of the men their mother thought Brianna would like were... interesting.

"Oh, yeah. This one, his name is Chester by the way, is a friend of a friend of Sharon's. As if it isn't bad enough I have Mom trying to set me up, now she's enlisted Sharon's help." The McBrides had lived next to them for his entire life and his mom and Sharon McBride were best friends.

"So, what does Chester do?" Brody poured the rest of the coffee from the tiny pot into his cup.

"He owns a Crossfit gym." Brianna shrugged her shoulders. "Which is like a thousand rungs up the evolutionary ladder from the last guy, but really, I don't need my mom in my love life."

"Then sit her down and tell her politely you don't appreciate it."

"As if that would work."

"It worked for me when I was dating Amber and Deb." The only serious relationships he'd ever had.

"What you fail to realize is Mom is on a mission, and it is to get all of us settled down. She wants grandchildren. Now that Brock is married, she's taken aim at me. Mark my words, once I find a man, you'll be front and center in her sights."

Well maybe Sunday would take some of the pressure off Brie. He snorted and shook his head. It would also put his mother's full focus on Amber and Gage. On that note... "Hey, when I was with Amber... was Mom... harsh to her?"

"Harsh? No, I don't remember that. I think she wanted to get close to Amber, but the poor girl was so out of her element."

"What do you mean?"

"I think Amber didn't know how to act when Mom hovered, prodded, and asked highly personal questions, you know? We've grown up around it, and we're used to it."

He didn't remember it that way, but... "Kallie didn't have any issues with Mom, did she?"

"Hell no. But take a look at the difference. Kallie had been through hell and survived. She wasn't going to let Mom push her buttons or intimidate her, and she knows when letting Mom have her way will make things easier. Amber was so young. We're loud, and add in the McBrides, and we're a lot to take in. I think Amber wanted to fit in, only she didn't know how, you know? It made her uncomfortable, and her being ill at ease drove Mom crazy—which made the situation even more uncomfortable." Brianna took a sip of her wine. "Why?"

"Something Amber said when we were visiting."

"Yeah, well I hope you forgive me if I don't feel sorry for her. She ripped your heart out and disappeared. You guys were living together, and she leaves? Shows up two months later? Yeah, no matter how young she was, that's cold as Antarctica."

He was going to need someone on his side on Sunday. Someone on Amber's side. Brie was the logical choice, but he needed her to drop the anger on his behalf. "Brie, she came to the hospital as soon as she found out about the accident and sat with me when no one in the family was there, and she'd tried to call my cell. I got a new number, remember? She said she filled up my phone with messages. She went back to the apartment and looked for me, but I wasn't there. She tried to contact me at Mom and Dad's. I didn't respond."

"Bullshit. If she'd wanted to reach you, all she had to do was contact any of us. You made us promise not to contact her, but if she'd tried to find you, we would have made it happen."

"She did try. Mom told her I'd call if I wanted to

talk to her. I was so messed up from the wreck and from my own anger and hurt, I didn't call her. I wish I had."

"Why did it take her two months to try again? What was suddenly so important?"

Brody reached into his shirt pocket and retrieved the photo. "He was." He extended the photo.

Brie took the picture. She gasped softly, and her hand went to her mouth. Her eyes filled with tears, and she glanced at him. "You have a son?"

"Gage. He's ten. I'm going to meet him Saturday, and if all goes well, I'm going to bring him and Amber to the house on Sunday. I need your help, Brie. You have to help Amber and Gage to feel welcome. Mom doesn't know yet."

"Oh God. I'm an aunt? You're a father?"

"Yes." He smiled at her elation.

"Okay, well he is definitely going to take the focus off me and my man-less existence. Thank you in advance for that." She chuckled and once again stared at the picture. "He's adorable. Did Amber ever get married?"

"No. She's a single mom. She, Gage, and her sister live together in the little house in Parkside."

"Damn, a DEA agent and a single mom? I bet

she's changed, too, hasn't she?" His sister stared at him and then smiled. "She isn't going to need my help with Mom. If she's grown up enough to raise this little boy and be a professional law enforcement agent, she's strong enough to be her own woman, but I'll be there to support all of you." She sighed and shook her head. "You had no idea?"

"No. She told me Sunday."

"Are you happy?"

"Wow, happy? Yeah, that's in the mix. I'm so out of my depth here. I was shocked, then pissed at her for keeping him from me, then scared, like terrified scared. How do you talk to a ten-year-old?"

"The same way you talk to anyone else. Look, you don't have to be everything all at once. Be yourself, get to know your son and grow into the relationship. You're dating, you know. You'll both put on your best fronts and then as time slips by, he'll see you for who you really are, and you'll see him that way, too. The important thing is you'll always be connected. You're his dad."

A smile split his face. "Damn, you've been hanging around Tara too much."

"Hey, I'll have you know I don't need my best friend to clue me in on this one. Besides, Tara

McBride has fallen for Carter. I hardly ever see her anymore."

"Carter Fiske is a good detective and a hell of a guy."

"Ha, McBride and King brother approved, huh? Did you do the macho face off you've done with all my boyfriends?"

"It needed to be done."

"You guys are so full of yourselves. The McBride and King women are capable of picking partners without your help." She lifted her glass to her lips, smiling behind the rim of the glass.

"Is that why Mom and Sharon are fixing you up?"

"Don't be a dick, Brody. Hey... Sunday, the call you got, the one that pissed you off, was it Amber?"

"Yeah."

She studied the photo for a moment before she asked, "What did Dad say about all of this?

He glanced at her. "Why would you assume Dad knows?"

"Because you tell him everything, and don't try to deny it." She pointed the picture at him as she spoke.

"He's concerned, and elated, and pissed that I

KRIS MICHAELS

asked him not to tell Mom. As far as I know, he hasn't let it slip."

"You're going to spring this little guy on Mom?" Brie cocked her head.

"Well, yeah, I was planning on showing up with them."

"No. That would be bad." She shook her head back and forth and her eyes rounded.

"Why?"

"Mom needs time to prep for this. She'll need to spin out of control for a while, and when she's past the initial shock, you can bring them by."

"So, I'll talk to her Saturday night after I meet him, and I'm sure they'll be coming with me on Sunday." He shrugged. It shouldn't be a problem.

"I want to be there." Brie leaned forward. "I want to watch the fireworks."

"You're sadistic." He snatched Gage's photo away.

She laughed and stood up. "Totally. But the more people there, the more ways to put out the flames if she explodes. Now get out of here. My people want to clear the table."

He stood and opened his arms for a hug. Brie slipped into his embrace. "Congratulations, Brody.

I'm so happy for you. I'm here if you need anything, and I can't wait to meet him."

Amber smiled as she pushed the button to end the call. She glanced at the clock. Damn, it was almost one o'clock in the morning. She and Brody had been talking for over four hours. She stretched, pushed back the sheet covering her, and headed into the kitchen. She opened the refrigerator door and grabbed a plastic jug of orange juice.

"You'd better use a cup, or I'm telling."

Amber jumped and gasped, "Holy Shit, Dawn!"

"What? I wasn't quiet. You were lost in your head. Must be all the late night talking with Brody." Dawn pushed past her and grabbed the milk from the fridge, putting the orange juice back. "Warm milk this late. OJ is going to spike your blood sugar."

"I don't like warm milk." Amber reached back in the fridge and grabbed the chocolate syrup. "Cocoa."

"Deal." Dawn poured milk into a saucepan and squeezed a long drizzle of chocolate syrup into the pan and then handed everything back to her to put away.

"So, every night this week, huh?" Dawn grabbed a spoon and stirred the contents of the saucepan.

Amber smiled and sat down at the little kitchen table. "Yeah, it's been... wonderful and so damn sad at the same time. I made such a huge mistake, didn't I?" Guilt had been beating her up. If bruises were visible from her mental slug fest, she'd look like a walking contusion.

"Well, obviously *now* I'm going to say, yeah. Two months ago? No. I wouldn't have agreed with you. You did what you felt you had to do. Did I agree with it? No, I was never comfortable with your decision."

Amber got up and fetched two cups for the cocoa. "Why?"

Dawn looked up at her and narrowed her eyes. "Honestly?"

"Always."

Her sister poured the warm mixture into the cups, and they sat down before Dawn said, "I can remember when you told me you were pregnant. I thought if what had happened to you had happened to me, I would probably have terminated the pregnancy."

She gasped and reached for her sister, placing a hand on her arm. "You never said anything--"

"Because it wasn't my place to say anything. Look, you made a big mistake by saying no and running away from Brody without discussing why you were afraid. It was a monumental blunder. I'm not going to downplay it, but when you sat with him in the hospital, called him, went to his parents' house to talk to him? He ignored you. Poof gone. Hell, he packed up the apartment and left your stuff. No note, no nothing."

The need to defend Brody reared its head. "Yeah, we both made mistakes."

"I'm not denying that, am I?"

"Well, no."

"And if I had been in your shoes, I don't know that I would have been willing to raise a child by myself."

The admission floored her. She shook her head and stared at her half sister. Emotion pooled in both of their eyes. She whispered, "I've never been by myself; you've always been here for me. I'd like to think I would have been there for you, too."

Dawn sniffed and nodded. "You would have stuck by me, but I meant raising a child without a partner. I know people do it all the time, but being that strong? Saying I'm having this baby, and I'm going to make a lifetime commitment to it and take on the responsibility of making a child a decent human being? Wow, it takes strength, and at that point in my life, I don't know that I would have been as strong as you were. So, I'm not going to sit here and judge you. Stop beating yourself up. You did what you felt was right for you and Gage. You stepped up when you thought his dad didn't want a thing to do with either of you. You had two ways to handle the pregnancy, and in my opinion, you chose the hardest one."

Amber shook her head. "The choice, it was easy. I loved Brody. His child? It was a piece of him I was able to keep."

"Loved or love?" Dawn took a sip of her cocoa.

Amber blinked and tried to catch up. "What?"

"You said you loved Brody. I've been listening to you every night this week. The soft laughter, the long hours of talk. You're still in love with him, aren't you?" Dawn set her cup down.

She took a drink of her cocoa to give herself some time to compose a response. Finally, she shrugged. "I don't know if I ever stopped loving him."

"Are you hoping for more than just Brody getting to know Gage?" Dawn took another drink.

"Maybe? I guess? I'm not sure that's what Brody wants, though."

"Have you asked him?"

"No!" She glared at her sister.

"Okay, okay, don't have a coronary and don't wake up Gage. He'll want cocoa and then food. That kid is always hungry." Dawn grumped, "You know communication between the two of you has been a stumbling block. Maybe you should work on that."

"We are. We're talking about how things were for me and for him. We've spent hours on the phone. At work things are good. We've been able to joke around, be together without the anger and the egg shells. He even called me after a work date this week."

Dawn stopped with her mug halfway to her mouth. "A work date?"

"Yeah, that's what I thought too, but he's trying to get funding for the team and a woman he used to date is the person who has access to the purse strings, or rather putting the information in front of those who control the strings."

"Interesting. Well, you need to figure out what

you both want and I'm going to make myself scarce on Saturday. Give you all some family time."

"You don't have to do that." She didn't want Dawn to feel like she was pushing her out the door.

"Oh, yeah I do. I'm going to go shopping, have dinner, and maybe catch a movie before I come home. If he's still here, I have an amazing book I need to read. You get those two guys together."

Amber lifted the cocoa cup and smiled. "A step at a time, right?"

Dawn snorted into her mug.

"What?" Amber blinked at her when she started laughing.

Dawn took her cup to the sink and rinsed it out. "Nothing... the two of you don't know how to take a single step at a time. You sprint and then crash. Don't crash this time, okay? It would break Gage's heart. Night."

She listened to her sister pad down the hallway. Unfortunately, if she didn't get it right this time, Gage's wasn't the only heart that would break. Again.

CHAPTER 11

B rody put Wilma into park and turned off the engine. Fuck, he was nervous. He was meeting his kid. *You can do this. Play it cool.* Yeah, right. Giving his palms another quick wipe against his jeans, he grabbed the triple chocolate brownies and a small gift he'd put together for Gage and got out of the truck.

Amber came from the back of the house, opening the gate, a smile on her face. "Nervous?"

"God, is it that obvious?" Brody drew a deep breath and handed her the pink box containing the brownies. He kept the small wrapped package.

"No, but I figured if I was nervous, and Gage was nervous, you may be freaking a little, too. Thank you for this." She peeked in the box. "Oh man, three more miles tacked on the end of my run tomorrow."

"You said he liked chocolate." He shrugged and peeked around her and froze. Amber glanced over her shoulder and smiled. "Well there you are. Gage, come here, bud." Amber held her hand out in invitation, and the boy moved toward them. He shoved his hands in his front pockets and examined him like he was a bug under a microscope.

"Gage, this is your father, Brody. Brody, your son, Gage."

"Hey." They both said the same thing at the same time, and Amber laughed. "Yeah, you two are most definitely related. Come on. I want to get the burgers on before you eat all the chips."

"We have two bags." Gage sent her a mischievous grin.

"Not my point." She motioned for Brody to follow them. They walked through the side yard and into the back. A nice sized concrete pad had lawn furniture arranged with an umbrella anchored in the middle of a table. A BBQ off to the side was hot, and the smell of charcoal was enticing. Music played softly from somewhere inside the house.

"This is very nice." He motioned to the set up.

"Thanks." She nodded toward Gage who was sitting at the table in the shade. "Go, visit."

Brody took a deep breath and nodded. He took a chair across from his son.

"You're like, bulked and tall."

Brody laughed. "Yeah, it runs in the family. You're good sized, too."

"I'm the tallest in my class. What's that?" He pointed to the small wrapped box he held in his hand.

"Well, I figured you'd have questions about my family, so..." He handed the container to Gage and watched the boy rip through the paper.

He lifted the lid on the box and opened the photo album.

"That is your grandma and grandpa on my side. My mom and dad."

Gage looked at the photo carefully. "Are they still alive? My Grandma Dot and Grandpa Wallace aren't."

"I'm sorry to hear that, dude. My mom and dad are alive. My dad is the Police Commissioner for Hope City."

"Like the Chief of Police?"

"Exactly, different title, though. He is in charge of all the police officers in the city."

"Cool. Cops are badasses."

"Language." Amber's voice spun both of them toward her for a moment. Gage turned back to him and rolled his eyes. The gesture reminded him of his sister.

Gage turned the page. "Who are they?"

"Those are your aunts and uncles. That is my brother, Brock. He's a homicide detective. This is my sister, Brianna. She owns a restaurant. This one is my brother, Blayze. He's a fireman."

"Blayze? And he's a fireman? Really?" Gage's suspicious question made him laugh.

"Yeah, we call him Blay, but his full name is Blayze Benedict King. He's named after some great grandfather on my mom's side." The kid wouldn't get the BB King reference, but that was another thing that Blay was teased with growing up.

Gage stared at the picture and then turned the page. "I know her! She's on TV!"

"That's my little sister, Bekki."

"That's cool." Gage turned the page and stared at the group King/McBride photo. "Dude, that's a lot of people."

"Those are our neighbors, the McBrides. Kyle, this guy right here was my best friend growing up. Sean and Brock are best friends. They're the same age, and Blay, Rory, and Erin—Rory and Erin are twins—are the three musketeers. Bekki and Caitlyn, these two, are the same age, too."

Those eyes that looked so much like his turned up and stared at him. "Did *you* always know your dad?"

"Gage!" Amber's shocked gasp didn't break their connection. He extended a hand, silencing whatever she was going to say. "No, it's a fair question." He knew the kid would be hard to win over, but he wasn't expecting the hard-hitting questions so soon, although he'd rehearsed several responses. He tapped the picture book. "Yes, I did. My mom and dad were married before my brother was born. Not like your mom and me."

"But you wanted to marry her. She said you asked, and she freaked." The kid shot a glance at his mom.

"Mistakes were made on both sides of that issue."

"Do you still love her? She said she's always going to love you because of me, but do you love her?"

"Your mom is special enough that I asked her to marry me. When I asked her, I loved her with all my heart."

"But you don't now?"

"I haven't seen your mom for longer than you've been alive. My feelings for her at this point are... complicated. Like your feelings about me. I bet you're kinda excited, a little afraid, and sometimes mad, aren't you?"

Gage shrugged. "Maybe. Is that how you feel about Mom, too?"

"Yes. You know what? All those emotions are okay."

"Mom said you were nervous. Why?"

Brody shrugged. "What if you don't like me?"

Gage looked up at him and narrowed his eyes. "Why wouldn't I like you?"

"Well, I could suck at baseball, or lacrosse, or football."

"Do you?"

Brody smiled. "Nah, I'm pretty da--, uh darn good at them." He glanced at Amber. She was smiling as she flipped the burgers.

"For reals? Football, too?"

"Yep. I played varsity quarterback in high school."

"So, like, we could throw the ball together?" Gage's body nearly vibrated to the front of his chair.

"Sure. I can teach you how to throw a tight spiral. Do you have a ball?"

"In the garage! Mom, I'm getting my football!" Gage tore around the side of the house.

Amber moved the cooked burgers to the side of the grill. "Very well done. Honestly, I'm impressed."

"Don't be. I nearly shit myself when he asked about my family."

"You did great. I'm putting the burgers in the house to keep warm. Everything will hold except his excitement."

"Here! Here it is!" Gage flew around the corner and slid to a stop in front of him. The boy pushed the ball at him and took off into the backyard. Brody smiled and waited for Gage to turn around, lobbing a perfect spiral straight at the boy. Gage tried to catch it, but it went through his grasp and dropped to the grass.

"Dang it!"

Brody trotted to where Gage was picking up the ball. "Hey, let's try something, okay? Catching it with your hands is a skill that you develop. Until you get there, and believe me, you *will* get there, you can use your body to trap it, your arms to hold it, and your hands to secure it. So, if it comes at you like this––" He held the ball and slowly pushed it toward Gage, folding the boy's arms with his free arm, as he instructed, "--what are you going to do?"

Gage made a perfect basket for the ball to fall into and then grasped it to his chest.

"Perfect. We're going to do that over and over until we can move further and further away. It's all about getting comfortable with the form of the ball and how it's thrown. Once you get that, you'll be able to catch it without a problem. Okay?"

"Yeah." Gage's smile split his face. "Thanks."

"You got it." Brody stepped back about six feet and threw the ball.

Amber sat at the table and watched her son and his father. They'd played ball all afternoon, talking between themselves as the ball went back and forth. Gage was catching everything Brody threw to him, and his return throws were getting better. They'd taken twenty minutes for lunch and were right back at it.

"It seems to be going well." Dawn slipped into a chair beside her with two glasses of wine, handing one to her. "Damn, Brody filled out, didn't he?"

"Yeah, he's like double the size he was when we were together, and they are doing really well. They've been talking all afternoon."

"About what?"

"Everything. Favorite colors, television shows, athletes, sports, food, his family, Gage's friends, his school, what he likes to do when he's not at school." Amber reached for her glass and took a sip.

"So, things are a go for the trip to Woodbloom tomorrow?" Dawn's question pierced her happy bubble.

"Yeah. I'm really not looking forward to that."

"Want me to come with?" Dawn took a sip of her wine and sighed contentedly.

Yes, she would love the moral support, but... "No. This is something I need to do. I'm not that girl anymore."

Dawn chuckled as Gage ran forward and tackled Brody. "You're right, you're not. You've got this." She stood and looked down at Amber. "You could have all of this."

Amber shook her head. "I don't know if Brody can ever forgive me."

"You don't know that. You could tell him what you still feel. Be vulnerable to him for once. You might be surprised what happens. I'm going to go inside and let you have the rest of your family time." She sauntered into the house and turned on the back porch lights, illuminating the yard.

Gage ran up to her. "Mom, can we go to Brody's house sometime? It's an old warehouse. He fixed it up, and his brother has video games."

"Sure, we can do that. Boy, you are a sweaty mess."

"Yeah, it was great." He turned and high-fived Brody.

"It looked like a blast, but I have to be the party pooper. You need to take a shower and clean up before dinner."

"Awww, Mom."

"Hey, do what your mom says. We'll have more opportunities to work on your skills."

"Tomorrow?" Gage's excitement poured off him.

Brody glanced at her and cocked an eyebrow. She gave him the slightest nod. He smiled at her and then winked at Gage. "How about tomorrow we have a football game with my brothers and sisters. It's only touch, but if the neighbors are around, it's a good time."

Gage spun around, "Can we, Mom?" His eyes were glowing with happiness and excitement.

"Sure."

He grabbed her around the neck. "Thank you, thank you, thank you!"

"Gah! Stinky boy pits! Go shower now!"

"Kay! See yah, Brody! Thanks!" He raced into the house.

Brody dropped into the chair and opened his mouth to speak, but Gage ran back to the porch. He grabbed his football and the photo album. "See yah!" He raced back into the house.

"My God, he *is* the energizer bunny." Brody dropped his head back in mock exhaustion.

"He always has been. It went well today, didn't it?" She took a sip of her wine. "Would you like a beer or wine? We don't have anything stronger in the house."

He motioned to the cooler that held waters from earlier. "I'll grab one or two of those." A groan came from him when he moved from the chair. "Damn, I think I used muscles that I forgot I had." He opened the cooler and fished for two bottles of water.

"Your arm's going to be sore. You had to have thrown that ball a thousand times."

"Yeah, but he was into it." Brody sat down and cracked the seal on the first bottle, drinking half of it.

"True. That photo album was a great idea." She drew her feet up into the chair with her.

"I saw that on a documentary once. A woman had lost her short-term memory, and they built her an album so she could remember who people were. I figured if he knew in advance who the people were he was going to meet, he'd have an easier time." Brody downed the rest of the water and crushed the bottle before capping it.

"Do your mom and dad know yet?"

"I've talked to Dad, and I've let Brianna know. She's going to be there. I wanted you to have someone besides me and Gage in your corner."

She stopped with her wine glass halfway to her lips. "Why?"

"You'd mentioned that you didn't think my mom really liked you. I asked Brie if she thought that was the case."

"And did she?" Amber put the wine glass back down.

"No. She thought you didn't know how to deal with Mom's hover-copter persona and that maybe the entire family was intimidating."

"No shit." She dropped her legs back down and sat up.

Brody laughed outright. "Well, tell me what you're thinking, why don't you?"

"I've no problem with that—now. Then? Well, I was different then."

"We both were." Brody knocked his knee against hers. "Still like popcorn?"

"Oh, God yes!" Amber groaned, "But I can't eat it for dinner now because I have a son. We have a protein, a starch, a veg and a fruit at every meal. Nutrition. It's a parent thing. What about you? Still living on pizza?" She nudged his knee back. His strong leg didn't even move; she kept her knee resting beside his.

"No, not at all. I haven't had pizza since Blay made some... hell that was a couple months ago."

"Blay is staying with you?"

Brody nodded. "When he's not at the firehouse or out with one of his women. That man has a stable full of ladies. But, I have more than enough space, and he cooks dinner when he's there, so it's a good swap. He's saving for a down payment on a house. Brock is the only one that isn't looking at putting down roots in the form of a house, but he and Kallie seem happy living downtown in their apartment."

"Where is the... warehouse?" She tried not to let the shock and disbelief tinge the question.

"Ha! You sounded so much like my mom right there. Seriously, it was a great investment even though I didn't know about the revitalization of the inner harbor that was starting when I bought it. The place was structurally sound, was coded as residential and business, and has a water view. Well, it has a water view now that I installed windows and sliding glass doors."

"How could you afford to buy an entire warehouse?"

"When my grandfather passed, he left each of us kids some money. Not much, but enough to put a down payment on the place. So, I bought it, and I squeezed every dime from my paychecks for the last eight years to refurbish it. At first, I built one room that I could lock and lived in it. Each paycheck, I'd buy what I could afford, and I've refurbished the entire building. What I didn't know how to do, I hired out. The electrical and plumbing were the most expensive. It took two years to pay off the debt those two jobs put on my plastic."

"Sounds like a huge project."

"It keeps me sane. Gave me something to do. So now I have rentals, apartments that are below mine. They pay the mortgage for the building, and I'm able to breathe... finally. I pinched every penny, but it was worth it."

"Sounds nice." She reached for her wine again.

"It is. I've been meaning to ask, do you need anything, I mean for Gage? I've been looking at my financials, and I can start making payments, you know for support. Back pay I'll have to work on. My savings is gone, but I have equity in the property now. I could get a loan."

"No. We don't need anything. Eventually, Gage is going to want to go to college. I'll take help paying for that." She chuckled. "We don't have riches, but what we have is enough."

"I'd still like to help out. Something every month." Brody opened his other water.

"You do what you feel you can do. Every penny will go to him or into a savings account for him." She ran her finger around the rim of her glass. "I wish I'd been braver back then."

"I do too, but we can't change the past. We can only live in the present."

She drew a breath and held it for a moment.

"Yeah, I know, but if I would have told you, then maybe we would be a family today."

He leaned forward, held the water bottle in his hands, and placed his elbows on his knees. "That would have been the dream, right?"

"A perfect dream. I miss you." She held his stare. Please God, let him see the regret and love she felt for him.

"A perfect dream." He echoed the words before he stood up and tossed the empty water bottle into the trash, not addressing her comment about missing him.

Well, that shut that door didn't it?

"I'm heading to the parents'. I'm telling Mom about Gage tonight, so she'll be able to land the hover-copter before we get there tomorrow. I'll pick you guys up at three?"

"Yeah, that'd be great. We'll be ready." She stood and walked him back to the front of the house through the side yard. They could hear Gage talking animatedly inside. "He's so excited."

Brody turned, and she bumped into him. He caught her, pressing her against him for a moment. His eyes locked with hers in the fading light. "Yeah, I know the feeling. I missed you, too. So damn much."

He eased forward, and then shook his head, pulling away. She could have sworn, for a second, he was going to kiss her. "'Night." He dropped his arm from her waist and spun, heading toward the front of the house.

"'Night," she called, and watched him walk through the front yard and drive away. She closed the gate and flopped back against it. Damn, what she wouldn't give to feel that man's lips against hers again.

CHAPTER 12

Brody drove into the driveway and smiled. He could see the lights on in the backyard. He, Blay, and Kyle McBride had strung small fairy lights this spring and his mom and Sharon McBride loved the effect. If the lights were on, that meant his parents and the McBrides were in the back, relaxing. He turned off the truck and headed to the backyard.

"Hey! What are you doing here on a Saturday night?" His mom sprang from her chair and hugged him.

"Well, I was wondering if I could talk to you."

"Oh, we can go back to the house." Sharon started to rise from her chair, motioning for Colm, her husband, to get up.

Brody stopped her. "No, it's okay. I'm sure Mom will tell you what I'm going to say anyway."

His mother laughed and swatted at him as she sat down by his dad. His father arched an eyebrow in question, and he nodded as he sat down across from his mom. "Mom, do you remember after my accident when Amber came to the house and wanted to talk with me?"

His mother's expression closed off immediately. "Yes. Why?"

"Well, I should have listened to you. I should have called her." He cleared his throat and removed the small stack of photos from his shirt pocket. "She was pregnant. I have a ten-year-old son. His name is Gage, and I met him today."

The sounds of nocturnal insects filled the vast expanse of silence after his mother and Sharon gasped in unison. Brody held the photos out to his mother. Sharon gripped Colm's hand, and his father placed a hand on his mom's back as she reached forward to take the pictures. She gasped again when she saw Gage.

"Oh, he is the spitting image of you!" She wiped at tears but didn't say anything else until she'd finished looking at each picture. She handed them to Sharon and drew a deep, ragged breath before she looked at him. "How did you find out?"

Brody braced himself and launched into the retelling of the story. Four sets of eyes stared at him when he finished.

"She should have told you. It wasn't right to keep him from us." His mom's tears streamed down her face. "What have I ever done to make her think I didn't like her?" She looked from Brody to Sharon, Colm, and then to his dad. "Am I such an ogre?"

"No way, you're a fantastic mom, but you have to remember she was young and brought up in a vastly different way than we were. Her mother wanted nothing to do with her. She thought Amber ruined her life so Amber had no real foundation. You're a great mom, but you do tend to..."

Hannah finished his sentence, "Stick my nose into my children's business."

Sharon added, "And hover."

Colm fake-coughed his comment, "Dominate the conversation."

Brody nodded. "You do tend to take over."

His mom's mouth dropped open, and she stared at the people surrounding her. "Really?"

"Yes, but in the best possible way." Sharon smiled, leaned in, and hugged his mom.

"Am I really that much of a busy body?"

"No, dear, never you." His dad's over-the-top denial provided the comic relief the night desperately needed.

His mom swatted his dad, and the man drew her into a hug, kissing the top of her head. "When can we meet him?"

Brody smiled and looked directly at his mom. "Well, if it is all right, I can bring Gage and Amber tomorrow. We could maybe have a family football game in the backyard and cook out? Something casual, so everyone feels comfortable?"

"That's an excellent idea." His mom stood and extended a hand to Sharon. "Come on, we need to decide what to cook. Oh!" She spun toward Brody. "Does he have any allergies?"

"Not that I'm aware of, and he loves chocolate."

"Wonderful!" Sharon clapped her hands. "I can make my Death by Chocolate Trifle!"

"Perfect, let's make a double batch. We need to call the kids and invite them. Goodness, maybe a triple batch. Oh, let's do steaks," Hannah added as they walked toward the house.

"Baked potatoes or potato salad?" Sharon opened the door as she asked.

"Salad has mayo, and it is supposed to be hot tomorrow, but we can put it on ice or in a cooler--" The door shut behind them.

"Well, that went better than I anticipated." Brody released a long exhale.

"Wait for it. She's excited now. About two o'clock this morning, she's going to wake me up and start asking me the hard questions." Chauncey chuckled. "How was today?"

Brody smiled at his father and Colm. "It was amazing. He's a fantastic kid. My God, the energy that boy has is ridiculous. I taught him how to catch a football, the right way, and he's got a good sized hand, so his spiral is going to be awesome with some practice. He's smart, and he asked a thousand questions. We talked and threw that damn ball all afternoon. I'm going to need a couple muscle relaxers tomorrow."

"How are you and Amber getting along?" Colm rose from his chair. "Wait, don't answer that. I'm getting a refill. This has turned into an interesting evening. Chauncey, Brody, can I pour you one?"

His father handed Colm his rocks glass. "Small portion, please."

Brody nodded. "Small also, please. I need to drive home."

"Will do." Colm strode to the back door. His mother and Sharon's excited voices filled the air for a moment.

"You're pretty protective of Amber. That's a recent change." His father crossed his legs and leaned back in his chair.

"Every time I've mentioned her name, people get hostile. I mean, I appreciate the support, but she wasn't the one who caused that accident. I could have driven slower. Hell, I could have let her have time to settle down without following her. She wasn't responsible for what happened any more than I was."

Chauncey smiled. "That's a revelation, isn't it?"

He nodded. "Yes. I guess it comes with examining the past rather than ignoring it." He knew all the facts now. He still needed to wade through all the emotions, his attachment to Gage, and yes, his feelings for Amber because he still had them. The tough part was trying to determine if what he felt for her was an echo from the past or feelings that had lived through the annihilation of their relationship.

"Funny thing about the past. The further away

from it we get, the easier it is to look at." His dad reached toward him and put a hand on his shoulder. He immediately felt the warmth of that big hand. "Make sure you don't romanticize it, though. You both made mistakes. Make sure you examine them. Drag them out into the light of day and talk about them, otherwise you could make the same ones again."

Brody angled his head to look into his father's eyes. "I still care for her."

"I know you do. You never stopped."

Brody drew a deep breath before he asked, "Am I being a fool?"

"No son, you're not."

Colm came from the house carrying three glasses and distributed them before he sat down. "So, what are we talking about?"

"Fools and women." His dad lifted his glass, and he and Colm followed suit. "To the women in our lives who tolerate fools like us."

Brody took a sip of his bourbon. He didn't want to be tolerated. What he wanted hadn't changed in ten years. He stared at the tumbler in his hand. Yeah, he was a damn fool.

~

Gage padded down the hall to the front room and sat down on the sofa. His hair was wet and going a million different directions, and his pajamas rode up to his ankles. He grew so fast. She needed to buy him some new ones. "Did you have a good day?"

"Yeah, Brody is cool. He's really good at football. Whatcha watching?"

"Reruns. You want the remote?" She'd let him watch a few minutes of television to help him unwind. He'd had an emotional day even though he didn't know it.

"Nah. This is okay." He flopped onto his side and propped his head up on his elbow. "It was weird."

Amber leaned back in the couch and plopped her feet onto the cushion. "What's that?"

Gage moved his head in his hand so he could see her. "Meeting him."

"Why's that?"

"Cause we're strangers; well, not now, but we were." He turned back to the television and smiled at the sitcom.

She sighed. It was hard for everyone, but Gage seemed to like Brody. "You seemed to get along well."

"Yeah. I like the photo book he gave me. That was cool." Gage yawned and his entire body shuddered.

She gave a hum of agreement and watched the show until it went into commercial. She muted the television. "What do you think about going to meet your grandparents tomorrow?"

Gage lifted up. "Why? Did you change your mind?"

"No, I wanted to make sure you really wanted to go and weren't caught up in the moment."

Gage sat quiet for a while. "Do you want to go?"

"Sure, it will be fun." *Interesting, nerve-wracking, terrifyingly awkward.* "We don't have to go if you don't want to. No pressure."

"I want to go, but..."

"But?"

"What if they don't like me?"

"What? Why wouldn't they like you?"

"They didn't like you."

She sat shell-shocked. "Who told you that?"

"I heard you and Aunt Dawn talking. You said that Brody's mom didn't approve of you."

"Oh honey." How the hell did she explain her relationship with Brody's mom? "You know maybe she didn't, but maybe that is on me."

"Why?"

"Lord above, that's your favorite word isn't it?"

He smiled and nodded.

"Well, I think I was more afraid of not being what she *expected* me to be, rather than being myself."

His face screwed up. "What's that mean?"

"I tried to be someone I wasn't. I was pretending because I was afraid that his family wouldn't like me. I felt, I don't know, out of place I guess when I was with them. They are a big family, and maybe I was intimidated. I don't know. But I do know that I acted differently when I was around them. Maybe that is why your grandma and I didn't really hit it off."

"So, she doesn't like you?"

"No, we like each other. We weren't really close, though, you know?"

"Like friends, but not best friends." Gage yawned again.

"Right. Like that." She flicked the remote at the television and turned it off. "Come on Mr. Football Star. Bedtime."

Gage got up off the couch and padded ahead of her to his room. He slid into his bed and she kissed him on the forehead. "'Night kiddo. I love you."

"Love you, too." Gage snuggled into his pillow. "Hey, Mom?" She stopped at the door. "When do I call Brody Dad?"

Her heart skipped a beat. "Whenever it feels right to you."

"Okay. 'Night."

"'Night." She shut his door, leaving it open an inch or two. She wandered down the hall and sat down on the couch. The silence of the room surrounded her in a soft cocoon of solitude. The magnitude of today settled in the middle of her chest. Her son had met his father. She'd imagined how such an event would play out. A smile tilted the corners of her mouth. Never in a million years would she have thought they would have literally played and talked for hours on end. There were no awkward silences between them after they started to play. None. They slotted together as if they belonged together. Well… they did, didn't they?

A tiny niggling of jealousy ate at her, and she batted it away with a firm mental slap. She wouldn't begrudge either of the males in her life the time to get to know each other. She'd done enough to keep them apart. Damn it, she wanted there to be a bridge, some way to negotiate the past and have a future. She closed her eyes and shook her head. A foolish desire, and yet it burned hot and bright.

CHAPTER 13

"Are you sure?" Brody asked her again as they waited for Gage to use the restroom before they headed to his mom and dad's house.

"I'm positive. It was nice of Brianna to agree to be my buffer, but I don't need one." She hoped. Brody's mom had always intimidated her, but it was time for her to lift her head up and be proud of her son and herself.

"She said she'd try to get someone to come down and watch the plumber."

Amber chuckled. "I'm okay, honestly. Brianna needs to take care of her restaurant, and taking care of a backed-up drain in the kitchen is way more important than standing guard over me. I'll be fine."

"Ready! Oh, should I bring my football?" Gage stopped two steps from them, his eyes wide as he waited for an answer.

"That would be great."

"Okay! Be right back!" He tore off down the hall.

"He's excited."

"He's also scared." She'd fielded a hundred questions, most of them variations of 'what if they don't like me?'

"Of what?"

"That your family won't like him."

"Why would he think that?"

"Because he's ten? Even though he's bigger than most kids in his grade, he's still young. He's worried, so anything you can say that would ease that fear would be--"

"Got it!" Gage barreled toward them again.

"Okay, then let's head out. I know your grandma and grandpa are so excited to meet you." Brody opened the door for them.

"They are?" Gage nearly twisted in half trying to see Brody.

"Of course. My brother, Blay, the fireman is going to be there and so is my little sister, Bekki. You said you've seen her on television, right?"

Amber ushered Gage into the truck and helped him connect the middle seat belt. "Yeah, she's a reporter."

"Right. Do you want to know a secret about her?" Brody waited for her to get in the truck, holding the door open for her.

"What?"

"She stinks at football. Never get put on her team." Brody wiggled his eyebrows and shut the door, jogging around the front of the truck.

Gage laughed and glanced up at her. She winked at him and smiled. "See, I told you, they are excited to meet you."

Brody opened the driver's side door and jumped in.

"Who else is going to be there?" Gage rolled his football in his hands as he spoke.

"Well, I know our neighbors will be there. We grew up with their kids. Between the two families, there were eleven of us kids."

"The picture. That's a lot of kids." The awe in Gage's voice was almost comical.

"It got kind of crowded at times, but it was always fun. My older brother and his new wife are stuck at work. They went on a honeymoon, and now they are both catching up, but they want to meet you. Brock and Kallie are police officers, too. Homicide detectives."

"Really?"

"Yep."

"And your other brother is a fireman."

"Correct." He held up his fist, and Gage bumped it with his.

"Why did he get named after a fire again?" Gage rolled his football in his hands.

"He didn't, actually. Blayze is my great great grandfather's name on my mother's side. Or something like that. An old family name."

"Oh, yeah, I remember. Why does everyone's name start with a B?"

"That's a family tradition on my dad's side. I have three sets of cousins, and all their names start with either J, N, or K."

"That's cool. Where did you go to school?"

Amber listened as Brody and Gage talked. The conversation was happy and easy. She was delighted and at the same time a little envious at how easily Brody accepted Gage into his life when he'd let her go so long ago. And of course, then she felt *guilty* about feeling *envious.*

"Right, Mom?"

"Sorry, what?" She zoned back into the

conversation.

"I was supposed to go fishing with Johnny and his dad."

"Right, but something came up." She smiled at him and drew a deep breath.

"No! Stop!" Gage put his hand over her mouth. "You don't wanna hear her sing."

Brody laughed and turned into the driveway of his parent's home. "Oh, believe me, I've heard her sing. Does she still sing in the shower?"

"Yes! It's so embarrassing."

"Hey! I can sing." Amber tried desperately to look offended, but anyone who'd heard her knew she couldn't carry a tune in a bucket.

"No, you can't." They both answered at the same time. Gage and Brody high-fived and laughed as they clambered from the driver's side door. Oh God, her heart swelled ten times the size it was two days ago.

"Come on, Mom," Gage called.

She shook herself from the moment and followed them into the backyard.

The swarm of people she'd expected didn't happen. Hannah and Chauncey King were on the back porch with Blay and Bekki. She was so proud of Gage. He was such a little man. He pulled out the 'Yes, sirs' and 'No, ma'ams' and charmed everyone with his mischievous smile. The neighbors migrated from their home about ten minutes after they arrived. She recognized Kyle McBride, one of Brody's best friends. She was reintroduced to Erin and Rory McBride, the twins who were the same age as Blay.

It took about an hour longer than she figured it would, but Hannah wandered out to where she sat, watching Brody and Gage play football with the host of Kings and McBrides.

"May I sit?" Hannah indicated the grass next to her.

"Please." Amber moved her soda can as Hannah sat down.

"Oh Lord, I may never get up from here." A small chuckle fell from Hannah's lips. "He's a wonderful young man, Amber. You should be very proud of him." Hannah's attention was on the game, too. Maybe because it was easier than looking at each other.

"I am. Very proud." She refused to apologize for her decision to raise him by herself.

"May I ask you something?" Hannah glanced at her.

Oh, boy, here it comes. She mentally steeled

herself for the barrage of questions, accusations, and anger-laced barbs she'd been expecting from not only Brody, but his family. "Sure." She drew her knees up and wrapped her arms around them, recognizing her body language was defensive.

"Would it be all right if we helped by taking care of him?"

Amber's head whipped around. *Take care of him?* "What?"

"Oh, that came out wrong. I'm so afraid of making a mistake... Can we help babysit him when you're working? I know he's ten and probably doesn't think he needs a babysitter, but if your sister ever needs help, we'd be willing to watch him. We'd like to get to know him, and let him know us."

Amber tracked through Hannah's rushed explanation. "You want to help watch him?"

"If you'd allow it. Brody told me when the two of you were together, you thought I didn't like you. I never meant for you to feel that way." Hannah plucked a dandelion and twirled the stem in her fingers. "I don't know why we had a strained relationship, but I felt it, too."

"Did you?" Amber asked and gave the woman her full attention.

"I did. I couldn't shake the feeling that you'd rather be anywhere else but where I was. I'm not sure what I did to make you feel that way, but I'd very much like to start over if we could." She nodded to the melee in the backyard masquerading as a football game. "For Brody and Gage, we should make the attempt."

"I never felt like you approved of me." Amber laid her cards on the table. "I tried to act in a way I thought would be acceptable to you."

"Approve of you?" Hannah repeated the words.

She nodded. "The whole time we dated, I had the impression you thought Brody could do better. The last time I spoke to you, the day I came looking for him… well… you said—" She stopped. She was not going to speak the words that had eaten at her for years. "At any rate, they simply confirmed my fear."

"I didn't like how you hurt Brody, but I never disliked you." Hannah gasped. "Oh, no, I'd never think that." She turned on the grass and faced Amber. "After we got married, Chauncey and I moved to Hope City to get away from Chauncey's mother. His brother Chance had married a lovely woman, Amanda. We all loved her. You remind me a lot of her, now, I mean. Strong, competent and not looking for anyone's approval. Anyway, Chauncey's mother disowned Chance for marrying Amanda because she didn't approve of Amanda's background. She came from a very humble past. Lord, that mean old woman won't listen to anyone, and once she gets something into her head, she is steadfast. But Chance truly loved Amanda and walked away from his family because he loved his wife. I watched that woman tear her family apart with her judgmental attitude. I swore I would never, ever, do that to anyone my children dated. All I've ever wanted for my children is for them to be happy and loved. I earnestly pray if I ever made you feel less than welcome that you'll forgive me."

Amber stared at Hannah before she nodded. "I've had a lot of time to think about it, and I was as much a part of the problem between us, if not more. I was so desperate for your approval that I couldn't relax or be myself."

"You never need to be desperate for my approval, Amber. You already have it. You always have. I wish we would have had this conversation ten years ago." Hannah patted her hand.

Amber chuckled and held Hannah's hand for a moment before she released it. "I don't know if I would have been able to have this conversation then. I've done a lot of growing up."

"Ah... being a mom does that to you, doesn't it?" Hannah smiled at her.

"Boy, that's an understatement. Does the worry ever stop?"

They both turned when Gage shrieked.

Brody hoisted him up and flung him over a shoulder. "Hang onto the ball!" Brody ordered as he laughed and spun away from an exaggerated slow-motion tackle from Kyle.

Gage laughed and bowed his back, lifting the ball higher, away from the ill-fated swat that Bekki attempted, although it looked like Bekki had actually *tried* to get the ball.

They both cheered as Brody carried Gage into the end zone, demarcated by two plastic garbage cans. Brody dropped Gage to his feet, and they both did a touchdown dance.

"You never stop worrying, but you learn to trust they know how to take care of themselves." Hannah chuckled. "I know they call me the 'hover-copter,' and I do enjoy checking in on my children, but I only want them to be happy."

"That's all you can hope for, isn't it?" Amber agreed.

"Indeed. Say, would you like to come to girl's night next week? Whoever is available, between the McBrides and us, get together every now and then and have some wine and gossip. Nothing formal, but Kallie will be there if she doesn't have a case. I know you'd like her. She's Brock's wife and a detective, too."

Amber smiled at Hannah. "Thank you, if I'm not needed at work, I'd like that."

"Work comes first. Between the two families, we usually have four or five that make it. Can I get your phone number from Brody? I'll text you with the details."

"That's perfect, but I can give you my number, now."

Hannah chuckled. "I'd love to jump up and get my phone, but I'm going to need a tow truck to come pull me off the ground."

Amber popped up and extended her hands. "I've got you, Grandma."

Hannah's eyes misted, and she grasped her hands. "I'm a grandma! I'm so happy."

Amber helped her up and swallowed back her emotion. As Hannah stood, she whispered, "So am I."

Brody flopped down on his side on the grass beside Amber. "I'm dead."

"Dead people don't talk, or play football, or eat two steaks." She patted his stomach.

He caught her hand and squeezed it before he released it. "God, don't remind me, but damn they were good." He rolled onto his back and scooched closer to her, and they gazed toward the yard.

Gage was having the time of his life and from the looks of it, so were the adults. Blay raced across the lawn and grabbed Gage, lifting him away from Bekki so she couldn't reach the bandana tucked in his back pocket. The kid had been manhandled like that all day and was eating it up.

He popped to his elbows and bellowed, "Blay, he ate a lot; he may puke on you!"

Gage's laughter echoed in the backyard when Blay faked dropping him only to catch him, hoist him in the air again and run across the grass for a touchdown. Blay dropped to his knees, put Gage on his feet and face-planted in the grass. Gage dropped on top of him and pounded the ground next to Blay's head. "One, two, three! I pinned you!"

Blay rolled suddenly and buried his fingers in Gage's ribs. The boy's laughter dissolved into hysterical shrieks of laughter. "Mom! Mom! *Daaaddd*! Help!"

Brody's heart launched the same time he did. He sprinted across the grass and tackled Blay, rolling him off Gage. "Come on, payback time!"

Blay was majorly ticklish, and he held the man down digging his fingers in, showing Gage where to attack.

"Not cool!" Blay laughed while Gage tickled him. "Uncle!" Blay shouted his surrender.

Brody rolled off him and stared up at the blue sky. Gage fell down between them and rolled onto his back. "I like this yard. It's huge."

"Your grandma and grandpa tore down the fence between the houses before your dad was born." Blay nudged Gage. "That's a long time ago because your old man is older than dirt."

Gage laughed and shook his head. "No one is older than dirt."

"Dessert!"

Brody groaned when Gage popped up at his grandmother's words, using his stomach as a landing place for his elbow.

"Chocolate Trifle!"

Gage was up and over him before he could blink.

"Damn, man, that kid has no give up in him." Blay flopped both arms above his head. His back popped, and he groaned.

"Told you."

Blay snorted. "I thought you were exaggerating."

"Nope."

His brother tipped his head and looked at the picnic area. "He called you Dad."

He nodded. The word made him feel twenty feet tall, though Gage had probably said it without thinking.

"Incoming." Blay rolled up and jogged across the lawn to the picnic table.

"Hey, coming to check if you'd actually died." Amber appeared over him, her ponytail hanging down as she bent over.

"Not yet. Soon." She reached down to help him up, but he tugged her down to the ground.

She laughed and then sat up, cross-legged. "Seems to be going well, huh?"

He rolled to his side, facing her, and not the crowd of people diving into dessert. "Saw you talking with my mother today. You have a good visit?"

Amber gave him a sad smile. "That talk was about twelve years overdue."

"Did it clear the air?" He plucked a blade of grass from the lawn.

She sighed and then shrugged. "It was hard, but we agreed we needed to try again. Next week, if we don't have something going on at work, I'm going to girl's night. The McBrides, the Kings —and me."

"You don't have to go if you don't want to." He'd damn sure have words with his mother and sisters before next weekend, too. He didn't want anyone laying blame on the woman for her actions. They hadn't walked in her shoes; they had no right to judge her.

"No, I want to. I think it would be good for us. The talk today was cathartic. Hard, but cathartic. It cleared the air, although I'd wager she's still hurt by my decisions."

He heard Gage laugh and looked over. The boy sat between his grandma and grandpa with a heaping bowl of chocolate trifle.

Amber chuckled. "He's going to be wired."

"He called me Dad." His whisper was reverent. It was a moment he'd always remember.

"Last night, he asked when he should call you that. I told him when he felt like it. Obviously, on the losing end of a tickle fight was the right time to call in the big guns." Amber plucked a blade of grass and examined it.

"It would seem." He yanked on her pant leg, drawing her eyes to him. "Thank you. For being here and for trying again."

"Trying again?" Her brows furrowed together.

"To get along with my mom. When we were together, I honestly didn't realize you two were having problems." He sat up and crossed his legs, facing her with only a couple inches of grass between their knees.

"Hindsight being twenty-twenty, it was mostly me. I wanted her to like me so much that I tried to be someone I wasn't. I wasn't comfortable around her or your sisters, and because of it, they weren't comfortable around me."

"Why didn't you say anything?" Brody took her hand in his.

She stared at their connection. "I was afraid of losing you." She gave a humorless chuckle. "And that's exactly what happened, but it wasn't because of my relationship with your family, it was because of my past with *my* family."

Brody squeezed her hand gently. "Did you ever love me?"

Her eyes rose to his. She nodded and whispered, "I've never stopped loving you."

He held her gaze. So much history to sort through and examine. Maybe too much. "There is so much damage to repair."

A tear slipped down her cheek. "I know."

He swallowed hard as he once again made himself vulnerable to the woman he'd once loved and still cared for. He wiped off the bead as it traveled toward her chin. "Where do we start?"

"I don't know." She reached a trembling hand to his. "Maybe being friends and getting to know each other again?"

Gage shouted from the porch, "Mom! Dad! You want dessert?"

"Your dad does! Just a minute!" Amber called back.

He chuckled. Although moving from this spot was the last thing he wanted, he always enjoyed dessert. "You know me so well."

"I want to know you better."

"We'll need to file paperwork with HR. I don't want this to come back and bite either of us."

"This?"

"Us."

"God, I never thought there would be an us again." She closed her eyes for a moment.

He traced his thumb across her cheek. "I always hoped there would be."

Brody drove up in front of Dawn's house. The front porch light was on.

"I better wake him up." Amber opened the truck door and turned toward Gage.

"Let him sleep. I'll carry him in."

"Are you sure? He's really heavy."

"Yeah, my back reminded me of that today when we scored the tenth touchdown. I've got him. You go open the door." He nodded to the house and slipped from his side of the truck, trotting around the hood of the vehicle to get to the passenger side. He unfastened Gage's buckle and slid him over. "Come on, dude, let's get inside."

"Huh?" Gage's eyes opened slightly. "I can walk."

"Nah, let me give you a lift." He slid the big guy from the seat and hefted him up. Gage weighed a good eighty to ninety pounds. He was tall and solidly built for a fifth grader. His long legs dangled, and he dropped his head to Brody's shoulder. He was definitely going to have to step up his strength workouts.

Amber had the door opened and pointed down the hall. "First room on the left."

There was enough light from the hall to illuminate his son's room. He smiled at the small desk and single bed. There were posters of superheroes, a two-foot-tall model rocket in one corner, and several model airplanes suspended from the ceiling. He put his son in his bed and watched Amber tug off his shoes, socks and jeans, leaving him in his t-shirt and boxers. She covered their son with a sheet and light blanket before she leaned down and kissed his forehead. She nodded to the door, and they both exited soundlessly. Brody backtracked to the front door.

"Would you like a drink or something?" Amber gazed up at him.

"If I stay, it won't be for a drink." Brody cupped her neck with his hand and placed his forehead against hers. "And I want to stay so damn bad."

"Not a good idea in the living room, but you could get away from here." Dawn's voice split them apart. She stood in the doorway to the kitchen.

"What? I was getting a drink of water when you came in."

"Wh-what?" Amber stuttered in her surprise.

"Look, you're adults, right? This isn't rocket science. I'm taking Gage to school in the morning anyway. Go on, head to Brody's and get your freak on. I know you have a travel bag in your SUV. Gage'll think you had to go to work."

"But..." Amber glanced at him.

"It's fast." He'd offer her the out.

Dawn snorted a laugh. "Yeah, what has it been, ten years in the making? God forbid. No, no, you're right. You should wait another ten years, no eleven. The kid will be able to drink then." She walked past them. "I'm going to bed. If you're here in the morning, you're here. If you're not, I've got Gage covered. 'Night."

He lightly wrapped his arms around her waist. "You don't have to make the decision tonight. We have a lot of things to work out."

Amber nodded and shuffled closer. She ran her nose along his neck. "But this isn't one of them, is it? Do you want me as much as I want you?"

Brody moved back far enough to see the desire in those beautiful eyes. "Yes." There was no other answer. Yes, he wanted her. He always had.

"Okay. I'll follow you to your place. I do have a travel bag in my car, but I'll need to get my service weapon." The small weapon in her purse was her secondary that she carried whenever she was off duty and out of the house. She tugged him along toward the kitchen. She reached up to the top shelf and removed a small gun safe with a handle on it. "I can't take any chances with it. Boys are very curious, especially when they've been told no." She unlocked the box and removed her shoulder holster and weapon.

"There's so much I need to learn." He had weapons throughout his apartment. It was something he'd address before Gage came to hang with him.

"You know everything you need to know. The things like this?" She examined her weapon and shrugged. "Keeping him safe from himself and things that can hurt him will become second nature. Until they do, I'll remind you." She threaded her fingers through his. "Are you ready?"

Damn, wasn't that the question of the decade? "Probably not, but I think we need to take a leap of faith." He leaned forward and tasted her lips for the first time in over ten years. She sighed and curved into him. Memories triggered by her feel and scent flooded by as he opened her mouth and slowly indulged in the decadent and delicious feast he'd thought he'd never taste again.

The kiss lingered; her response heated as his desire became harder to harness. He put a small amount of space between them and dropped his forehead to hers while they both panted for air. "We should go."

She stepped back from him, walking backward and leading him out the front door. She locked it behind them, and after another long, delicious kiss, he took her to her car.

He jogged to Wilma and started the old lady up. Damn, the trip across town could be the longest drive of his life—but it would also be the most careful.

CHAPTER 14

Amber followed Brody's truck to the inner harbor area. The revitalization of the harbor was spreading further and further south, bringing new businesses down to the waterfront. They passed through upscale restaurants and boutique shops and drove south along the shoreline. With each passing mile, doubt edged further and further into her thoughts. *Were they moving too fast?* The tapping of her fingers on the steering wheel stopped when she watched Brody pull into a parking slot in front of a nice-looking building. She could see where it had once been a warehouse, but the exterior was painted a dark beige, and the white and dark brown trim around the doors and windows made it inviting and attractive. She maneuvered into the vacant slot next to him and put her crossover into park.

She got out of the vehicle, grabbing her overnight bag when Brody opened his door. "Is this building yours?"

"Yeah. I still have some work to do on the third apartment. It's livable but not high end, and it needs to be down here. I think I have another six months or so to scrimp and save."

He extended his hand to her and she took it, grateful for the warmth of the connection. Touching his hand grounded her nervous thoughts. "I thought you said the apartments paid for your mortgage?"

"They do."

"Then why do you have to save?" She walked beside him until he reached the door, which was locked. She could see a small clean lobby area. Crown molding framed the ceiling and the floors were hardwood.

"Well, I have a son to help support, now." Brody unlocked the door and ushered her into the small but well-appointed lobby.

She spun toward him. "I told you, we don't need the money."

"And I told you it was something I want to do.

The third apartment can wait for its finishing touches."

"Wouldn't life be easier for you if you rented it out?"

Brody shrugged and motioned toward the stairs. They started climbing together.

"I think you should finish the apartment. If Gage needs anything, I promise I'll let you know, but finishing the apartment puts you in a better position financially to help if he does need something that I can't provide. I promise, right now, all he needs is your time."

"Which I won't have if I work on the apartment."

"Can't he come and help? I mean, you could teach him things about carpentry or fixing stuff that neither Dawn nor I could teach him. Lord knows if we can't get a repairman to come in and fix something, it stays broken."

He chuckled as they passed the second floor.

"There's three apartments? One on each floor?"

"No, four apartments, if you include mine. Two on the second floor. One on the first floor. The remaining area on the first floor is partitioned into storage rooms for the four apartments."

They emerged from the stairwell into a small

foyer. He unlocked the door and turned on the light. "Wow."

Her eyes were drawn to the wall of windows and the absolutely beautiful view of the harbor. Lights danced on the shore across the expanse of water. To the far right was the industrial port and the bright lights illuminated massive ships. To the left, the city rose away from the water like a sentinel. "This is beautiful," she whispered as she made her way into the vast living area.

The dark leather furniture popped against the soft beige carpet. Carpet that Gage could destroy with a juice pack and muddy feet. There was a massive television on the far wall, but who would ever want to watch television when they had a view like this? Brody grabbed her overnight bag and slid his hand under her shoulder holster, taking the weapon with him. She watched him place her weapon and his on a high shelf on the far side of the room, but she couldn't resist one more look at the magnificent view.

Brody came up behind her and wrapped his arms around her waist looking at the view with her. After a moment he whispered, "Are you afraid we're making a mistake?"

She nodded. "I am. I seem to make a lot of them where you're concerned."

"Then let me make the decisions for us." He shifted away, and her heart stopped. He turned her around and wrapped her in his arms once again. His lips found hers, and the hunger that had abated during the trip across town rippled to the surface, slicing through the waves of self-doubt and whirlpools of guilt and regret. He held her as he backed up. He guided them deeper into his apartment, but his mouth and hands eliminated any concern that had been building. When they stopped moving, her shirt hit the floor. She found his warm skin under his t-shirt and peeled it over his head. They toed off shoes, and jeans slid to the floor.

Amber brushed her hair from her eyes and gasped softly, "Oh..."

Tattoos that weren't there the last time they were together now adorned his chest and arm. She traced the writing on his bicep that told of his salvation and hope. The Bible verses were unexpected.

"You weren't religious before." The words were the last thing she'd expected on his body. He was raised in the church; she wasn't, and Brody never mentioned his beliefs.

He placed a finger under her chin and elevated her face. When her eyes locked with his, he whispered, "I found my faith when I hit the bottom."

"As did I." She reached up and pushed his long bangs from his eyes. "We hurt each other."

"We did. But never again. Never." His head shook slowly as he spoke.

Those beautiful eyes were focused on her and only her. She felt cocooned in the man. "I promise to talk to you if I'm afraid or confused, not to run away."

The corners of his lips ticked up for a second. "I'll come after you if you do."

She cupped his face with her hand. "Will you forgive me?"

"If you want my forgiveness you have it."

"What if I want your love?"

"I'm here." A soft smile on Brody's face was the only warning she got before he swept her off her feet and walked her to the king-sized bed by the wall of glass.

She sighed as he lowered her onto the bed and found his way between her legs. His lips traveled the length of her neck, and he paid particular attention to the sensitive spot at the base, swirling his tongue and sucking the skin into his mouth. Ten years disintegrated as they came together. The time that separated them turned to dust and was swept away on the fresh breath of desire and the warm breeze of renewal.

He lowered down her body, finding her bra clasp and eliminating the impediment. She ran her hand over his hot skin as he feasted on her breasts. Sensations lapped at her, building inside. He lowered further, trailing hot kisses down her abdomen to her hip. The elastic lace of her underwear snapped under his grasp and the material fell away, replaced by Brody's lips.

She arched into his touch. One hand stayed in his hair, to guide him, as if he needed the help. The second grasped the soft comforter under them, as if the act would ground her to the bed, but it couldn't. Not when Brody reclaimed every fetter that had bound her to him for the last ten years. His feel, his scent, and the way he instinctively knew what she needed, perched her on a cliff with only one way down. He spread her sex and lowered his mouth. The warmth and softness of his touch soon gave way to a fast-paced race to the end. She tipped her head and glanced down at him.

His hips moved against the bed in the same manner hers moved against his lips. His hand traveled over her body and cupped her breast. *Oh God. Yes.* His fingers rolled her nipple at the same time as the fingers of his other hand entered her and curled. He sucked her into his mouth and used his tongue to excite her clit, moving her past the ledge he'd placed her on. Her body seized and exploded. His actions detonated her orgasm, and she shattered into a million pieces.

She felt him climb her body. His kisses sent shivers through her. When she felt him above her, she opened her eyes and beheld the man she'd loved and then lost. She twined her hands through his hair and brought him down to her. He kissed her and rolled to his side, bringing her with him. She felt him reach and move away. He opened his bedside table drawer and removed several condoms. She took a packet from him and opened it with shaking hands.

Brody caught her hand as she moved toward his hot, rigid cock. "Don't play. I'm not going to last."

"No, no playing," she reassured in the same pained, panting breath he'd used. She carefully pinched the end of the condom and rolled the thin sheath down his shaft. The soft skin that covered the iron was like warm velvet in her hands. When they'd satisfied their initial lust, she was going to have that cock in her mouth again. She could make Brody lose his mind and planned on doing that as soon as possible.

He rolled her onto her back as soon as the condom was in place. His knee moved her leg up, and he lowered, placing his cock at her center. They stared at each other as Brody moved forward and retreated. He worked himself into her and with one final thrust buried himself deep inside. She gripped his biceps and panted. The fullness and heat of him was a sensation she wanted to log in the annals of her mind, somewhere where she would never forget this moment, this feeling.

"I'm not going to last." Brody dropped his head to her shoulder, his hot breath fanning the skin of her neck and breast.

"Take what you need." She wrapped her arms under his and grabbed his shoulders.

He shifted away slightly and looked at her. "You're what I need. What I've always needed."

"Then make me yours again." She wrapped her legs around him and pushed him forward. His hips moved into a driving rhythm, forcing her back up to that precipice. His thrusts became erratic, but it didn't matter. She tightened as he thrust forward, and they both shouted as they came. Brody groaned and continued to thrust, riding through his orgasm. He dropped on top of her, and she panted shallowly as he recovered. Regardless if she drew her last breath under him in this moment, a blissful feeling consumed her. She was back where she belonged. Back with the man she'd never stopped loving. God, please let her get it right this time. *Please.*

Brody woke when he heard Blayze come into the apartment. Or leave it. No, he was coming in. He heard the water run in the kitchen. Damn, he should have shut his door. Not that Blay had ever come back to his room, but still. Amber's body stiffened next to him. She was awake, too. They both glanced to the window. The sun had started to rise on the horizon.

"What time is it?"

Brody shifted and looked at his nightstand. "Almost six." He looked down at her and dropped a kiss on her forehead, remembering her aversion to kissing him without brushing her teeth. "Good Morning."

"It is, isn't it?" She snuggled closer to him and dropped her arm on his waist. "Can we play hooky?"

"What kind of example would that be for our son?" Brody dropped his head back on the pillow and brought her closer to him.

"Don't know." She yawned so hard she shook against him. "Shower."

"Together." It wasn't a suggestion.

"Absolutely. Water conservation."

He threw the comforter and sheets off them and stood up. There were clothes everywhere. A smile of satisfaction perched itself on his face and stayed there. They'd made a huge step toward returning things to the way they'd been ten years ago. But this, what was between them now was... calmer and deeper. At least for him. He needed to make sure they were on the same page before he gave himself permission to think things were going well. Still.

He turned back to the bed in time to catch Amber stretch. Oh, lord. Those long, lean muscles and peach color skin. She was beautiful and so much more than the girl he used to love. He extended his hand, and she grasped it. He helped her from bed, and they wandered into the master bath.

"Dang." She blinked when he turned on the lights. "That shower big enough for you?" Her eyes squinted at the corner of the room.

It was a massive shower with eight massaging shower heads. He'd helped the plumber with every part of the project. It brought down labor costs and taught him what he needed to know to do minor installations. However, minor had never featured in his vocabulary. This shower was his reward after he'd paid off the plastic he'd used to finance the initial plumbing of the building. He'd tiled it and installed the glass walls and doors. Yeah, it was big enough.

She pointed to the far side of the room, and he nodded before he started the shower. Waiting for her to finish, he made a quick search of his cabinet and produced a new toothbrush. He tossed it to her and grabbed his from the cup, doing a quick job on his fangs before he took care of business and joined her in the shower.

Her long hair slicked down to the curve of her back, and the water sluiced over her skin. Her hard nipples enticed him as he stepped into the warmth of the jets. She slid up next to him and urged him down for a long, searing kiss.

"Good morning," she husked when he finally moved away.

"It is indeed." He moved back in, but she shook her head.

Taking a washcloth off the bar, she dropped it to the floor and lowered to her knees. "I promised myself the second I could do this, I would."

Her hand circled his cock. What had been a slow and steady rise turned into steel in the time it took her to circle the head of his cock with her tongue. God, the woman had always been able to drive him insane with her mouth. The perfect, wet, heated slide of her tongue and mouth around his shaft, coupled with the way her hands stroked his lower half and fondled his balls, was killer. Deadly and so damn good.

He placed his hand on the back of her head and dropped his head back between his shoulder blades. The perfection of being with her again, feeling the chemistry between them, and knowing it could all be his again, was too much. He tightened his grip on her hair. She wouldn't pull off, but he'd always give her the opportunity. She moaned and doubled her efforts. His thigh shook and a blaze of heat shot up his cock. He felt her suck it down and keep going. She loved this last little bit of torture, when the suction became exquisite and yet almost painful. He shuddered and shifted away. She let his cock slide from her mouth and rested her cheek against his thigh. He stared down at her as she looked up.

"I love you."

Her words floated up to him on the steam and wrapped themselves around the cold dark place that had filled his soul for the last ten years. He helped her up and wrapped his arms around her. Against her ear, he whispered the knowledge of his heart.

"I never stopped loving you."

Brody entered the kitchen after taking Amber's overnight bag back to the bedroom. She had to deal with all that hair, so he offered to get coffee.

Blay sat at the kitchen table reading his tablet. "Coffee is done," he grunted while wrapping himself around his cup as if Brody was about to swipe the cup from Blay's hand. His brother had one cup every morning. How the man lived on such limited caffeine was a mystery. Brody grabbed two cups and poured coffee into them. To one cup he added a small amount of cream and a packet of sugar, before he took a big swig from the black coffee he adored.

Blay stared at him, one eye closed, the other eye narrowed. Brody looked down. Nope, all tucked in, buttoned and zipped. He glanced back at his brother who was now frowning. "What?"

"Who is that for?" Blay nodded to the cup on the counter.

"Me," Amber said as she entered the kitchen. "Wow, this is nice!" She walked to him and elevated on her toes, giving him a kiss. "I love the granite."

Blay swung his gaze from Amber, who was roaming the big kitchen and looking at the appliances, to him. The man's eyebrow rose, and he shook his head back and forth. He smiled and took another drink of his coffee, holding Blay's stare. The little manwhore had absolutely no right to condemn the relationship he was regenerating with Amber. None whatsoever.

"Blay?" They both turned at Amber's question.

"I'm sorry. What?" Blay blinked at her innocently.

"I was wondering if you are on shift today?"

"Ah, no. I traded a forty-eight with Reno so I could meet the little man yesterday. I'll pull four straight, starting tomorrow night."

Amber returned from admiring his appliances and leaned her back into his front. He rested a hand on her hip and smiled at his brother.

"Thank you for that. I know a double shift has got to be exhausting," Amber said.

"Actually, I think I worked out more yesterday playing with Gage then I would during a double." Blay chuckled. "That kid is awesome. You did good with him."

"Thank you. Hopefully the next time you two meet, he won't exhaust you." Amber took a sip of her coffee and glanced at her watch. "Well, Sergeant King, we have to get to work, and you have paperwork to complete with your HR department."

"Don't you mean our HR department?" He chugged a couple scalding hot gulps so he could top off his mug.

"No. I'm DEA. My HR doesn't give a shit as long as I'm not dating someone in my chain of command—" she pointed at him when he opened his mouth "--in the DEA." She pushed her cup across the counter to him. "Will you top me off? I need to go grab my bag and weapon."

"Bring mine?"

"You got it." Amber headed to the living room.

Blayze hissed, "Seriously, you're making this mistake again?"

He spun and glared at his brother. "Repeat that and you're going to be bloody."

Blayze shook his head. "Whatever, man. What are you going to do when she leaves again?"

"I'm not going to do that. I'm not that person anymore." Amber walked into the kitchen and handed him his weapon. "You don't have to take my word for it Blay, but I'd appreciate a chance to prove people can grow up and change."

Blay's eyes bounced between them. "Not sure I can do that, but I'm going to make it easier for you two to figure it out. I'll grab my shit and bunk somewhere else. Don't want to impede the groove."

Brody took his weapon and slid it on. "Amber, grab your bag and we'll head to work."

She glanced between brothers. "All right."

Brody waited until he couldn't hear her footsteps down the hall. "Blay I don't know what crawled up your ass, but you don't have to leave unless you are going to continue to be a dick. This is your home as much as it is mine. Hell, you helped me refurbish damn near every inch of this place. If you don't want to stay with me, take the third apartment. It's yours."

"You're making a mistake, Brody. Just because you have a kid together doesn't mean you need to take *her* back," Blay whisper-hissed and shook his head.

"Did you ever stop to think that I still love that woman?" He returned the hiss and pointed back toward his bedroom.

"Why? What has she ever done but hurt you? She didn't tell you about your son for ten years, Brody. Ten years! Do you think she's going to stick around when the going gets tough? She's proven she's a runner. Leopards can't change their spots and become tigers. It doesn't happen," Blay spat but managed to keep the words low and quiet.

"You know what? I was wrong. You can't stay here. Take the third apartment or don't, I don't care, but you're not staying in my home. I really hoped you would support us. We're trying to find a way forward." He grabbed his coffee cup and Amber's, anger making him spill some on the counter.

"You're not going forward, Brody. You're

reaching into the past for something that *died*. Do you think you can resurrect what you used to have?"

"No! But I can damn sure live in the present and be thankful for what is in front of me. I have a son, and the woman who gave him to me is the woman I have *never* gotten over. She has *always* been the one for me." He saw Amber out of the corner of his eye. Her eyes were huge. With no idea how much she'd heard, he headed her way. He grabbed his keys and opened the door for her.

On the stairs heading down she cleared her throat. "He hates me."

"He has no reason to." Brody ground the response through his teeth.

"No, he does. He saw you go through some serious pain. He's not trying to hurt you. He's trying to help you."

"He can keep his help to himself." Brody stomped down the stairs.

Amber turned and stopped him. "Every person in your family, heck in your life, will have an opinion. Everyone. I'm going to have to deal with that. You don't need to draw a sword and chase after windmills for me. They will either accept that I'm back in your life or they won't. You getting into it with them isn't going to change anything. Not a thing."

"What is between us is none of Blay's business." Brody stepped down to the stair above where she was standing.

"He's your brother, and he cares for you. That makes it his business."

He slid his hand around her neck, brought her closer and kissed her. "No, that makes it our business. The rest of the world be damned. This time we're going to make it work."

"We are. When we've been married twenty years and have grandchildren, you can ask those nay-sayers for an apology." She laughed until she saw the look on his face.

He waggled his eyebrows. "Did you just ask me to marry you?"

Her eyes widened, and she shook her head. "I meant..."

"I know what you meant." He grabbed her hand, tugging her into step with him. She meant living the rest of their lives together, and he couldn't agree more.

CHAPTER 15

Amber followed Brody to work. Conflicted thoughts flowed as she drove. Brody and Blay's argument today wasn't unexpected. Well, that wasn't exactly true. She'd expected that argument from his mother instead of his younger brother, and wasn't that something? She shook her head. She had been expecting it, but still it hurt. His family had lived the last ten years thinking she ran away... and to a degree she had. The skepticism and doubt were something she'd have to work on, but trust would only come with time.

They parked next to each other, and he waited for her to walk to the building. "I'm sorry again about Blay." He glanced at her and shrugged. "He didn't seem to have any problems yesterday."

"Ah, but did he have any clue we were going to try a relationship again?"

"Probably not."

"So my being with you this morning was probably a big shock."

He slowed, and she matched his gait. "Brie got defensive, too. Maybe it was something I said or did. I don't know, but every time I brought your name up, it was as if they were ready to go to war."

"Is Brie still upset? You said she wanted to be at your parents' house."

"No, once I told her the entire story, she understood."

"Did Blay know the entire story?"

He glanced at her. "Ahh... I don't know. I assumed Mom and Dad told him."

"But you don't know for sure. He could have been blindsided this morning."

"True." They walked up the steps together. "Last night was really good." He stopped with his hand on the door.

"Better than that." She smiled up at him and waggled her eyebrows.

He smiled and a slight blush rose up his cheeks. "You realize once I complete the paperwork, either you or I will be removed from this op."

"Figured, but I'm new, so I can float, and you're a pilot, so you're the logical one to stay on the case."

The door opened and Terrell stuck his head out. "If you two would stop yakking, we have an update in the conference room." He spun and walked back into the building.

She glanced at Brody, and he shrugged. Obviously, it wasn't anything out of the normal for Terrell. Maybe someday she'd get used to the shouting, goofing around, and friendships that dominated the team atmosphere here. In the DEA, things were more buttoned up. More conservative, polite, quiet, office demeanor ruled during all disagreements, and meetings that could become contentious were held behind closed doors. Hell, wearing jeans to work would have been a quick way to get your ass written up, but not on the JDET team. Thank God.

Amber smiled at Rayburn and Watson who were sitting at the conference room table. The now familiar grease stained bag was in the middle of the table. Rayburn reached in and threw a biscuit to her, Brody and Terrell.

"You're buying tomorrow." Watson pointed to her.

"Deal." Even if she wasn't on the team, she'd make a stop for them. She liked the two men. They were crazy, but their crazies matched hers. She unwrapped the biscuit and dropped into her chair, sending a glance to Terrell who was doing the same thing.

He took a bite of the food and opened the file in front of him. "Good news," he said around his food and swallowed hard. "Thanks to some magic, we've got good fortune heading this way. The FBI is unassigning a confiscated aircraft that won't go to auction for a while, and we can use that for the undercover op up north."

"What about the house?" Brody asked, probably because he was the only one who didn't have a mouthful of food. Amber chewed and listened.

"We struck gold there. I know a person who owns a real estate brokerage company. He knows the small agency that has the listing for the house we want to occupy. He's gone out on a limb for us and is in the process of purchasing the house from the agent. He assures me it is a good business deal as he is going to update the house, or flip it, as he calls it, and sell it for a lot more than it is currently worth. He's asked for a rent-back situation until closing. The smaller agency has agreed. The only thing we need to worry about is the appraisal, and Cooper doesn't think that will be a problem. He's pulling strings to get that done in the next three days. After that, we have carte blanche to do whatever we need to the house in regard to ensuring observation of the two homes that have recently been sold." Terrell took another bite of his breakfast sandwich.

"Hell of a friend." Watson muttered.

"Relatives are all right." Terrell groused back.

"That covers the plane and the house. What about the man-hours?" Brody took his first bite after he asked.

"We'll work that as it comes." Terrell shrugged. "The board meets tomorrow."

"Board?" Rayburn chimed in.

"Above your paygrade, Rayburn. King, you and I need to talk about a few things. Rayburn, Watson, Swanson, you get the blueprints for that house and head to Briar Hill. Tech should be able to outfit you with wide angle cameras for the outside of the house. Make sure you get enough, and if you have to sign for them, make sure those serial numbers match. Last time I had to pay for equipment Morrow swears we never received."

"Roger that." Rayburn got up and tossed his wrapper in the brown paper bag and held it open for Watson to toss his garbage in. "Come on, woman, you're holding up the show." He jiggled the bag from his fingertips.

"Sorry." She shoved the last bite of her sandwich into her mouth and crumpled the paper. She shot it, and held her hands up in the air as it went into the trash bag. Her exclamation of 'score' sounded more like a toad croaking because her mouth was stuffed full of greasy, cheesy heaven.

Watson gave her a high-five, and Rayburn pitched the bag into the trash can. "Who knew a DEA agent had game?"

She grabbed her purse and headed to the door with her teammates. Damn, it was good to fit in. Too bad she'd be reassigned soon.

Brody tossed his wrapper toward the trash can, rimming it in with ease. "What's up?" He leaned back in his chair waiting for his boss to finish his biscuit. Terrell pushed another folder toward him. He opened it and read the three statements that were stashed inside. Each statement said basically the same thing. He shut the folder and sighed. "Damn it."

"Yeah, that covers it." Terrell leaned back in his chair. "I'm sending those and Swanson's statement up the chain. Anderson has been harassing our females, and they haven't said a word. That shit stops now." His captain slammed his fist down on the table. "I have to talk to him this morning, but I need a sanity break before I do."

"Have you talked to HR?"

"Yeah, I just got off the phone before I saw you two standing at the door. They said he needs to be removed from his supervisory position, and because I can't trust him, I'm transferring his ass off the team. With four corroborating statements, he's going to get paperwork, and possibly a demotion."

"Damn it."

"You already said that."

"Still seemed appropriate." Brody chuckled even though there was no humor in the situation. Terrell's chuff of laughter followed.

"We'll need a new lieutenant." He wondered who was next up on the list with the right credentials.

"You're on the list."

"Yeah, but I'm *way* down on that list. You'll have to offer it to what, ten or fifteen people before you could reach me?" There was no way that many people would decline a promotion.

"Some don't have the qualifications." Terrell opened another file. "Three have what it takes. One is homicide, but word is that there is an opening coming up. Lt. Davidson is up to fill Captain Reisner's billet, so the candidate there will probably slide into Davidson's position."

"Okay, that still leaves two above me. They'd be stupid to turn down the promotion. Look, I'm honored, really I am, but if you don't do this by the numbers, people will scream nepotism."

"Yeah, I know. Theron and Brantley are good candidates. Brantley was groomed in the Desert, and Theron has experience with task forces, plus he has five years of SWAT under his belt."

"That could be helpful. Either would be great in that position."

"Yeah, and what sucks, is a year or two from now, after one of those two settle in, a billet will open up for you somewhere else."

"New blood is a good thing, but don't send me down the river, yet. I fought hard to make it here, not planning on leaving anytime soon." Brody leaned forward. "Unless you think it's for the best."

Terrell's forehead crunched down, and the captain glared at him through narrowed eyes. "Why the hell would I think that?"

"You know that shit I said I was working on last week?"

"I seem to recall that conversation."

"Agent Swanson and I have more in common than a simple past. Turns out she and I are parents." He waited a heartbeat and then launched into the specifics of the last week.

Terrell leaned back in his chair and rubbed his chin. "Have you filed the paperwork with HR yet?"

"No, sir."

"Okay. Good. I'm going to ask you not to do that."

The words sat him on his heels. His captain followed every rule, every time. "Excuse me?"

"I'll put it in writing, so you don't take any heat because of it. Don't go to HR and report your relationship, yet. We have this surveillance gig almost lined up. I want you and Swanson to act like a couple and actually inhabit the house. We'll do the remote monitor from the truck. We can park it outside the housing area and still monitor the cameras. That way you and Swanson can sleep, but during the daylight hours, I want you and her out and about and seen by the neighborhood. I need you to be accepted so the occupants of those two houses feel like you're a part of the environment. If you file HR paperwork, I can't put you on the same operation, and I need two people who those suburbanites will believe are a couple."

He and Amber could sell the relationship, but Terrell was putting his ass on the line ordering him not to report a relationship. "That could come back to bite you."

Terrell shrugged. "You get to play house with Swanson for a couple weeks. File the paperwork after you finish. Undercover hookups aren't unheard of and ideally at the end of this, we'll have Peña's supply pipe throttled."

"I'll play ball, Cap." His old man would have a cow if he discovered they were going around the directives, but he'd have Terrell to act as a buffer. Not that he'd ever use it. He was well aware not filing the paperwork was wrong, and he was doing it anyway.

Terrell sighed and leaned back in his seat. The

old grey metal groaned under his boss' muscled bulk. "Good. The hot sheets recorded three deaths at the Cardboard Cottages last night. Suspected overdoses. Don't know if those three are related to Grey Death yet but the coroner had two John Does OD this weekend. Both are waiting tox, but according to witnesses, they bought GD, split the buy and died within minutes of toking up. Who do you know in the Southwest District?"

"Detective Kyle McBride. Straight shooter. He's been a detective working Southwest Vice for about five years now."

"Can you trust him?"

"Absolutely." His best friend had always had his back, and he had Kyle's.

"Take a trip, do this in person. I want to know what the scoop is with those three that OD'd and if their deaths are related to what we've got coming in from Peña's airmail delivery."

"You got it. Do we have background on the people who bought the two houses we are putting under surveillance?"

"No. After they pull up the blueprints, I'll put the three stooges on that." Terrell chuckled. "She seems to have gelled with Rayburn and Watson well enough."

"She's good with people."

"Must be if you're walking up to the plate and swinging that bat again."

"Plan on making a home run this time." Brody was going to do his damnedest to make that happen.

"Well hell, I'm rooting for you, but don't strike out and throw a temper tantrum in my ball field."

"Never happen, Cap." Brody smiled and stood up. "Heading to the Southwest."

"I'll send you that email directing you to stand-by on that paperwork. If you don't need it, delete it."

"Roger that." He watched his captain open the file holding the statements before he headed down the hallway to the bullpen. That email would be deleted the second he saw it in his in box. Standing on his own decisions was a lesson he'd learned early and well. The captain had enough to worry about. HR forms were the least of his issues. There was the upcoming "talk" with Anderson. He didn't envy the man. Being a leader was a balancing act. Balancing respect, authority, both earned and given, and the demands levied upon his shoulders by his superiors wasn't easy. Terrell was an excellent leader, and the pressure he protected the team from was unrelenting. Such stress would lay lesser men to waste.

He made eye contact with Amber. A slight nod in her direction was all he could do, but it was enough. She smiled and turned back to her animated conversation with Rayburn. A laugh from Rayburn and Watson tipped his lips north. The three stooges. Yeah that fit.

He called Kyle as soon as he started his truck.

The man picked up on the second ring. "What up?"

"Hey, do you have any intel on the three suspected ODs at the Cardboard Cottages last night?"

Wind crackled through the phone. "I'm there now. Why?"

"Give me time to get there, and I'll let you know."

"Damn it, Brody, these people don't need any more shit to deal with. Please tell me you're not going to bust up their encampment with some massive multi-jurisdictional sweep."

"Nah, nothing like that. I'll be there in thirty."

"I'll still be here. Lots of eyes and nobody has seen shit."

"Isn't that the way it always flows?"

"True. True. I'll see you when you get here."

Brody shoved his phone back in his pocket and rubbed his face as he waited for the stoplight to turn from red to green. On impulse, he grabbed his phone again and hit up Blay.

"Sorry, man." Blay's comment was out as soon as his phone stopped ringing.

His shoulders relaxed, and he nodded even though his brother couldn't see him. "Yeah, me, too. You know you have a place with me as long as you want, right?"

"Yeah, but if you were serious about the third apartment, I'll take you up on it. I can work on it while I'm saving for my own place," Blay's voice echoed.

"Are you in the apartment now?" Brody hit his blinker and merged onto the interstate on ramp.

"Yeah. Wanted to check it out. Real nice." Blay whistled. "When did you tile the shower?"

"Two weekends ago. You were working." Brody accelerated onto the interstate and merged into the middle lane.

"Nice. Maybe I'll buy this from you and forget about looking for a place."

Brody blinked and then smiled. "Dude, that's a great idea. It's the largest of the three apartments. The other two take care of the payment on the building. I'll cut you a break if you agree to help me with the upkeep of the building and do the rest of the work on the apartment yourself."

"Man, if you are pulling my leg, that shit ain't funny."

Brody let himself get excited about the possibility. "No, really, it makes sense."

"We could buy the lot behind us, make it a backyard for the entire building. Dude, I could get a dog."

"Who would watch him when you have to pull shifts?" Brody shook his head. Blayze was an animal lover with a big heart. When he was a kid, he'd pick up strays and bring them home. It drove their mother crazy.

"Yeah, I'll figure that out. If you're serious about this, I'm in."

"I'm serious."

"Good. And it wasn't my place to say anything this morning. I'm sorry for that."

"Who'd you talk to?"

"Mom."

"She told you to say that, didn't she?"

"Well, hell, I was going to say it anyway, but yeah." Blay laughed and mimicked their mother. *"Blayze Benedict King, you know I love you. You're my youngest son and your brothers let you get away with a lot, but you had no right to insert yourself into Brody and Amber's business."*

Brody barked a laugh. "She said that?"

"Serious as a fucking heart attack man."

"Dude, we may need to stage an intervention. Aliens have snatched Mom and replaced her with a pod-person. Come to think of it, she hasn't called me today." He glanced at the old analog clock in Wilma's dash. "When did you talk to her?"

"About an hour ago. She was going to go into the city and help Brianna buy new tile for the restaurant."

"New tile? Does Brianna know about this?"

"Hell if I know. I had to tuck my tail and listen to her fuss at me. I'm not going to stick my nose in anyone else's business today."

"Smart man."

"I can be taught, or so I'm told."

"Don't listen to lies." Brody laughed when Blay hung up on him.

Ten minutes later, he was bumping down a pothole strewn road that fed back under the freeway. As he rounded the corner, the shunned microcosm of society filled the view from his windshield. The homeless, who couldn't get into shelters, the mentally ill, social outcasts, runaways, and drug addicts, had built a community of cardboard homes. Occasionally tents popped up between the shelters. Pieces of rusty, jagged, corrugated tin, old broken plywood, and cardboard of all shapes and sizes, made up small shelters for the residents to get out of the weather, but most of them sat outside in the sunshine today. There were at least fifteen burn barrels scattered through the assembly. Kyle wasn't hard to pick out, neither was Kyle's partner. He waved to Alex and headed deeper into the community where Kyle was talking to three men.

The scared, the paranoid, the hopeless, the criminals and those who were high or holding, moved away from him as he strolled through the filth and stench. He scanned the area. Communal living with no sanitation facilities. Families seemed to congregate together on the edge of the settlement. The children huddled beside adults. There was no running and laughing, no backyard football game, or a grilled meal to share. Here the barren future held no happiness, only fear and anxiety.

He reached Kyle as the men he'd been talking with shook their heads.

"Are you sure?" Kyle asked the men again.

"Didn't see nothing." Said one of the men. He looked young, maybe twenty, but this life aged people fast. He glanced up and eyed Brody, not missing the badge or gun, both positioned in plain sight. "Nothing." He turned and hurried away. The other two older men shook their heads.

Kyle nodded to him, and they fell into step, walking further into the community. "Amazing how three people end up dead by this burn barrel, in front of all these people, and no one saw a thing." Kyle shook his head.

"Safer for them not to get involved." He glanced at the crime scene. "Who has the death scene?"

"Homicide detectives were here and did the initial canvas. Crime scene techs got what evidence they could, but the bodies had been rolled. No shoes, clothes, nothing of value left on them. It sucks. So many people, so little resources to help."

"Hey, people like Tara and Brianna are doing everything they can."

"True, but what brought you here?" Kyle

snapped off his latex gloves and dropped them into a nearby burn barrel.

"We've got good intel that Peña's cartel is bringing in Grey Death. Two ODs are suspected already. Was there any indication that these three were using GD?"

Kyle shook his head. "One died with a dirty needle in his arm. H is my guess. The other two were meth heads. If they had the money, they'd buy more crank."

"One of GD's primary components is heroine, but they cut it with elephant tranqs."

"Are you serious?" Kyle blinked up at him. "I've heard about GD, but I haven't seen it on the streets. Not here at least. Thank God."

"Do me a favor and keep your eyes open. When the tox comes back on that H user, let me know what it says?"

"Yeah, I've got a good working relationship with Miller and Tripp. I'll give them a call and give them a heads up."

"Thanks, but keep it quiet for now. We don't need anyone talking. If Peña gets wind of us working to close down what we suspect is his pipeline, we're screwed."

"Gottcha. I'll call and make an inquiry then. Casual."

"Perfect. You have much business in the Cottages?" He pushed his hands into his jean pockets so he wouldn't touch anything.

"Always. Cheap drugs cut with everything from baby powder to drain cleaner tend to eliminate the poor suckers that are hooked on the shit, but I'm tracking an anomaly. Prescription drugs."

"No kidding?"

"Yeah."

"Let me know if I can help. We can put out feelers if you have anything to go on. Oh, and thank you for coming to the 'rents' yesterday."

"I'll take you up on that offer, and dude, mini-you is a great kid. Sorry I couldn't stay longer." He nodded toward his partner, Alex. "We had a call out."

"No worries. I'm glad you made it over."

"Hell, I wouldn't miss it." Kyle glanced at him. "You were getting pretty close to Amber. That on again?"

"It is."

"Be careful."

He groaned, "Man, not you, too."

Kyle chuckled. "You're my best friend. Yeah, I'm

going to tell you to be careful. I'm also going to tell you to go for it, because that woman and that kid are worth the effort. I tried to kick your ass into going to see her after the accident."

"Yeah, I remember. Wish like hell I'd taken your advice back then."

"So... you're saying..." Kyle's smile spread across his face.

"Fine. You were right." Brody laughed when Kyle punched the air in front of him.

"Damn, that hurt didn't it?" Kyle's eyes caught on something across the way.

"It did. I'm leaving now."

Kyle blinked back to him; his brow furrowed. "Yeah, okay."

"What? What did you see?"

"Someone that doesn't belong, which makes me edgy. Let's go to the Celtic Cock this week. You owe me a drink or ten for being right."

"Deal. Take care."

"You too." Kyle tossed the words toward him before he headed across the encampment, zeroing in on a woman wearing a backpack. She really didn't fit in. New clothes, nice backpack, and... was she wearing earphones? No wonder Kyle was making tracks that way. The woman was going to get herself robbed or worse.

He threw Alex another wave as he headed back to his truck. With Kyle and Alex keeping an eye open for GD in this district, it wouldn't take long to get notified if the drug had started making it to the inner city and the homeless population.

CHAPTER 16

A mber held the ladder for Brody. The small camera he was mounting to the eaves at the corner of the house masqueraded as a flood light. They'd arrived about ten this morning and made a show of pulling up the SOLD sign that hung in the front yard.

Brody had wheeled in several suitcases that held nothing but monitoring equipment. She'd toted in several boxes with extra pots and pans they'd scrounged from their kitchens over the last two days. Dawn and Hannah were taking turns picking up Gage from school this week. Gage was thrilled he could introduce his grandmother to his friends at school. She grabbed Brody's jeans when he leaned forward on the ladder. "Don't you dare fall off this thing."

He chuckled and leaned even further. "Yes, dear." He leaned over. "Heads up." He grabbed the cap that would hide the small camera and snapped it into place. The lens of the camera looked like a sensor, not the wide-angle lens that would record the comings and goings of the people in the two-story colonial next door.

"Hi!" A beautiful, dark haired woman strolled across her manicured lawn and headed their way. "Are you moving in?"

"Hi!" She held the ladder until Brody was no longer standing on the top rung. "Yes, we are. I'm Amber. This is my fiancé, Brody."

"Clare Edelman." The woman extended her hand.

"Nice to meet you. Your yard is absolutely beautiful." Amber nodded at the vast expanse of perfect green.

"Thank you. It was a mess when we moved in about four months ago, but I have a green thumb and love to dig in the dirt. Erik, my husband, built me a greenhouse." Happiness shone through her smile, and she spun and looked back at her house.

"You can't see it, but it's between the house and the hangar."

"I'd love to look at it sometime." Amber pointed to the pathetic flowerbeds that rimmed the ranch style house they'd 'bought'. "I'm not sure what's a weed and what's supposed to be there."

"Oh, I can help with that. I've been itching to get my hands on these flower beds, but Erik thought maybe the new owners would object."

"No objection, I'll take all the help I can get. I don't have a green thumb."

"Perfect, anyway the reason I stopped by is my husband is due back any time now. Would you like to have dinner with us tonight? I know you probably haven't had time to go shopping yet. You've been working on your lights most of the afternoon." She pointed at the camera system they'd installed.

"Well, I guess that's on me." Brody laughed. "I wanted them installed before I brought the plane in. I'm also going to make sure the lighting in the hangar is up to par."

"Oh no, are you an airplane widow, too?" Clare's hand went to her chest in mock horror and then a blazing smile appeared.

Amber's genuine smile spread fast. "I am. I

admit it. Before we've even tied the knot, I've become a widow." Amber pushed her hair back and smiled.

"Don't worry. I'll keep you busy gardening when your man and mine are lost in the clouds. Unless... you're not a pilot, are you?" Clare arched an elegantly tweezed eyebrow.

"Me? No. I tend to get airsick in small aircraft." Amber screwed up her nose at the memory of her last ride. She'd lost lunch and breakfast during that flight.

"I did too until Erik got the new plane. It has a pressurized cabin. But I don't travel with him much. My plants get more flying time than I do."

Brody put the last of his tools in the toolbox and closed the lid. "Plants?"

"Erik is the best. He travels to Jacksonville three times a week for work, and he's such a sweet man that once a week or so he brings me back a small pallet or two of flowers or plants. She pointed to the blooming color around her house. "I'm going to try to grow some of the sturdier plants in the greenhouse through the winter. Listen to me rattling on, I came to invite you for dinner, not go on about my flowers."

"Dinner sounds wonderful. What time?" Amber

gave a mental fist pump. Contact with one of the two neighbors they needed to get close to, and they hadn't even finished setting up their equipment.

"Erik is due to land at six-thirty. Why don't you come to ours for drinks about then, and we'll grill since it is such a beautiful day."

"You sure your husband won't mind?" Brody closed the ladder as Amber asked.

"Not at all. I'll have a drink waiting for him, and he and your fiancé can go kick the tires on the plane while we get the grill going."

"That sounds perfect." Amber genuinely smiled. She really liked Clare and hoped for the woman's sake that her husband wasn't involved with the Peña cartel.

"Wonderful. We are casual. I'm wearing this tonight, so don't worry about putting on airs." Clare nodded to the other house they were watching. The Dawes residence. "I invited the Dawes for dinner and didn't tell them not to dress up. Needless to say, I was in capris and Erik was in khaki shorts. They arrived buttoned up and pressed."

"Oh wow, I bet that was uncomfortable." Amber watched Brody head to the garage with the ladder.

"It was! Erik and I laughed about it after they

left. Olivia and Samuel are nice people, but they're older and from a different era. We like to have drinks on the back porch, grill and visit."

"That sounds heavenly actually." Amber glanced at the Dawes' home. "Does she fly?"

"Yep. She and her husband are lawyers, and they fly to different cities to consult. I used to see that plane coming and going all the time. Not lately though. What is it that you do?"

"We own and operate a couple of web design platforms and recently added a digital information storage business platform." It was an excuse that allowed them to be around the house all day without anyone thinking it was abnormal.

"Gah, computers. I don't know a thing about them. Erik uses them for work, and he's always checking his email on his phone."

"What does Erik do?"

"He's a business consultant. He's responsible for ten or fifteen companies at a time. His company moves in when a business is in trouble and helps them streamline, remove the dead weight and trim to become efficient and effective again."

"Wow, that sounds interesting. No offense, but I hope we never need to call in his company." Amber made her eyes cross.

KRIS MICHAELS

"Oh, Amber, we are going to get along fine. I'm so glad." Clare made a big production of looking to her right and to her left before she leaned in and whispered, "Most of the women around here have a stick up their ass, or so many kids they'd give anything to have a stick up their ass."

A shocked laugh erupted from her before she could stop it. "Well, I'm not a fan of sticks." She was damn proud of Gage, but she wouldn't bring him into an operation. Keeping him safe was paramount and making sure potential suspects didn't know about a personal vulnerability was absolutely essential.

Brody came back out of the garage and dropped his arm on her shoulders.

"Well, I'll let you two get back to moving in. See you at 6:30, and come straight to the backyard. I won't hear the doorbell and there is no sense going to the front of the house when you can walk through the yard."

"Thank you again." Brody extended his hand and shook Clare's.

"No problem, welcome to the neighborhood!" Clare waved and headed back to her immaculately pruned and groomed yard.

~

Brody watched the woman walk across the lawn. Amber leaned into him. "I really hope she's not smuggling dope. I like her."

He chuckled and turned her toward the house. "Smile and flip off the camera."

"How about we don't and say we did?" She elbowed him in the side, and they both meandered back into the garage and then into the house. They were lucky. The house had been staged to sell, so there was a couch to sit on. They'd brought an air mattress and bedding. The bedrooms hadn't been staged except for a few plants. Tonight, the surveillance van would start its coverage. The city utilities van they'd commandeered three years ago would once again be a set up for utilities work that never actually happened. The bullpen had drawn straws for shift coverage as the houses would be monitored 24/7, even when Brody and Amber were there.

Amber brought him a cold water as he worked on the computers they'd set up in the office. They had two monitors each, and the cameras were sending the stream into the cloud. They would be able to monitor take offs and landings from the security system already installed on the hangar by the previous owner. The hangar was alarmed, but not the house. Brody shook his head. Whoever lived in this house had their priorities wrong.

He picked up his earwig and hit the mic key on the computer. "Do you have us?" He glanced at the feeds he had on his screen and then looked over the top of his monitors to Amber. She nodded that she had all the feeds.

"Roger that. We have nine feeds. Three on House A, three on House B, and three on the hangar. We can see down the entire flight line. Those are good cameras."

"Installed by the previous owner." Brody continued to work through the program his cousin had sent him. He hit the small icon and instantly both screens flashed black before a myriad of pop-ups appeared.

Amber pushed away from the computer and held her hands up. "I didn't do that!"

He chuckled and hit the icon again, sending everything back the way it was. "That is a gift from my cousin, Jewell. If we have unannounced guests, click on the black treasure chest at the bottom of the screen."

"Here?" Amber clicked and both sets of screens once again flashed black and populated the nonsense they'd seen before. "Wow. That's impressive."

"It doesn't do anything but run on a loop, but if anyone was to come into the house, they wouldn't see our surveillance feed, they'd see our 'work'. The van has the same program installed. It has saved our bacon a time or two when nosy city workers showed up."

"Okay, so we're set?" Amber pushed away from the desk and looked at him.

"I believe we are. Control, do you need anything?"

"Negative. We have food, drink and a porta-john outside. Life doesn't get any better than this." Anvi Patel's voice through the earwig made him smile. He was damn glad the woman had their six. She was razor sharp and a great asset.

"Roger. We have a meet and greet with the neighbors at 6:30. You'll see us head to their residence through camera three." Brody waited for acknowledgement before he removed his earwig and put his mic on mute. He pushed away from the desk and stretched.

"You clear?"

She clicked off her mic and took out her comms. "Clear. What's up?"

"Shower time." He held his hand for her and helped her from the chair. "Do you want to check on Gage before we get ready for the night?"

She glanced at her watch. "No, but if we get home in time, I want to call him and tell him good-night. Get the rundown on his day."

"We can do that." Brody leaned down and kissed her.

The feel of him so close sent a shiver through her. She reacted not only to the sexual chemistry, which they had in spades, but to the emotional closeness that enrobed her in warmth, security and a sense of purpose. His presence in her life filled a dormant need in her soul. She'd closed the door on the hope that the love that had once grown there would ever revive and flourish again. However, life had given her a second chance, a re-emergence of what had once been, coupled with what was yet to be. Together.

"*We*. I really like the sound of that."

"So do I." He took her hand and led her into the master bedroom. She'd unpacked their toiletries earlier, and she'd made sure to set up his sink the way he liked, or rather the way he used to like it.

His razor on the left-hand side. Toothbrush and toothpaste on the right. Comb behind the tap along with his deodorant and cologne.

He turned and enfolded her into his arms. "When we're done here, will you and Gage move in with me?"

Whoa. "What? Are you sure?" A host of thoughts hit in a gale-force slap of reality. She wanted nothing more, but she needed to make sure he was certain.

"I am, and I think you are, too."

He dipped down and took her lips, but she leaned away. "What about your family?"

"I told you Blay was buying the apartment on the second floor."

He lowered again, and she bent backward to avoid the kiss. "But Gage's school, you're not in the same district."

"We can drive him and pay tuition so he can finish the year. Then transfer him next year."

"Dawn?"

"Is a big girl who probably would relish her life back."

Oh. True. She'd actually worried about that for years, but... "I can't. I mean, what is Gage going to think?"

Brody held her with one arm and reached into his pocket. He extracted a dark red ring box from his pocket and flipped it open with his thumb. "He'll think his Mom and Dad have finally figured shit out and decided to get married." He held the box so she could see the ring.

"It's not the same one." Why those words fell from her lips was beyond her, but the ring situated on the blood red cushion wasn't the small solitaire he'd offered her ten years ago. This ring had two sapphires on either side of the square cut diamond.

"I sold the other ring. I thought it was cursed. I picked this one yesterday and had it sized." He took her hand and slid the ring on her finger. "Amber Swanson, will you finally marry me?"

She waited, but none of the terror, none of the claustrophobic loss of freedom, and not a whisper of her mother's voice pierced her happiness. She removed her hand from his and placed it against his cheek. "I'd be honored to marry you."

Brody's smile was huge, "If Gage agrees."

"Gage doesn't get a vote on this one, I'm afraid. If there is one thing I've learned it is when the man you love asks you to marry him, you say yes." She pulled him down and whispered the yes against his skin. The kiss they shared buoyed her heart as it healed and promised, fed and nourished the parched place at the very core of her being. There was no rush, no desperate scramble to find skin; only a slow, gentle love. The kind of love she'd never thought she'd have again. They slide-stepped to the corner of the room, and as one, they slowly lowered to the air mattress.

Long, deep kisses broken by a slow slide of fabric filled her with a single fixation. Brody. He swamped her senses. His taste and smell surrounded her as certainly as his hard muscles surrounded her and shielded her from the outside world. How had she ever doubted this man or his love? Unbidden tears flooded her eyes.

"Hey, what's this?" His fingertip traced an escaped tear.

"I'm so sorry." The emotion of this second, with him, splintered her into a million shards.

He pushed her hair back away from her face and his eyes penetrated her soul. The honesty of his searching stare took her breath away. "We're past that. All is forgiven. We have each other. We have our future. We live in the here and now."

"Then no condom. I'm on the pill. I want all of you." Pieces of the past evaporated in the moment; carried away on his absolute forgiveness and love.

He lowered to kiss her and entered her at the same time. She clung to his shoulders and arched under him. Oh, yes. This was heaven. Her heart shattered, but not in pain this time. Brody had obliterated what remained of her heart, but with each touch, kiss, and breath he restored her. Each fragment built on the next. The past annihilated, the future renewed.

His breath left goose bumps when it moved across her overheated skin. There was an absence of words, but not a lack of communication. He spoke in the way he touched her, and her answers were composed by her responses to those gentle hands, lips, and tongue. Unfettered and unrestrained by the past, she focused all her attention on the man who *still* loved her.

They climaxed together and, completely spent, drifted for several long moments before he whispered the words that set her world on its axis and made the stars shine in the heavens.

"I loved you then; I love you now, and I'll love you and Gage, unconditionally, until the day I die."

CHAPTER 17

Brody shook Erik Edelman's hand. "Nice to meet you."

The guy was as tall as he was, and he looked damn tired. The luggage he was toting under his eyes could be used as steamer trunks.

"And you." Erik returned. "Sorry for being late tonight, but business has been crazy. The boss is in a snit, which makes telling him things he doesn't want to hear difficult." The man rolled his eyes. "He's on a tear, and thankfully, I made it out of the meeting intact." The man downed half his beer in one go.

"I take it his bite is worse than his bark?"

"Oh, hell yeah. But, enough about me. What is it you do?"

They moved to a large wrought iron table and scooted the chairs away from the table to sit.

"We have a couple businesses. Digital storage and website design." He took a drink of his beer and prayed Erik didn't have a clue about either.

Erik shook his head. "I use computers as a tool. I can muddle through all the programs, but if you ask me to go farther than that, I'm lost."

"Which keeps me in business." He hoisted his beer in Erik's direction. "So, what do you fly?" He pointed to the hangar.

Erik's face lit up. "My Piper? Clare calls her my girlfriend. She's a beauty. Would you like to see her?"

"Definitely." He caught Amber's eye as she talked with Clare and nodded to the hangar. Amber smiled and waved at him, drawing a knowing smile from Clare. The women laughed as they headed down the flagstone path. Erik had a spring in his step as they walked toward the flight line.

"Ah, is that the famous greenhouse?" He pointed to a large glass or Plexiglas building, perhaps sixteen feet long and ten feet wide.

"Yes, it is. It's a kit, believe it or not, and it only took three weekends to put together. She loves her plants. Hell, she can plant a dead stick and make it grow. That's her hobby, and this is mine." Erik disabled the alarm and opened the door to the hangar. He reached in and flipped on the overhead lights.

He whistled. "Nice." He walked up to the plane. "Three blade, constant speed propeller?"

"Damn straight. She's got a 350 HP engine and pressurized cabin up to twelve thousand feet."

Brody nodded. "Light emitting diodes." He indicated the exterior lighting. "Exterior storage?"

"Some in the underwing radome and another in the tail, but I don't need it. Take a look at this." Erick opened a clamshell door and motioned for him to enter. He used the stairs Erik retrieved from the cab and entered the aircraft. Tan leather seats, cream carpeting, and bonus points, the seats were adjustable.

"She's a sweetheart, isn't she?"

"Oh, yeah, definitely. Did you modify the seats?" Brody could actually sit up straight in them, which at six-foot-five was unusual. Most seats in these smaller planes were manufactured for a shorter person.

"You know your stuff. Yeah, I did. There is a modification kit for this baby, otherwise I wouldn't have bought her. I can't fly her if I can't sit down comfortably."

He admired the interior of the plane. "What is your maximum?"

Erik smiled even wider, if it was possible. "I can go thirteen hundred nautical miles if I have no passengers and full tanks, but I've never had to stretch it. It's a good jaunt from here to Jacksonville or Atlanta, but she handles it fine."

"You work in both cities?"

"Yeah, mostly Jacksonville now. The boss has a special project he's trying to get off the ground and I'm his conduit. Shit the man comes up with." The last words were mumbled as Erik pointed to the multi-function display. "Instrument approach, which is invaluable. I don't ever want to fly a fixed-card ADF approach again. Not after this little beauty."

Brody laughed with Erik. "She's gorgeous. Do you put plastic down when you bring Clare the plants?"

"You bet. I know she loves those things, but I'm not going to let anything dirty touch my plane."

"Erik! Brody! Dinner!" Clare's voice from the doorway swung both their heads.

Erik raised a hand in acknowledgement. "Let's get going. Clare makes the best grilled fajitas."

Brody disembarked and waited for Erik to close up his aircraft before accompanying him through the yard and back to the patio.

"So, what do you fly?" Erik handed him a plate.

Brody grabbed a couple of tortillas and answered, "I have a SF50 Vision."

Erik stopped with a tong full of grilled chicken halfway to his plate. "A Vision is a two million-dollar jet."

"I got a good deal on it, and it was used." Brody shrugged and nodded to the chicken. "You going to eat that or suspend it in mid-air."

Erik blinked at him but dropped the chicken on his plate and then likewise dropped the tongs. "Why are you living *here*?"

Amber snorted. "Because he has a million-dollar plane."

Clare's laugh was contagious, and thank God, Amber kept the conversation rolling. The FBI's little gift of a *jet* could have put a serious rift in the new 'friendship'. Some people can't see their way past money. Thankfully, Erik and Clare didn't seem to be that type.

Brody sat down and handed the coffee around the table. The meeting was the second one they'd had with their team as others monitored the neighbors from the van. The last twenty-one days had been productive, but the productivity wasn't on their case. Together he and Amber had been going through information the JDET personnel had mined from the streets, interviews, and testimony in court cases involving their collars. They'd carefully pieced together two viable leads, and Terrell and the rest of the team had moved forward on them. At least they were advancing the team's objectives while playing house, but their case was going nowhere.

"It's been three weeks." Captain Terrell spoke as he reached for the cream. "We have nothing on the Dawes couple. They do pro bono work, but it would seem they have taken a hiatus there as well. They bought a puppy and are walking it twenty times a day." He snorted and stirred his coffee. "They are vying for the most boring couple on the face of the earth."

Rayburn grabbed one of the scones he'd bought. "Edelman flies all the time."

Amber took a sip of her coffee and glanced at him. He passed her the biscotti he'd bought for her before Rayburn or Watson could grab it. A quick-silver flash of a smile was his reward. He internal-ized their secret connection as he turned to Rayburn.

"He does. Mainly to Jacksonville. So far, our contact in Jax hasn't been able to validate where he's landing. We only have two more airfields. We knew it would be a process of elimination."

"Did digging into their background show anything?" Amber asked.

Terrell shook his head. "Not much. Clare Edelman was Clare Washburn. She was raised by her parents until they died in a factory explosion down state. She had no family, so she spent four years in foster care. She stayed with the same family for all four years. She went to college on scholarships, worked at a large nursery for four years before she married Edelman. Erik was born to an upper middle-class family. His parents are still alive. He works for T-7 Consulting and has for the last four years. Recently promoted and moved to this new housing area. He is in debt to his eyeballs, or he was, until recently."

Brody stopped his boss. "How did you get a look at his financials without a warrant?"

"I didn't." Terrell leaned forward. "You can learn a lot about a person from his or her mail carrier."

Watson leaned forward, "Say what now?"

"I happened to run into the postal worker and struck up a conversation. I told her I was thinking about moving to the area but wasn't sure about the neighborhood. We talked for fifteen minutes. When the Edelmans first moved here, a lot of past due and last notice mail was forwarded from their last address, but they don't receive them anymore. The Daweses are staunch Democrats, and their next door neighbors, the Logans, are huge Republican backers. She didn't know anything about you, thankfully."

"Damn, Captain, I forget you were a good detective before you started flying a desk." Rayburn's comment earned him a middle finger from his boss.

"Speaking of flying, have you flown the FBI's plane yet?" Watson asked before he took a sip of his coffee and literally moaned in appreciation.

He chuckled at the man's orgasmic expression. He got it. Coffee was what jump started his heart every morning. Well, that and fantastic morning sex. He capped the thought right there. He wasn't going to have lewd thoughts about the woman he loved in front of his team. He leaned forward and answered Watson as he reached for an apple fritter. "No, I'm not rated on this particular aircraft, and it was only supposed to be a stage prop."

"It's going to be suspicious if you don't fly it pretty fucking soon." Terrell sighed. "Damn it, I'd hoped we'd have more information before now."

"I can call someone I know. Someone who is rated and can fly it. Legally." His cousin Jason would know if there were any pilots in the local area who could go up with him. He needed someone in the co-pilot seat who was rated, so he could log hours and let his neighbors see him fly the damn thing.

Terrell picked a bear claw. "Call them. We need to find something soon or we're going to have to pull the plug. In the last three weeks, we have forty-seven confirmed overdoses, all pointing to this shit Peña is bringing into the city. Fenton is telling anyone who will listen that JDET is ineffective and inept."

"Yeah, and Detective McBride said there are a rash of deaths at the Cottages from the shit. It started with the one user they assumed died from

H. They confirmed Gray Death." Brody added the information from Kyle's latest call.

The table was silent for a moment. "Fenton is pissed because we're starting to get some of the money from the shit we seize, isn't he?" Rayburn asked.

Terrell narrowed his eyes and glared across the table. "Where did you hear that?"

"From Merlene Talbot in Public Relations. She said the board unanimously approved the allocation. They're going to run an article about it in the *Hope City Journal*. Bet the memo sent Fenton over the wall." Watson answered for his partner who'd stuffed half a cinnamon roll in his pie hole. Odds were good Rayburn could have stuffed the entire thing in his mouth.

"He's not happy." Terrell leaned back in his chair. "This is the skinny. We need to put Edelman with Peña, or we need to move on. I've been given a week. This time next Wednesday, if we don't have anything, we're pulling up stakes and moving on."

Damn it. He knew Peña was bringing Grey Death into the city. This had been their best lead and although he loved playing house, they needed to push on if they couldn't tie either the Daweses or the Edelmans to Peña. For all intents and purposes, the Daweses had been eliminated, although they were still being watched. The pup was kind of fun to watch, but the older couple were as Terrell had said, boring as hell. He glanced at his boss. "I'll call in a favor or two, take up the jet. Probably Friday. I hope." He could explain the urgency to Jason. The man would get it.

"Has this guy Edelman done anything, anything at all, that pings you as cartel related?" Terrell took a bite of his bear claw while staring at him.

"No. All appearances make him a hard worker and a great husband. He brings home trays of flowers for the wife."

Amber added, "He's every wife's dream. According to Clare, Erik does dishes, helped with her gardening hobby by building her a greenhouse, does all the shopping and makes a weekly run to the recycle center because there is only a garbage service in the housing area."

Rayburn chuckled, "A regular Ward Cleaver."

"Ward didn't do housework." Amber reminded him.

"Fine. He's Mrs. Doubtfire." Watson chimed in.

Amber shook her head, "No dresses."

"Burt in *Away We Go*?" Terrell countered.

Every eye at the table turned to Terrell. The man arched an eyebrow. "What? I have a life outside of the office."

"Since when?" Both Rayburn and Watson said at the same time.

"Fuck you. Get out of here and go back to work." Terrell tossed a wadded-up napkin at Rayburn.

"See, that's not fair, they get to stay." Watson picked up his coffee, gave them a two-finger salute and turned toward the door as he reprimanded his partner. "See what your mouth gets us? More work."

"Me? Dude you said the *exact* same thing as I did at the *exact* same time." Rayburn nabbed a jelly doughnut and chased after Watson.

Terrell waited until they'd left the coffee shop before he turned his attention to Brody and Amber. "I know this operation is lasting longer than anticipated. I am aware you have a son. If this is causing undue stress, I can cut you loose, Swanson. We can spin it as you leaving for a work commitment elsewhere. It will give you a couple days at home."

Amber's eyes widened. "No, sir, that's not necessary, but thank you. My son is used to me being gone. Believe it or not, being in the same city is better than what I've had to do in the past. Plus, Brody's family is picking up the slack when my sister can't manage. Gage is having the time of his life."

Which was true. The 8:30 call every night was one of the highlights of his day. Sleeping every night with Amber, rediscovering their love, and using the last three weeks to reconnect, to talk, and to acknowledge mistakes, while working on communication, had been another gift. As a couple, they'd found solid ground, and his mother was in heaven. She sent pictures of every outing, every dinner, every first she had with Gage. Brianna had even commented their mom hadn't had time to set her up on another date, which spoke volumes. Brock and Kallie had met Gage, and they'd taken him to the amusement park. Brianna said both Brock and Gage got sick on the spinning teacups. Kallie had pictures which would humiliate Brock for years to come.

Terrell nodded. "That's good. This op will be ending in the next week. We have to find who is bringing the drugs into the city and close them down. Get at least one flight in on the FBI's plane, and make sure Edelman sees you do it. I want him, and if the plane will smooth the way, we're going to use it." He stood up ending the meeting. "Be careful. Remember, they may look like suburbia, but we're dealing with the cartel." The man spun on his heel and left.

Amber took another drink of her coffee. "Who are you going to call? Your old flight instructor?"

"No. I'll call Jason."

She slid him a sideways glance. "Your cousin?" He nodded before he took another sip of his coffee. "Don't you think he's a little busy running a billion-dollar company?"

"While Guardian is a Fortune 100 Company, I'm not sure it makes billions... yet. He will know of pilots in the area who can be trusted, and besides, I have an idea."

"What's that?"

"The jet flies higher than Erik's plane."

Amber blinked and then rolled her hand indicating he should continue. When he didn't, she narrowed her eyes at him. "You're going to have to give me a bit more, Detective King."

"I could take off ten minutes or so before Erik. His schedule doesn't really fluctuate much. He'd see me taxi and take off, but I circle the field and wait for him to take off. We could shadow him to

Jacksonville. There is enough fuel in the jet to make it there and back. We'd know where he was landing."

"Then we could have Terry follow him the next time he lands. See where he goes."

"That's the plan." He boosted his cardboard coffee cup and tapped the rim against hers. Now, could they implement it before the plug was pulled on the op?

CHAPTER 18

Amber watched the huge SUV pull into the driveway. Black, with tinted windows and expensive looking rims. Damn, either the person inside was a rock star, or POTUS was in the neighborhood. "Ah, Brody? I think your cousin's man is here."

The guy who exited the vehicle was striking and not just because of his strawberry blond hair and wide shoulders. She chuckled as the man ambled up the sidewalk, cowboy boots and all. Dang, she'd never seen a real-life cowboy before. From his salad-plate-sized, shiny belt buckle, to the polished boots with worn down heels, and the starched white shirt with creases down the sleeves, the man read cowboy from the top of his very high head to the toes of his pointed boots.

She hurried to the door and opened it before he had a chance to ring the bell. His smile was dazzling. "Hi. Amber, right?"

He extended his hand, and she grasped his in a firm, warm shake. "Yep. Brody will be here in a second. Come on in." She shut the door behind him. "Can I get you some coffee?"

"No, thank you. I've had my limit today. I'm Dixon Marshall, by the way."

"Dixon, it's nice to meet you. So, you're a pilot?"

"Yes, ma'am. I fly about anything with wings or rotors. Do you fly?" He trained his intelligent light blue eyes on her and smiled again.

"I fly a desk. It's safer for everyone. Evidently my inner ear doesn't like little planes. It tends to get messy when I go up."

The man was a looker, and if she wasn't head over heels in love with Brody King, she'd be throwing her hat in this cowboy's corral. Speaking of rings... the thick, dark metal band on the man's left finger would be the cause of many a single woman's tears, or maybe underhanded schemes. She sure hoped whoever had landed this man was strong enough to endure the come-hither looks and telephone numbers he'd attract

Dixon laughed. "Well, thank you for the heads up."

Brody walked in and extended his hand. "Hey, Dixon, right?"

"I am. You're definitely a King. I could put you up against any one of your cousins and see the family resemblance. Your eyes are different. Most of my Kings have green eyes or variations of green."

"These blues actually come from my dad's side. My mother said my cousins take after my Aunt Amanda. Are you ready to take a look at what the FBI is letting me play with?"

"Absolutely. I need to log some flight hours. Where are we heading?"

"Well, that's what I wanted to talk with you about." Brody stopped as they approached the back door. He leaned in and gave her a kiss. "See you soon."

Amber drew a worried breath. "Be safe." She reminded herself that even if *she* didn't like to fly in small planes, it didn't make the event itself dangerous.

Brody squeezed her hand and whispered,

"Always." He opened the door and the men started talking as soon as they cleared the doorway. She leaned against the casement and watched the men walk to the hangar. Not a minute later, she caught sight of Erik drinking a cup of coffee and staring at the hangar Brody and Dixon had entered. To say the man wanted to go up in the plane was an understatement. Erik practically vibrated whenever he and Brody talked about the jet, and when Brody let him sit in the aircraft, the man had practically orgasmed he was so excited.

She closed the door and moved her observation of her neighbor into the office. She clicked on the right camera angle and zoomed in, watching her neighbor's back porch. Clare came outside and handed a piece of paper to Erik. He didn't look pleased but nodded. The two of them stood side by side and watched as Brody opened the main hangar door where the FBI's jet sat. With one of the hangar cameras, she could watch the men perform a preflight inspection. She ping-ponged her attention between Erik and Clare, to Brody and Dixon, but her attention was soon focused solely on the couple next door. Clare shook her head when Erik said something. She pointed a finger at him and stabbed him in the chest. The man slammed his cup down onto the table, and his coffee splashed on the tabletop. Clare threw up her hands and got in her husband's grill, her movements punctuating whatever she was saying. Erik stood with his hands on his hips, and they exchanged what looked like heated words.

Clare stormed back into the house. Erik grabbed his briefcase from the patio table and headed to his aircraft. The engine of the FBI's loaner started. The high-pitched whine of the jet was distinctly different from the smaller propeller aircraft. She watched the single-engine jet taxi and then take off. Her stomach lurched at the thought of flying in such a small plane. Erik's Piper trotted from his hangar about five minutes later. He made the trip to the end of the runway, and she watched until the plane jogged down the stretch of cement and elevated into the air.

Hopefully, Brody and Dixon could manage to shadow Erik's flight. She wished them luck, loads of luck, but if what she saw this morning was an argument, she was going to try to get closer to Clare. People talked when they were upset. She would pop by and offer to help Clare when she saw the woman go to her greenhouse. Maybe suggest a midday glass of wine or two, and then talk. The perfect couple had a wrinkle. The argument this morning indicated not everything was as blissful as they'd like people to think. Until her neighbor headed to the greenhouse, she had plenty of work to do to keep her busy. The JDET work continued outside this case. They had a crew of people who worked as eyes on the street, and with cultivated confidential informants, the team gathered information at an astonishing rate.

Amber tapped on the greenhouse door. "Hello?"

Clare jumped and spun around. "Oh, hey. What are you up to?" The large black rubber gloves she wore went up to her elbows and there were several empty planting crates stacked on top of her work table.

"Not much. I needed a break from the computer, so I thought I'd stop by and see what you're doing?" She glanced past Clare to the raised planting beds.

"I'm cleaning up a bit. I've been so focused on getting the plants started, I'm afraid I've let things stack up around here. She waved a gloved hand toward the crates she'd seen Erik bring home to her.

"Oh, I can help. Do you want me to throw those away for you?"

"No, I'll use them to start my own seeds." She stacked the trays on her workbench and took off her gloves. "How about a glass of lemonade?"

"I'd love one. Brody is flying one of our clients to New York today, so..."

"While the cat's away, the mouse is going to play?"

She laughed and nodded. "He keeps me focused. I love what we do, but I'm not much of a nose to the grindstone type of person." She followed Clare into the immaculate white on white on white kitchen and sat at the counter while her neighbor poured two glasses of what looked like hand squeezed lemonade. "Thank you."

"You're welcome. I was going to come see you today or tomorrow and talk with you about planting an evergreen hedge at the back of both of our properties. When it comes in, it would obstruct the view to the tarmac. We could do matching arches over the walkways to the hangars so the backyards are defined, and the ornamental arches will provide a relief from the massive hangars in the background."

"Wow, well sure, tell me what I need to do."

"I'll get prices and then once we've agreed on the type and number of plants and design of the arches, we'll split the cost. We plant, the men install the arches, presto the start of a hedgerow. We can do it--"

Amber jumped at a knock at the back door. "Hang on for just a minute, okay?" Clare smiled quickly and then jogged to the door. The unexpected visitor didn't wait long before he knocked again, and louder. Clare opened the door and pushed a man back, shutting the door behind her. Amber leaned back and caught a good look at the man's profile. It was one she'd seen before. Paul Desoto. Desoto had never been officially connected to the Peña organization, but as with all of Peña's upper echelon, the men and women he employed were usually above reproach and members of good standing within the community. Desoto was a prominent businessman in Hope City, but he'd caught both JDET and DEA notice. Their suspicion of the garbage company's owner was based on his proximity of far too many incidents involving Peña.

Clare moved them down the stairs and out of view. Amber slid off her seat and edged to the window. Desoto's stance was rigid, and his arms crossed over his chest as he glared down at Clare. He glanced at his watch and glanced right and left before he spoke a few words. She couldn't hear what was said, however the tone left little doubt of his current mood. Desoto wasn't happy. Careful to stay behind the lace curtains, she got an up close and personal view of Clare running her hand up Desoto's chest before she stepped in closer to the man. Her hand landed on his cheek, and she raised up onto her toes.

Desoto's arms shot around Clare's waist, and he yanked her into him. The kiss wasn't nice. It was hard, almost like a punishment. Stunned, Amber stood motionless for a moment, and then carefully made her way back to the counter, and chugged the remaining lemonade in her glass. She trotted to the refrigerator and opened the door as she heard the back door reopen. She grabbed the pitcher of lemonade and spun around with a wide smile on her face.

"Hey, I hope you don't mind, but this is some of the best lemonade I've ever had."

"Ah, no problem. Sorry about the interruption."

"I didn't mean to get in the way of anything." Amber filled her glass. "A neighbor? I still haven't met everyone. Always behind the computer screen." She put the glass pitcher back in the fridge and made her way back to the counter.

"No, an old business acquaintance."

"Am I keeping you from visiting with him? I'm so sorry! I can leave." Besides, she wanted to make sure the cameras caught Desoto's image and needed to ensure Terrell got the information quickly.

"Oh, he just stopped by. We'll visit again another day, but I do need to get back to work in the greenhouse." Clare waved toward the building's location.

"And I do need to go back to work. Thanks for the lemonade and the break. Sorry to interrupt your day."

"Really, it's no problem, one of those days. Started out bad and isn't getting better."

Amber took another long sip of her drink to see if Clare was going to share more. When she didn't, Amber prompted with a sigh, "Yeah, Brody and I have our moments. It doesn't mean I don't love him, but sometimes I'm glad he flies, if you know what I mean. We all need our space."

Clare chuckled and rolled her shoulders. "Space in my life is at a premium, that's for sure. Maybe someday we can go to the city and shop, have lunch and do girl things, tips and toes, or a spa day."

She carried her glass back and placed it in the sink before she walked around the counter toward Clare. "Or a spa day. One including tips and toes." Amber laughed and waggled her fingers in the air. "I haven't had a mani-pedi in almost a year."

"Then we're due." Clare moved across the floor with her and opened the door.

She skipped down the steps and turned to walk backward, taking in the yard. She saw someone in the greenhouse but didn't draw attention to the fact. "Call me about the shrubs and the day out."

"I will." Clare raised a hand and waved before she turned toward the greenhouse.

Amber forced herself to walk in a leisurely, meandering fashion to her house. She stopped to look at a couple flowers. Clare had told her the name of the bush, but the information had gone in one ear and out the other. She ambled past the flower beds Clare had helped her weed and plucked a couple of stray green shoots from the dirt. She waved at Mrs. Dawes and her puppy.

"Hello, Amber. It's a beautiful day, isn't it?" The older woman held the leash of the little puffball as it walked a thousand steps to Mrs. Dawes' one. The thing was nothing but fur, a black button nose, and a tiny pink tongue.

"It is! A great day." She watched the puppy for a few seconds before she wandered into the house. The second the door was closed, she raced into the office and put in her earwig. "Please for the love of everything holy, tell me you got the man on film."

"Paul Desoto." Rayburn confirmed.

Amber was busy pulling up camera screens. "Did he go into the greenhouse?"

"Yes, he did. Did you get a load of the kiss he put on her?" Watson's voice came through the comms.

"They're more than old business associates."

"Is that what she claimed?" Rayburn asked.

"Yeah." Amber clicked on the cameras angled toward the Edelman's. "Do we have any better angle on the greenhouse?"

"Try the camera on the hangar."

Shit, why hadn't she thought of the higher angle? She selected the camera and directed it toward her neighbor's house. "Not great, but I can see the door."

"Yeah, we got it."

"This is going to the cloud, right?"

Rayburn snorted.

"Not an answer." There was no way she was going to lose this connection because someone didn't double check to make sure the recording was being saved.

"Yeah, it is an answer. It is going to the cloud, and we hit record here in the van as soon as we saw him get out of the car." Rayburn huffed.

"Don't get your panties in a wad, big-boy. I wanted to make sure." Amber chuckled at Watson's outright laugh at her comment.

"My panties are the least of your concern. What is he carrying?"

At Rayburn's questions her eyes popped to the screen. "I think those are the planting pallets Clare uses."

"Why the hell does he need planters?" Watson's question was the one which was on her mind, too.

"Do we have a list of his businesses? Someone please get Terrell on comms." Amber scrolled her mouse to her second screen and hit up the DEA database. She input Paul Desoto's name and brought up his criminal history—three speeding tickets and a misdemeanor possession charge when he was nineteen years old. She dug as deep as she could, but she didn't find anything more. On a whim, she entered Clare Edelman and requested all known aliases. She wasn't prepared for what she saw.

"Oh shit."

"What? What did we miss?" Watson's question was asked about two seconds before Terrell came on the line.

"Captain, Paul Desoto just left the Edelmans' residence." Rayburn filled him in as Amber kept typing.

"That's the connection."

Amber nodded in agreement and added, "Yes, sir, it is, but the connection runs deeper. Desoto was in foster care the same time Clare was, and guess who lived with Clare for the first two years of her time in the system?"

"Desoto." Terrell made the leap easily.

"Yes sir, and we have another connection. Aarón Rubio was a foster in the same house at the same time."

"Rubio, as in the right hand of Peña?"

She nodded and breathed, "One in the same."

"Are you accessing this information legally?"

"Yes sir. Public documentation obtained

through the Freedom of Information Act in a massive foster care fraud filed by the FBI three years ago. It was gathered for that case, and I appreciate the hell out of whoever did the legwork, but it's all here on the DEA's database." Free and for the taking. Well, free if you were a DEA agent, which she still was, technically.

"Why didn't this information come up on our background searches?" Terrell growled.

"This database isn't connected to the NCIC checks. If you aren't DEA with a reason to search it, there is no way you'd know about it." Hell, she'd only checked it on a hunch.

"So, we have our connection. Great work." Terrell's voice held a hint of relief.

"Our focus needs to shift to the wife, and what's in the greenhouse. We need to find out what Desoto had sandwiched between those crates." Watson put in his two cents.

Terrell agreed. "Unfortunately, we can't stop him from taking the lady's trash out."

"That's the thing though, she didn't want me to throw them away. She said she was going to reuse them, so why did she let Desoto take them?"

"Was there anything unusual about the crates?"

"No. They're those hard, black, rubber contain-ers." Amber wished like hell she'd looked closer.

Rayburn hummed into the mic for a second before he interjected, "Maybe it's under the soil?"

"It could be, I guess. She was wearing heavy duty rubber gloves today. Not the cloth and leather ones she uses for planting. She said she was clean-ing. Come to think of it, I spooked her when I popped in this morning. Maybe she was working with the stuff? But I didn't see a damn thing that resembled drugs."

"You'll need to get a closer look inside the greenhouse."

"Yes, sir." Her mind and Terrell's ran on the same track.

"Has King checked in yet?"

Amber glanced at the time on the computer. "No sir, they should be landing soon if everything goes like he'd hoped."

"I'm going to get a tail put on Desoto. He's cagey as fuck, and I don't want to blow this case now that we have a link. Give me a call when King is on the ground. We need to work a game plan. Don't go to the house without having King as a backup. You hear me?"

"Loud and clear, sir." She waited for Terrell to

clear before she asked, "Rayburn, can you please play back the footage of Desoto leaving the house? How many crates did he have?" She watched the screen and waited until the rewind stopped and Desoto left the house. "He's wearing gloves like the ones Clare was wearing."

"Are the trays empty? Maybe he has the GD inside the little cups in the trays? Remember it could be in pellet or pill form."

"I can't tell. The video is too grainy. It doesn't look like there is anything in the top one, but it could be sandwiched between the layers. I can't tell how many he has. Three, maybe four?" Watson said.

She stared at the best shot of the man. "Do you think the tech lab can enhance the digital?"

"I'd have to get clearance from Terrell. If we take it outside of the unit, gums will start flapping." Rayburn cautioned.

"Damn, that's right. Ok, let's hold off, and make a note to brief Terrell that an enhanced digital may give us a lead on how they are transporting the dope."

"If they're transporting dope. The guy could be visiting his girlfriend, and the woman could be a bored suburban wife who wants a little mid-morning delight." Rayburn's comment tightened her jaw. Not because it was crude, but because he could be right. They could be spinning themselves up because of coincidences. The only thing that kept her dogging this trail was her training. There was no such thing as a coincidence. Not to this extent, and not this closely linked to the upper echelon of the Peña cartel.

Brody brought the small jet into a final descent for Hope City.

"There you go. You've got this. A couple more flights, and I'd be comfortable with you as my right seat." Dixon's words came through the headphones.

"Thank you, I take that as a compliment." The man had listed off the aircraft he'd flown and the ratings he held. It was amazing someone so young could have accrued the hours in the air that he'd chalked up.

"I'm heading back to DC and then home. If you need another alibi ride, give Jason a call, and he'll find someone to come up."

Dixon's hand was on the stick, but the man let

him correct his descent and bring the nose up a bit more. Brody concentrated on the landing and was rewarded with a murmured, "Good. Damn good," from Dixon when he reversed the engine and settled the little plane on the short suburban airstrip.

They taxied to the hangar and parked the plane outside. After he shut down the single engine, both he and Dixon attached a tow bar to the front of the plane and used a small tractor to back the aircraft into the hangar. The tractor was, once again, parked alongside the aircraft shelter, and the doors were rolled down and buttoned up. Dixon shook his hand and headed straight for the SUV parked in the drive. He watched his Guardian chaperone drive away and opened the screen door.

"Did you find Erik's airport?" Amber's question met him as soon as he shut the door.

"Kresley Field. I gave the information to your contact in Jacksonville. He was at Jackson-Dehnam, across town."

Amber leaned against the archway leading from the kitchen into the formal living room. "Guess who came to the Edelmans' house today."

"It's too early for Santa." Brody walked up to her and wrapped his arms around her. "The Easter

Bunny has already been here. A leprechaun carrying a pot of gold?" He dropped a quick kiss on her lips.

Her smile was brilliant. "Nope. Paul Desoto."

It took a couple of seconds to make the connection. "As in...?"

"Yep and there's more. Come here." Amber urged him into the office. "I saw Clare and Erik have a spat this morning as you and... Dixon, right?" He nodded. "Yeah, well when you were in the hangar doing the airplane thing, Erik was outside watching, or drooling, dealer's choice, but Clare came outside with a piece of paper, and they had words. It was obvious they were having a heated discussion, so, after he took off, I decided to see if Clare needed to get something off her chest."

"Did she?"

Amber shook her head, her ponytail waving behind her. "No, she talked hedgerows and arches, but then we were interrupted by a knock at the door. I had a perfect profile look at Mr. Paul Desoto."

Desoto had always been in the pool, but never in the deep end, and never wet enough to give the cops probable cause to get a warrant, or hell, for that matter, to focus manpower chasing him. "But it doesn't necessarily tie them to Peña."

"Maybe, but Desoto and Clare have a past and are tied to someone else who is a known associate of Peña." She showed him the monitors and walked him through the afternoon's events. "Captain Terrell wanted us to call when you got back. I think he wants to talk about how we are going to get a look at what's in the greenhouse."

"Damn, then Clare Edelman is the key, not Erik."

"We think so. She knows Desoto in an up close and personal way, and they both have a connection to Aarón Rubio."

"Rubio is directly tied to Peña. We need to get a better look at the greenhouse."

"Yep. But how? She barely let me in the damn thing when I stopped by today, and she's never offered to give us a tour, other than in passing."

He snapped his fingers. "Erik."

Amber blinked at him and cocked her head. "Excuse me?"

"He's proud of what he built. If I tell him I'm going to build you one as a surprise, he'll want to show me what he's done. I'll ask him to take me for a tour, and you can keep Clare busy so she can't run interference."

A smile spread across her face. "I know how to do it, but we'll have to wait until Saturday. I can make an appointment for Clare and me at a spa. She mentioned it today. We'll be gone for hours."

"Perfect. In the meantime, let's call Terrell."

CHAPTER 19

Amber stretched and smiled. Brody was wrapped around her back, spooning her tight against his body. She loved this time of the morning, when the worries of the case weren't foremost. Brody's hand splayed across her abdomen, and he moved his hips against her.

"Morning." His deep voice was a few octaves lower first thing in the morning. The rumble went through her back and deep into her soul. It was a sound she never thought she'd hear again and one she prayed she never took for granted.

"Good morning." She pushed back into him and was rewarded with another rumble of sound. This one was a needy growl. His morning whiskers scraped against her shoulder. The stark contrast between his warm lips, soft tongue, and scratchy whiskers sent a shudder of anticipation through her. They'd made love every night, several times a night, and almost every morning, too, but the love they shared now was different than it was ten years ago. At least for her it was. She was happy in her own skin, content in the new relationship which was regenerating from the disaster of the past, and pleased they'd cemented the remodeled connection with communication. The sex was fantastic, but more than anything, she cherished the friendship, trust, and forgiveness that supported what they were building between them.

She rolled onto her back and Brody covered her, moving between her legs. She ran her fingers through his bed head hair and smiled at the sexy man who looked at her like she'd placed the sun in the sky.

"What time do you have to meet Clare?"

She groaned. "Nine. We're driving into the city. It will take at least an hour to get to the spa and then we have four hours booked. Mani-pedi and a massage, plus an hour drive back after we have lunch."

"Then we have time." Brody lowered to her breast and circled her nipple with his tongue. She arched into him and held his head down to her sensitive skin. He took her into his mouth and hummed. The vibration and suction traveled in currents through her body. Under her skin, her muscles contracted, sending the pulsing currents along a familiar corridor of building tension and need.

Her hands traveled along the divots and ridges of his shoulders and back. His skin prickled under her exploring fingertips. The tactile need to reinforce her connection to him peaked as she gripped his hard ass cheeks and arched her hips. Her breath released in a sigh as he entered her. The feel of his hard sex exponentially multiplied the threads of yearning that weaved a tightening pattern deep inside her.

He moved his arms under her and joined their bodies from shoulder to toe. They moved together, bound by not only the physical sensations, but by their commitment to each other, to Gage, and to the future.

His pace quickened and his hips thrust harder. The increase shifted her past the cliff, and she shattered into a thousand brilliant pieces of erotic stimulation. As she held Brody to her, she felt him as he chased his release. He shouted her name and slammed into her two... three times before he stilled above her.

She pushed his hair from his face, and he kissed her palm. God, he was majestic in his masculinity, and he was hers. She held her regrets at bay. She'd always have them. It was something she'd need to deal with as they moved forward, but they would move forward. Together, as a family.

Brody watched as Amber put on her makeup. "Text me if you're getting back sooner." She glanced at him and blinked her eyes. The 'no duh' was left unsaid. Yeah, it was a stupid thing to say. "Sorry."

"I'll be fine. We're getting our fingernails painted. As far as we know, she isn't a threat."

"As far as we know." He reiterated that portion of her comment.

She put down her mascara and turned around, leaning on the sink. "I am a full-grown DEA agent, Detective King. I can handle myself. I don't take unnecessary risks, and I have my weapon in my bag." She nodded toward the massive straw tote she was going to take with her to the day spa.

"Desoto and Rubio are not people to mess

around with. If she's got a connection with them, she's dangerous."

"Really? I had *no* idea." Sarcasm dripped from her comment and landed on the floor between them like a flopping fish.

He put his hands on his hips and drew a deep breath. "Look, I'm trying. I understand now why we shouldn't be on this operation together. It's hard to let you go with her, knowing what we do."

Amber took the two steps forward to put herself in his arms. He enfolded her into him.

"I appreciate the concern. Let's look at this from another angle. We are both highly trained. How about we trust each other to do what we know how to do and promise each other we will be as safe as we can be. After this operation, we won't be in this position. You'll never know when I'm in danger."

He recoiled and stared down at her. "That doesn't make me feel better."

"It's the truth, and we've promised to ground this relationship in the truth, right?" She stared up at him waiting for his answer.

"Yes, we did. The truth is I don't like it, and I probably won't ever like it." He dropped his forehead to hers. "But I'll deal with it."

"It's all we can do."

"Still sucks." He tipped her chin and kissed her tenderly.

"It does. Now I need to finish getting ready before Clare gets here. I'm taking one for the team today. A massage, a mani-pedi, and lunch out. How much do you want to bet those receipts get tagged for an audit when I submit my expense reports?"

"Almost guaranteed. I can see Terrell explaining them to Fenton." Brody grimaced. Fenton was an absolute dick. He took every opportunity to call Terrell to the carpet. It sucked his old man couldn't do something about the jerk.

"Wow. Didn't even think about Attila. I hate the guy, and I've never even met him."

"Lucky you." He heard a horn blast.

"Clare's here. I'll be safe. You go find us something that links her to the drugs."

"I'll get into the greenhouse and take a long look." He opened the front door and gave her a quick kiss that Clare could see. Amber skipped from the house, and he waved at Clare. She returned the wave, and he watched the women back down the drive and head out of the development.

He headed to his computer and brought up the

camera screens as he plugged in his earwig and activated the mic on his computer. "Good morning."

"Are you ready?" It wasn't a surprise to hear Terrell's voice through the comms. The man tried to be present at every major point in his team's investigations.

"I am." He unlocked the desk and hiked up the leg of his jeans. The small holster for his secondary weapon went around his calf and was cinched tightly against his leg. He checked his weapon, making sure a bullet was in the chamber. The safety was on the handle of the automatic. When he applied pressure to fire, it eliminated the gun's firing safety.

"I have a tail on Clare and Amber. Nothing close, and they know the final destination so if they lose them in traffic, they can find them again, but if shit goes down, I want her to have back up not too far away."

"Roger that." He respected the hell out of his boss, and things like this were the reason.

"Speaking of which, we've moved to the first cul de sac of the development, so if you need us, we'll be there in short order." Terrell's voice brokered no discussion on the matter.

"Dude is on his back porch." Watson's voice came through his earwig. "Coffee and the paper."

"Same as the last two Saturdays," Rayburn announced. "I want a life like that. Same old thing, day after day."

Watson snorted, "You'd die of boredom."

"Probably." Rayburn chuckled.

"All right. I'm heading over." Brody waited to get an acknowledgement before he dropped his earpiece into his desk drawer, brought up the fake screens which masked what he and Amber were actually doing, and headed into the kitchen. He poured himself a cup of coffee and ambled into the backyard. He pretended not to notice Erik and walked into the expanse of lawn at the rear of the house. He stood staring at the carpet of green and then moved and stared at a different spot.

He heard Erik's chair slide against the flagstone as he got up. It was working. He moved to another spot and stared at the grass intently.

"So, watching the grass grow?" Erik came up beside him and stared at the same patch of lawn as he was looking at.

Brody pointed to the far corner. "What do you think about a greenhouse, right there?"

Erik narrowed his eyes and then swung them

to the other corner. "That area has direct sunlight. It would be better there."

Brody's head snapped around to blink at his neighbor. "Is sunlight important?"

"Well, yeah." Erik chuckled his response.

"Shit. I don't know anything about building a greenhouse, but Amber is researching plants, and has bought some seeds. I think Clare has rubbed off on her. She's mentioned wanting a greenhouse so she could grow her own plants."

"Ah, it's started. Yeah, Clare has definitely rubbed off on her."

"Hey, would you mind if I took a look at how you built the one you constructed for Clare?" Brody took a sip of his coffee after he popped the fifty-million-dollar question.

"Clare really doesn't like anyone going inside, but since she's not home, she'll never know." They turned and walked toward Erik's backyard. "I had to get the city to put in a new water meter, and then I had the irrigation system professionally installed, but other than that, I did it all. The kit is pretty straightforward. Damn, I wish you'd been here when I was trying to get mine together. It probably would've taken half the time. Four hands are better than two."

"How's this, I'll buy a steak dinner if you help me with mine." It was a dinner he'd never buy and a construction project which would never see the light of day, but his neighbor didn't need to know that.

"And drinks, man."

"Deal." Brody laughed as they approached the greenhouse.

"This is Clare's pride and joy." He opened the door using a key on his key ring.

"She locks it?"

"Hell, it's alarmed at night, too." Erik laughed. "She has some pretty special plants in here. I disable the alarm when I get up in the morning. I made the mistake of coming in to get the garbage once without turning it off. I had a headache for a week." He reached up and tapped a foghorn shaped piece of metal. "The damn alarm speaker is right at the door."

"Ouch, man, that had to suck."

"No worse than trying to get Clare to stop fussing at me. The woman does not like anyone in her space." Erik stood inside the door and stared at the raised beds.

"How does she reach the panels in the ceiling?" Brody walked into the building and his eyes scanned everything. There were a couple bags of natural fertilizer stacked under a workbench and three of the empty planting pallets sitting on top.

Erik glanced up. "With this." He reached to the back of one of the raised beds and grabbed a long stick to demonstrate how to open a venting panel.

Brody took the time to duck down and inspect the lower shelves. There was nothing he could see. "You said you had irrigation?"

"Yeah, over here." Erik showed him the small control panel and the hose system which worked through each of the beds.

"This is amazing." Brody stood with his arms crossed.

"And it isn't hard to do. You can get smaller ones, but you've met Clare. Only the best will do." Erik shrugged and glanced at the house.

"I'm that one in our relationship. Amber was content living in a tiny ranch-style house. The backyard was the biggest thing about the place where she used to live." He smiled at the memory of Gage catching the football. Damn, he really wanted to see his son again in person, not on Face-Time or a voice call with him on the phone, although he was seeing sides of Gage it probably would have taken a few months to discover. He was a good kid, watched out for his friends and had his priorities right. He loved to play, was a good student, and was good to his family. He knew this because his entire family had been texting him. And it chapped his ass. He wanted to be the one spending time with Gage, but work kept him away. Hell, he didn't know how Amber had done it for so many years. Her sister was a champ, but she was also happy to let others help out. Thankfully, his family, and even Sharon McBride, had taken turns picking Gage up from school and watched him on the weekends so Dawn could have some free time.

"I didn't mind where we were living before, but Clare hated it. When the opportunity for this promotion came up, and I was asked to submit for it, I didn't think I stood a chance to compete, let alone get the promotion. I think the fact I didn't mind flying as long as the company reimbursed me for my fuel was the thing which finally won the boss over. Having boots on the ground is important."

"It is. That's why I've got the Vision. Sometimes you need to see for yourself where people are landing."

Erik nodded toward the door. "I know exactly

what you mean, although I have no idea why my boss pays me so much to do the same thing I used to do. He only needed to pay for my fuel and a per diem so I can keep Piper healthy."

"Good raise huh?"

"God, I'll say. We were neck deep in debt, you know? Like I said, Clare only wants the best. I mean take these trays of flowers. I have to make a special trip to pick them up and they bill her for them. I'm so damn glad I don't see the price. As long as we are in the black, I'm happy."

Erik picked up one of the trays and turned it over in his hand. "Crazy about these plants..." He spoke to himself as he held the tray.

"Hey, would you mind if I used one of those? Amber has some seeds. Maybe I can convince her to start simple and see if she has a green thumb. If she kills the plants, I'm off the hook as far as a greenhouse goes."

Erik glanced from the trays to him. "I don't see why not. Clare should have about fifty of these things somewhere. Probably in the garage. She says she'll repurpose them, but I never see her using them." He handed the tray to Brody.

Erik shut and locked the greenhouse door behind them.

"Hey, when are you taking the Vision up again? I'd love a chance to go up in her."

Hell, probably never. "Maybe next weekend. I was thinking of taking Amber to Miami. Maybe you and Clare would like to come along?"

"That would be awesome, but I thought Amber didn't like to fly."

"She doesn't, but her doctor prescribed a scopolamine transdermal patch. I was going to test it out." He was relieved to remember the medical term for the motion sickness patch. He'd seen a late-night documentary on a murder case where scopolamine had played a role and had been fascinated by the concept. That rabbit hole cost him an entire night's sleep, but it came in handy just now.

Erik chuckled. "Maybe we'll pass until the experimental stage is over. From what Clare told me, the last time Amber went up it was ugly."

"Dude, she painted the cabin in puke. Nobody and nothing was left unscathed." Brody laughed at the gagging sound Erik made.

"Yeah, we'll definitely wait until you know those patches work. Want another cup of coffee?"

"Nah, thanks, I'm actually waiting for the city to show up. I think I have a problem with my water meter. My bill is outrageous, so I asked them to come and look at it."

"Man, if it isn't one thing it's another. The joys of home ownership." Erik picked up his paper. "Wait, the city sending someone on a service call on Saturday?"

"Yeah, surprised the hell out of me. I called them after getting the bill yesterday. I guess they figure there might be a leak or a break some-where." Brody huffed a laugh. "That would be my luck. Anyway, have a great day and thanks for the growing tray." Brody raised said tray as he headed back to the house. "No worries." Erik sat down in his back porch chair and flipped his newspaper with a quick motion of his wrist.

Once back in the house, he headed into the office. It took less than ten seconds to put his earwig in and unlock his computer. He hit his microphone enabling him to speak to his boss. "I have a tray."

"We saw it. How do we get to you?"

"I told Erik I was having problems with my water meter."

"Smart." Watson pimped him some praise.

"We're on the way." He heard the motor start as Rayburn said, "Captain is driving. Pray for us."

Brody chuckled and turned on the overhead lights so he could examine the tray. "What is so special about you?" Why would Desoto take three or four of them? The man owned a huge garbage company, but it wasn't like he'd be hauling away junk from his married girlfriend's place. There had to have been something sandwiched in between the trays.

"We're here. Any idea where the hell the water meter is?" Watson asked as a flash of light from the windshield tracked across the wall. "On the right hand side of the garage. I'll open the door and let you in through the other side of the house. Edelman won't be able to see you enter."

"Perfect." He heard doors slamming and hustled to the garage through the kitchen. He flipped open the lock to the outside door and stepped back to allow his boss and teammates through the door.

"We can't spend too much time here without raising suspicion." Terrell got down to business immediately.

"This way." Brody showed them through the house. Both Rayburn and Watson whistled at the rather opulent spread.

"Here." Brody waved to the tray. "I just started my examination of it when you drove up."

He and Terrell leaned down together, and he moved the tray, tipping it to catch the light.

"Huh... it looks like shrink wrap," murmured Terrell.

"Yeah, probably pressed cardboard underneath. It's not very heavy." He hefted the tray.

Terrell stared at the thing. "Rayburn, get me an opioid test kit."

"Got it right here." Rayburn dug around in what looked like a toolbox and produced a metal tube which held an ampule, a small spatula, and a zip bag to contain or trash the test results.

"Carefully cut through the shrink wrap." Terrell nodded to the tray.

"You think the bastards are coating the cups in the shit?" Watson asked as he handed Brody a razor blade cutting tool from the drug testing kit pouch.

"Wait." Terrell cautioned. "Put something over your mouth and wear gloves." He glanced around. "Everyone."

Brody hustled into the kitchen and grabbed some linen hand towels. He tied one over his mouth and nose as Rayburn distributed a pair of latex gloves to each of them.

"Okay, King, cut the wrap and scrape a sample

of whatever is under it. Put the sample into the ampule." He crushed the chemical held in the ampule and nodded for Brody to continue.

He took a deep steadying breath and carefully scored the film at the very corner of the tray, then used the knife to keep the cut open. With his free hand, he scratched the inside of the container and watched as it crumbled easily. The outside was black, the inside––gray. He took the tiny spatula and transferred a minute sample to the ampule his boss was holding. Terrell carefully closed the tube and gently shook the chemicals to mix them.

"Son of a bitch."

"Would you look at that?"

"Holy hell, look at the color."

"Yellow. It's heroin."

"This entire tray is pressed heroin." Watson whistled.

Terrell shook his head. "No, I think this entire thing is pressed Grey Death. How much does this weigh?" Terrell carefully assessed the tray. "Four, maybe five pounds?" His captain glanced at him in question.

"Yeah, about two and a half kilos." He confirmed his boss' guestimate. He did the math in his head. "Fuck, this one tray has a street value of

$750,000 *if* they package it into gram bags *as is* and don't cut it down further. If they have someone cutting it before it hits the streets, each one of these trays could be a million dollars on the street." Brody leaned away from the innocuous looking planter. "We need to seal this shit up. I don't feel like OD'ing today." He nodded to Rayburn. "In the kitchen, in the cabinet under the island, there's black electrical tape."

Rayburn hustled from the room. Watson glanced from him to Terrell. "So, we know the woman is definitely involved. What about the husband?"

"My gut is telling me no. He has no idea what he's been transporting up here. Hell, there is no way he'd give up a cool mil to the next-door neighbor. Nah, he doesn't know anything. He's guilty of bringing his wife the flowers she ordered. She knows, though. She gave Desoto four of these."

"It was five." Watson clarified. "I was able to run the recording through an over the counter digital enhancer. Five trays."

"Five million dollars of Grey Death on the street." Brody closed his eyes.

"That we know about. Who knows how much Edelman has flown up here." Watson added.

"But we have a way to Peña now." Brody glanced at his boss.

"We need to get to the husband before the wife comes home."

Brody glanced at the digital display of the time on his computer. "We've got three hours, maybe a little longer. I can text Amber to stop and pick up something on the way back. That might gain us a half hour or so."

"What do you have planned, boss?" Rayburn handed him the black electrical tape as Watson asked the question.

"We're going to catch Clare and Desoto and work them for a lead to Rubio and Peña. King, get Mozinga on the horn. I want the entire team in the briefing room in less than an hour. Rayburn, call Judge McClure, we need to put a tracer in the tray, and we're going to do it legally. Watson, help me seal this so King can get it to the greenhouse before Clare Edelman gets home. King, when you come back, bring Edelman with you. He's in for one hell of a Saturday.

CHAPTER 20

"Hey man, what's up?" Erik glanced through the screen door at the tray he was carrying.

"Yeah, dude, I went to put this in the garage and found Amber already had like five of them."

"Figures." Erik chuckled and stepped from his house. They both headed toward the greenhouse with the tray they'd sealed *after* Terrell had a warrant. Once they had the verbal authorization, Mozinga dealt with the paperwork, and they placed a GPS tracker inside the shrink wrap. The black electrical tape they used to seal the tiny cut blended well with the black tray and unless someone inspected it closely, they shouldn't notice the small square which sealed the corner of the tray.

Mozinga assigned two teams to the tracker and both were positioned and waiting outside the housing area. The tail would leap-frog in traffic and keep Desoto from knowing he was being followed. Of course, if things went as planned, the units and the GPS chip wouldn't be needed, but there was no way in hell they'd let almost two million dollars in drugs sit in a greenhouse or drive away with Clare's lover. Technology was great, but failures in equipment happened, so four detectives lived and breathed this shift for the sole purpose of keeping an eye on the damn GPS beacon embedded in this tray. If the GPS blacked out before they could execute the plan, they'd have to regroup. Until then, the detectives watched the blinking light on a screen.

Brody put the tray back where he found it, and Erik locked the greenhouse after him. "Hey, what do you say we take a ride in the jet? I figure since the girls are having a day, we can too." Brody shoved his hands in his pockets and nodded toward his hangar.

Erik's eyes widened, and he glanced at Brody's hangar. "Dude, you mean it?"

"Sure. I need a break and nothing urgent is happening at work. What do you say?"

"Deal. Let me text Clare we're flying. She worries."

"Perfect. Tell her we won't be home until late. I have baseball season tickets. Atlanta is playing Chicago this afternoon."

Erik stopped texting and looked up at him. "Damn man, how much money do you have?"

"Meh, the tickets were a gift from a grateful client." Brody started walking toward the house they were using. Erik fell into step with him and pocketed his phone. "Come on in. I need to grab my wallet and do one last check on the weather around Atlanta."

"Sure." Erik followed him into the house and shut the door.

Brody stopped and turned. "Erik Edelman, you're under arrest for transportation of opioids across state lines."

Watson and Rayburn walked into the kitchen; their badges hung around their necks on chains.

"What?" Erik's eyes grew huge, and he spun toward Brody. "Is this some kind of sick joke?"

"I wish it was, man." Brody removed his badge

from his pocket and motioned toward the interior of the house. "We need to talk."

"I want a lawyer." Erik crossed his arms.

"You can ask for one when we read you your rights. Right now, you're going to sit down in there, and you're going to listen." Brody held up a hand when Erik opened his mouth to talk. "The only question we are going to ask you is, 'Do you understand your rights, and do you want a lawyer?' but, let me tell you, Erik, you need to listen to what my boss has to say before you make that call."

"His entire world just shattered." Captain Terrell leaned against the wall and stared into the office where Rayburn and Watson were taking Erik's statement. They'd been up front with Edelman. Told him the facts as they knew them and watched the guy silently fall apart. Faced with the facts and the video of his wife and her lover, he waived his right to an attorney and answered every question they had.

Brody glanced at his pseudo-neighbor. "It did. Fourteen or fifteen trays in the last four months.

ODs are going to reach an epidemic level if we don't get the shit off the streets."

Terrell nodded. "That's why we're going to put pressure on Clare and Desoto. We're going to play hardball. They're going away for life. Interstate drug trafficking with intent to distribute." His boss shook his head. "This guy had the world, and his wife took it away."

"He had an illusion. It wasn't real." They both leaned against the wall and, except for a few murmurs from the office, silence settled through the house.

"This thing you have with Swanson. Is it real?" Terrell didn't look at him when he asked.

Brody drew a breath and released it. "It is. I told you we had a past. The way we ended was ugly and difficult for both of us. A myriad of miscommunication and boiling emotions. Now? Hell I have a son and the woman I've *always* loved. Good is an understatement."

Terrell nodded and stared at his shitkickers. "Keep that. Not everyone gets a second chance."

Brody sent a side eye his boss' way. The man's brows were drawn together, and he looked a million miles away. The professional distance between them lessened in that moment. His captain had always been a bit of an enigma. He was personable, not personal. Professional and distant, making appearances at get togethers, but not staying long. He was tough as nails and someone the entire team respected. In this moment, however, the man behind the badge stepped forward. Brody acknowledged the warning. "I know. I'm one of the lucky ones."

Terrell nodded and pushed off the wall. "What's the ETA on Swanson?"

Okay, so the conversation was over. His boss had shut the door, and he was okay with it. When it came to Terrell, getting to know him was a matter of progress by inches, not miles. He grabbed his cell and glanced at it. "Any time, now."

They'd relocated the van, and Mozinga had assigned two people to monitor cameras on the Edelman residence at the same time he'd set up the trail vehicles. The rest of the team were positioned inconspicuously outside the neighborhood but would move in as soon as Desoto made his way to the house. And *that* step was the gamble, the long pole in the tent which could keep everything from dropping the way it needed to drop. Would Clare call Desoto? With Erik absent, would she take the opportunity to contact her lover? Right now, they were playing a wait and see game. They'd wait as long as they could before they moved on Clare. Getting Desoto and Clare at the same time was paramount. Interrogation with leverage. Play a "he said", "she said" scenario. They had some of the best interrogators in the city on the team.

"Car in the driveway." Rayburn's voice straightened him away from the wall. He moved through the house and watched from the dark front room as Amber got out of the car. She and Clare visited for several minutes before Amber shut the door and waved when Clare backed out of the driveway. He moved so he could watch Clare's vehicle without being highlighted in the car's headlights. Clare backed out, drove to the next driveway, and then idled forward before disappearing back by the garage. The cameras would catch the rest.

Amber unlocked the front door and came in. She leaned to the side. The lights were on further in the house, and the sound of male voices let her know they had company. "Bring me up to speed." She dropped a couple bags on the floor.

Brody nodded toward the office. "Erik's in there. He let me borrow a tray. Pressed Grey Death under black paint and shrink wrap. From what we can ascertain, he had no idea he was doing anything wrong. He's cooperated fully. Terrell is recommending no charges. There was no intent. What about Clare? Did she give any indication what she was going to do tonight?"

Amber chuckled. "Netflix and chill. She probably assumed I didn't actually know what that means."

Terrell wandered into the darkened room. "I need you to get in contact with your counterparts in the DEA. We have the location where Edelman picked up the flowers. Either the containers are being produced at the nursery, or one of the employees is bringing them in and ensured Edelman got the right tray each time he came in to pick up Clare's order."

Brody shook his head. "It would be too hard for an employee to ensure they were there each time Edelman came in. The person is probably in management, if not the owner."

"Plenty of land at a nursery to set up shop and make the trays." Amber added.

"Yeah, and nurseries handle chemicals, so they'd have the PPE to prevent them from accidentally inhaling the product."

"Nurseries also tie into Clare's past. I'll have

Terry do some background on the owner of the nursery."

Terrell stopped her. "Swanson, let's make sure your contact keeps this close to the vest and at the recon level right now. We don't want anyone moving on the property and scaring our players."

"No problem. Where's the information?"

"On your desk."

Brody watched her walk away. Pride ran through him when she excused herself to work the case. She was professional, through and through— a damn good cop. Terrell would have no reason to suggest either of them be reassigned, not that he actually thought his captain would, but it was an option if officers who were a couple weren't professional or caused a disruption in the unit. Furthermore, her confidence was sexy as hell. He loved her intelligence and yeah, it turned his crank. For him, Amber Swanson, DEA agent, hard-ass cop, mother of his son and his lover, was the whole enchilada.

Everything about his present life with her eclipsed the shattering desolation he'd survived during the last ten years. Through time and trials of the heart, their love was consummated and forged in a maelstrom of mistakes, miscommunication, and missed opportunities. He glanced at his boss again. Everyone might not get a second chance, but he was damn sure going to grab his with both hands and hold on tight.

Erik glanced up at her as she entered the office. "You're a cop."

"DEA, actually." She sat down at her workstation and stopped the loop of fake screens. "What is the name of the nursery in Jacksonville?"

"Pretty Polly's Perfect Petals." She'd directed her question to Rayburn, but Watson answered. *Naturally.* She narrowed her eyes at him. "Are you screwing with me?"

"No. That's the name of the place." Erik answered. "She's been lying to me. How long, Amber? How long has she been with this guy?"

Damn. The pain the guy was feeling was coming off him in waves—tangible in a way she hadn't witnessed before. Normally, when spouses learn they've been cheated on, the response was one of anger and disbelief. Watson stood behind the guy and shrugged.

"I don't know."

"But you saw them together, right? The film, I couldn't see her. Was she being... forced?"

Amber sighed and turned to look at her 'neighbor'. Why did it feel like she was kicking the guy in the balls? "No, she initiated the kiss."

Erik closed his eyes, and his head dropped forward.

"You're doing the right thing here, Erik." The need to comfort him prompted her statement.

A huff of bitter laughter escaped him. "By what? Telling the truth? Real noble, aren't I?"

"Sometimes the only goal we can have is to live through the events that happen." The resonance of her voice stemmed from a one hundred percent belief in her words. That's exactly what she'd done.

Erik stared at her for a moment and then dropped his eyes to the carpet. His foot started tapping on the beige loops. Well, good. He should start to get irritated, mad, even downright pissed. Clare *was* cheating on him. She'd used him to transport some of the deadliest drugs known to law enforcement across state lines, and she was working with Desoto, Rubio and Peña.

She printed off a copy of Watson's notes, already added to their shared drive, and grabbed her cell phone from her purse. Before she went any further, she stopped and grabbed her shoulder holster from her lower right desk drawer and slipped it on. She fished for her badge, clipped it to the waistband of her slacks, and withdrew her .45 ACP Kimber 1911 from her purse. With practiced ease, she tucked it under her arm, securing the strap behind the hammer with a quick snap. "Heading to the master bedroom to make a call to my colleagues in Jacksonville. Come get me if there is movement."

"Roger that." Rayburn sat down at her desk and brought up the camera screens again. She glanced at Erik one last time before she walked back to the rear of the house and turned on the light in the bedroom she shared with Brody. Terry answered on the third ring. "Got something?"

"We do. Need you to do some very quiet and very low key surveillance and maybe some background on Pretty Polly's Perfect Petals." She rolled her eyes as she said the name of the business.

"The one off Interstate 10? Sure can. It's a massive place. Everything from palm trees to petunias." Terry chuckled. "Not that I'd know what the hell a petunia was, but they run a local advertising campaign. The jingle is catchy."

"Hmm... I'm starting to worry about you."

"Just starting? Girl, I thought you were one of my best students."

"I was your *best student*."

"Damn straight. I'll start looking into things. Do we think this is an origination or hand off location?"

"We don't know for sure, but if I follow my gut, I'm thinking processing, packing and hand off."

"Damn, making the drug would be hard when the place is open to the public." Terry's voice faded. "Guess it's time to take the missus to find some new bushes."

"Don't get your ass in a crack on this."

"Would never involve the missus, but if I let her drag me around the place, I'll have plenty of time to observe and perhaps see if there's a location which would favor what we're talking about. Don't worry. I still know how to do this job."

"I know you do, but please be careful."

"Will do, kiddo. Are you getting closer to making a bust up there?"

"Low level, tonight. We're hoping to get one or both of them to roll."

"Good luck with that. People who talk about Peña don't tend to stay alive too long." Terry's warning sent her eyes toward the front of the house where Erik was waiting for his future to implode. Damn, she probably needed to talk to Terrell about protective custody for both Edelmans.

"Thanks, Terry. I'll keep in contact. I'd say we are a day, maybe two, from going after bigger guns. We'll need to take down Polly's operation then."

"I'll get a walk through there tomorrow morning, and I have a few agents I trust to keep their trap shut. I'll bring them in when you tell me to do it. What about a warrant?"

"My boss will allow me to provide the information for a federal warrant as soon as he has enough actionable information."

"That works. I'll be waiting."

"Take care, Terry, and hug Marla for me."

"Will do, kiddo."

She ended the call and glanced up. Watson was standing in the doorway, leaning against the intricate woodwork of the door frame. "So, this is a really big house."

"Yeah? And?" She arched an eyebrow, daring him to say what she knew he was thinking.

"Only one bed in the whole house."

"Again... *and*?"

"Nothing." Watson's face broke into a huge

smile. "Absolutely nothing at all. If I were to have anything to say, I'd say I'm damn glad Sarge is *finally* happy. It looks good on you, too." He winked, and before her mind could form the words to put him soundly into his place, said, "Desoto drove into the housing area, but he parked the next block over."

"Why didn't you say so?" She hopped up from the bed and jogged past him.

"I just did." His words followed her down the long hallway. She stopped behind Brody who was at his desk, all the cameras focused on the Edelman house. She glanced at Erik. The man sat still in his chair, staring at the ground, as the rest of the people in the house crammed around the monitors on Brody's desk to watch for Clare's lover to arrive.

"There." Brody pointed to the corner of the camera. A man waited at the far corner of the Edelmans' property. "He's on his cell."

"There's Clare." She pointed to the back door of the home. The man started moving along the far hedgerow, heading toward the back of the house.

"On this camera." Brody motioned to the view of the backyard and clicked the lower left monitor, which brought it up to the center of the screen and enlarged the frame. Clare and Desoto met in a heated embrace. She felt Rayburn shift behind her, blocking Edelman's view. She threw him a quick, grateful smile. He shrugged as if it wasn't a big deal, but the compassion *was* a big deal. At least to her, and apparently Rayburn, too.

"All units stand by." Watson was working the comms and his words broke the silence.

"We're waiting for Desoto to leave with the trays." Terrell's words grounded the team, and Watson repeated the captain's decree.

The couple groped in the darkness for what seemed like an eternity. Finally, they started backing toward the greenhouse. Clare turned to open the building, and Desoto crowded up behind her. The obscene grind against her backside left little room for imagination as to what Desoto wanted.

The light in the greenhouse turned on. They watched, and yes, recorded Desoto spin Clare and pin her, face down, to the workbench. From the motion of Desoto behind Clare, it wasn't hard to guess what they were doing.

"Have the teams move closer while the suspects are... occupied. Close but not visible, we don't want to spook them." Terrell murmured the words to

Watson who repeated them for the detectives outside awaiting orders.

Amber looked across the room toward Erik. The man hadn't moved. God, she couldn't imagine what he was feeling. Used, hurt, cheated on, deserted? All of the above. She returned her attention to the silhouettes in the greenhouse. Desoto finished and slumped down onto Clare's back. They stayed that way for several long minutes until Desoto backed away. It appeared they reconfigured clothing for a while before Desoto drew Clare into his arms and kissed her. He picked up the trays and headed to the door. Clare followed him but didn't turn off the greenhouse lights, which only helped to capture their images. They spoke for a minute before he handed her an envelope, and she shoved it into the pocket of her slacks. Desoto pivoted and headed back to the front of the house.

Terrell snapped, "Take them down. Now."

"Go!"

"Everyone watch your six. These bastards are ruthless," Watson cautioned.

. . .

Within ten seconds the yard was swarmed with JDET team members. The camera witnessed the entire take-down, and Amber was impressed with her new team. They had Desoto handcuffed and the trays seized at the same time as Clare was put to her knees.

"Search her right front pocket. She has either money or directions for the next pickup." Terrell barked the order, and Watson repeated the instructions.

Patel did the search. The female officer stood from where Clare was kneeling. "Boss, we have money. A lot of money, and it looks like pick up orders." Patel's voice came through the radio.

"Copy that. Bring Mrs. Edelman first. Don't let Desoto or Clare Edelman see or talk to each other," Terrell said, and Watson repeated the words. "Rayburn, get Mr. Edelman out of here. Have a unit take him downtown to the office. We need to get the paperwork from the DA before we release him."

"I want to talk to my *wife*." Edelman spit the last word like it was dirt on his tongue.

"Now's not a good time, my man." Rayburn grabbed Edelman's arm and pushed him into the hall and toward the kitchen where he would exit through the garage. Amber followed Rayburn with Brody and Captain Terrell on her heels. They had a finite amount of time to work on Clare while the shock and confusion of the take down was foremost in her mind. Unfortunately, the detectives who hustled Clare across the lawn were quick about the task. Detective Patel opened the door, followed by Clare and Patel's partner, Thompson. Erik glanced back when he heard Clare's scathing accusations of abuse from the detectives. Clare saw her husband and immediately changed the tune she was spitting.

"Erik? Baby, what's happening? What did *you* do? Why did they arrest *me*?"

Rayburn handled the situation by propelling Erik through the door and slamming the thing shut behind him.

"What did he do? Why am I being arrested? Amber? Brody? What?" Clare's eyes fell on the badges and guns. "Police?"

"Have you advised her of her rights?"

Detective Avni Patel nodded. "On the way across the lawn." She pushed Clare into the kitchen and hooked a boot around the leg of a kitchen chair, drawing it out. Patel shoved Amber's neighbor into the chair.

"I want a lawyer. You can't arrest me!"

"Oh, but we can." Avni plopped the envelope down on the table. Thousands of dollars spilled across the walnut surface. Avni flipped the cream colored paper over. Six dates and the numbers of pallets to be picked up from Jacksonville.

Amber took a seat next to Clare. "You know, I've figured out almost all of the background. My only question is how you knew Erik would be flying to Jacksonville on these dates." She looked across the room at Brody and Terrell. There must be someone on Peña's payroll working at Erik's company. Brody nodded his head and called Watson, murmuring something to him. Watson headed to the office.

She turned her attention to Clare. "Life in prison."

"What?" Clare gasped.

"The going sentence for transporting millions of dollars of illicit drugs across state lines."

"Drugs?" Clare shook her head. Tears formed in her big brown eyes. "What in the hell are you talking about? I didn't transport anything!"

"I believe you requested a lawyer?" Amber smiled at Clare. "Unless you're waiving your rights?"

"I..." Clare's mouth snapped shut.

Amber reached her hand toward the cash and spread the money in a fan across the table. Nothing in the pile but one hundred-dollar bills. She did a quick calculation. "There's at least fifty thousand dollars here. You'd understand how we would believe you're involved in drug trafficking." She glanced up at Clare.

Clare made a high-pitched whine in her throat before she choked out. "I'm not trafficking drugs!"

"I'm sorry, did you say you waived your rights to a lawyer?" Amber flipped the envelope and scanned the information written in block print. "You know, Sergeant King, it seems like an open and shut case to me." Amber leaned back in her chair. "Clare's lover feeds her the pick up dates, and she sends hubby off to transport the drugs back here to Maryland."

"That's not what happens." Clare's tears were coming in a stream now. Her nose dripped onto the table, but the woman was oblivious.

"Too bad you can't tell me what actually happens. Imagine the stigma of being dragged downtown, booked and charged. Not to mention a trial. Having talked with Erik, I don't believe he's going to be too inclined to pay your legal fees." She waited for Clare to drop her eyes and then glanced at Brody. The man winked at her. She hadn't asked the woman a single question other than to ask if she'd waived her rights, but she was damn sure poking the woman with every pin she could use. Clare wasn't a hardened criminal. She'd break.

"I want to talk to you." Clare looked at Amber, pleading with her eyes.

"Do you waive your rights to your lawyer?"

Clare nodded.

"Sorry, you'll need to state it."

"Yes, I waive my right to a lawyer. You need to know the truth." She wiped her nose on her shoulder. The handcuffs cinching her hands behind her prohibited her from doing anything else.

Amber glanced at Terrell who displayed a handheld recorder. "So tell me what the truth is, Clare."

"I know Paul from when we were growing up."

"To clarify, you mean Paul Desoto, the man who came to see you tonight?" Amber leaned forward.

"Yeah. Paul Desoto. We were in foster care together. I ran into him about six months before we moved here."

"Where did you run into him?"

"The nursery where I used to work. Sometimes I could get plants that were dying or clippings I could re-root from them for pennies."

"Why were you counting your pennies?"

A harsh laugh came from Clare. "Erik's hours got slashed. He had a plane, and we'd bought new vehicles thinking he'd continue to get paid what he had been."

"But he didn't."

"No."

"And then what happened?"

"Paul and I went for coffee. I needed someone to talk to, you know? Erik worried so much, and he was looking for another job, for someone to buy the plane, a way to refinance the smaller house. He was trying, but the bills kept coming."

"What happened when you told Paul?"

"He said he could help." She shrugged her shoulders. "For a price."

"And the price?"

Clare slowly focused on her. "He could fuck me whenever he wanted, and I do what he said."

Amber drew a breath and asked, "Did you agree?"

"I was desperate. I made one stipulation. He could never use me when Erik was home. He made me call him every morning when Erik left and every night when his plane touched down."

"How long has this been going on?"

"Since right before Erik got the new job."

"Why didn't you stop when he got the new job?"

"Paul videotaped us engaged in... you know. Told me he'd tell Erik."

"And when did you know you were helping the man transport drugs?"

Clare sighed. "I didn't know for sure, but almost from the beginning. Paul made me wear gloves when I was handling the trays. He told me to touch them as little as possible. I assumed there was something. Drugs, poison, something. I kept everything Paul gave me. The instructions telling me what to do and when."

"Is it in his handwriting?"

"Yeah, the block print is his. He's always written like that. Even in high school."

"And he paid you?"

"Yeah. He paid me twenty-five thousand dollars for each flat."

"And how did you explain the money to Erik?"

"Paul told me to tell him my foster parents had died, and they'd left a couple of us the proceeds from life insurance and the sale of their house, but it was going to be paid over a period of years. I memorized the words from the instructions he gave me."

"And Erik believed you?"

"Yeah, because the day I told him was the first day Paul... used me. I was a mess. Tears, crying. I love Erik, you know?"

Amber didn't touch the last statement, continuing her questioning instead. "Do you know what Paul did with the trays?"

She shook her head. "I don't. He never said, and believe me, I didn't want to know."

"One more question. How did you think this was going to end?"

Clare shook her head. "I don't know. I got so I could endure Paul, and then... it wasn't so bad. Erik's gone a lot. When he's here, he's really tired." She shrugged. "I figured Paul would get tired of me. By then we'd be okay financially, and Erik could cut back on his hours."

"All right Clare, Officer Patel is going to take you downtown."

Clare's head whipped up. "You said if I told you, I wouldn't have to go downtown!"

"No, Clare. You heard what you wanted to hear.

We have our conversation recorded, and I can assure you I made no such statements."

She stood, and Clare lunged at her. The chair she was sitting on slid across the marble floor. "You can't do this! He'll kill me!"

"Paul Desoto? He's not going anywhere."

"You don't know who you're dealing with!"

"You mean Paul's bosses? Aarón Rubio?"

Clare's eyes flared. She snapped her mouth shut and glared at Amber.

"Or is Oscar Peña the one coming after you?"

"I want a lawyer." Clare spit the words at Amber.

"So be it." She nodded at Detective Patel, and the officer assisted the furious woman from the chair and headed for the garage.

"Avni, keep her in the garage until transport shows. We're going to need all hands to search the Edelman residence," Brody ordered.

"You got it, Sarge." Patel and Thompson closed the door behind them.

Terrell's voice rose. "Watson, have them bring in Desoto."

Watson nodded before he lifted his hand, catching everyone's attention. "Sir we have two blacked out SUVs outside the housing area."

Terrell's eyes narrowed. "What are they doing?"

Watson asked the question. "Nothing. They're parked about a block away."

"Keep an eye on them." Terrell's command sliced through the silence. Amber slid her gaze to Brody. She'd been in this position before. She nodded at his look of concern and he gave her the faintest of smiles. Damn, she loved that man.

CHAPTER 21

Brody rolled his shoulders. While the SUVs outside the housing development were concerning, he had a job to do. He was certain Desoto wouldn't be as uncomplicated as Clare had been. Clare was between a rock and a hard place, but millions of people handled financial troubles without turning to crime. She'd known what she was doing was illegal. She'd admitted as much, and thank God they had it on tape, both the confession and the waiver of her rights. Her statement tied Desoto to the transportation of the drugs. He was going away. The question was whether or not the man would take others down to mitigate his time.

Detective Rosen opened the door and a cuffed Desoto ambled into the light. His self-assured swagger and the 'fuck you' sneer he wore was completely inappropriate considering the circumstances. He glanced at Terrell. His captain's eyes narrowed. Yeah, his boss saw it, too.

"What am I being arrested for, Officer?"

Brody glanced at Harlow and Delgado. "Have you advised him of his rights?"

"Yeah." Delgado placed a not too gentle hand on the guy's shoulder and shoved him into the chair. "He didn't want a lawyer. Harlow witnessed."

"Mr. Paul Desoto, I'm Detective Sergeant Brody King. You were placed under arrest for interstate drug trafficking."

"Really?" The man drew out the word like it was elastic, and he was waiting for a snap.

"Where were you taking the trays?"

"To the dump. Like I do every time Clare asks me to take out the trash."

"At about million dollars per tray, I doubt you throw them away."

"I'm sorry, Detective, but I have absolutely no idea what you're talking about. I was taking out the trash for my… paramour."

"Well, your paramour has stated you told her when to have her husband retrieve the flats."

"Really? Got any proof there, Detective… King, was it?"

Brody mimicked the guy's eat shit and die smile. "Yes, yes we do."

The man's bravado waned. "Put up or shut up." The uncertainty Desoto felt was lodged deep and it showed in his eyes.

Brody leaned forward. "Clare kept all the envelopes you gave her with the dates of the pick-ups. How long do you think it will take Aarón Rubio to put a bullet in your head? You are now a loose end."

"Sir, we have movement on the SUVs." Watson's warning snapped Desoto's head in that direction.

"Stop them." Terrell growled the instructions

"There's nothing to those notes," Desoto said, but it was more to himself than anyone in the room. His frantic eyes skittered around the kitchen.

Brody glanced at Terrell. His boss was staring at Watson waiting for an update. Brody pushed on with the interview. "What about the instructions on how she was supposed to explain the money to her husband?"

Desoto's eyes found their way to him slowly.

"You have no idea what's coming for you, Detective."

"I'm not interested in your threats."

"You didn't think I came here alone did you? That much product without an escort? You're a fool, and unlike you, I'll be alive at the end of this." Brody moved away from the table at the same time a staccato burst of gunfire sounded from the front yard.

Instinct pushed him toward Desoto, but the man was fast. He jumped up and slammed his shoulder into Delgado who lost his balance and fell into Detective Harlow. As Brody gathered himself, Terrell was barking orders. He sprinted after Desoto who'd jumped through the breakfast nook's window. Desoto was struggling to stand as he hurdled through the windowsill and landed on top of the man.

"Two officers down!" Watson shouted.

"Take those bastards out!" Terrell shouted.

Brody and every cop in the house moved at once. A loud squeal of tires came from the street. The sounds of glass breaking were interspersed with rapid gunfire. It seemed to be contained toward the front of the house. Shouts from his fellow officers filled the air. Desoto spun to his back and kicked at him, catching him at the base of his chin and snapping his head back. Blinding pain dropped him to his knees, but not for long. He blinked to clear his vision and pulled his gun which he pointed directly at Desoto. He heaved to his feet and pushed Desoto onto his stomach. "Stay down. Move and someone is going to shoot you." He'd volunteer to imbed a bullet if no one else took on the job. He turned his neck gingerly. The bastard had a hell of a kick.

He kept an eye on Desoto and edged to the corner of the house. He snuck a peek and slammed back against the house. Two men were working their way along the side of the house to the back-yard. He glanced into the kitchen window of the house. No one. They'd all gone to the front to assist the officers involved in what sounded like one hell of a gunfight. He glanced at Desoto who stared at him; the suspect's eyes were narrowed and vicious. "They're coming for you too, mother-fucker." Brody warned the asshole, "Keep your mouth shut or I'll shut it."

Brody crouched and risked another glance around the house. The guns told him they weren't cops because the good guys didn't carry Uzis or Mac 10s or whatever the hell those guys were carrying. Going up against two submachine guns with his .45 was going to be tricky and, yeah, a suicide mission, but he had to protect the mother-fucking drug dealer on the ground next to him. He crouched down and braced, ready to launch from a three-point stance into the first man who cleared the side of the house.

A crash of glass and whoosh of flame at the Edelman house diverted his attention for a split second. Damn it. Molotov Cocktails. Two more crashes followed in rapid succession along with several sporadic bursts of gunfire.

He spun at a soft sound behind him and locked his gun on the target. Relief poured through him. Terrell had jumped from the window and was moving his way. He held up his hand, pointed to his eye and then held up two fingers. Terrell nodded. Brody pointed to himself and held up one finger. Terrell moved up behind him, his weapon raised and ready. Brody holstered his weapon. They were outgunned, but the element of surprise was their chance to walk away from this without becoming pin cushions. His boss nodded and placed his hand on Brody's shoulder. Brody bunched his muscles in preparation. When his boss tapped his shoulder, he launched forward.

The bastard didn't stand a chance. Brody was six-feet-five-inches and two hundred sixty pounds of flat out pissed police officer. His shoulder connected with the man's hip. A spray of bullets sounded as they collided. The man's reflexive pull on the trigger sent bullets into the house with a distinct whapping echo following the bullet's percussion. As soon as they hit the ground, Brody rolled and was on his feet. The man twisted; his arm rose in a perfect arch. Brody grabbed the gunman's wrist and twisted it one way while he twisted the burning barrel of the weapon the other. He felt the break and heard the man's scream. Turning, he drew his weapon to bear on two men running to the rear of the house.

"Halt! HCPD!"

The men dove in different directions, firing as they went down. Brody returned fire. He hit the first man and rolled to his right, drawing the fire away from Terrell. Brody glanced at the epic martial arts fight his captain was embroiled in before he located the second man. The bastard was on his stomach and low-crawled along the flowerbeds, headed toward the backyard. Brody was behind the man, and his position gave him a slight advantage. He rose to his feet and checked his six. The fight between Terrell and the unknown martial arts master in front of the gunman was occupying his attention. Brody sprinted forward in a crouch. He dropped on the man and placed the barrel of his gun at the base of the man's skull. "Move and you're dead."

He cuffed the man and hustled forward, sweeping the area. Terrell delivered a flurry of hits and dropped the bastard he was fighting using a roundhouse kick. His boss went down at the same time as the assailant. He hustled to help. Terrell groaned and hauled himself to his feet. "I've got these. Go!" Terrell pointed to the Edelmans' house. A fire blazed on the bottom floor. "Get the damn evidence! The notes! We need them to implicate Desoto and Peña!"

Brody sprinted across the lawn. In his peripheral vision he saw Amber running toward the kitchen, too. Another flaming bottle broke through the front windows of the Edelman house. Three detectives took the person throwing the Molotov cocktails down. They hit the porch at the same time. "Where would she keep the notes?"

"The greenhouse!" Amber pointed to the small structure which was almost entirely engulfed in flames.

"The workbench!" Brody sprinted forward. He kicked down the door and staggered back from the heat. "Get the hose!" He ran along the building and glanced in. The workbench was still intact. He flew back to the doorway.

"Douse me!" Brody called as Amber strained, pulling the garden hose toward him.

"What? Are you insane?"

"Do it! It is our only chance!" He grabbed the hose and saturated himself. He handed her the hose and looked straight into her eyes. "I love you!" He turned and sprinted through the flames.

His lungs screamed as he held his breath. The heat of the flames evaporated the moisture in his clothing immediately. He untucked his shirt and drew it up, covering his mouth and nose. He made it to the workbench and grabbed a drawer handle, singing his skin against the metal pull. He opened drawer after drawer, the heat and smoke making it hard to see and impossible to breathe. The bottom drawer had a metal lockbox. He grabbed it and used the handle on the top to swing it against the Plexiglas of the greenhouse.

Coughing, gasping for breath, he dropped to his knees, still banging the damn box against the wall of the greenhouse. His vision gone, he fell to his hands, the box still clutched in one. He tucked the damn thing against his stomach and rolled to his side.

He couldn't breathe. In sudden clarity, he understood he was going to die, but he was going to fight that motherfucker until his last rattling breath. He'd just found his family; Death could go screw himself.

Amber screamed for help; her radio forgotten. She saw him dash through the flames and moved on the outside of the greenhouse following him until he burst through the flames and crashed against the workbench. The smoke was so damn thick she could barely see him as he searched through the drawers.

The smoke obscured him. She screamed and pounded on the thick plexiglass. A sudden slam of a metal box against the plexiglass snapped her attention two panes down. Again. There he was, she could see his hands. She pulled her weapon and moved one pane further down. Praying he hadn't moved she pointed at the center of the bottom pane and emptied her clip through the thick membrane. She launched back and slammed her foot against the window. It gave slightly.

"Move!" Captain Terrell bellowed, as he ran toward the greenhouse. She spun away as the man left his feet and drop kicked the pane. It snapped in half, pinning the captain between the two halves. His great arms spread the warping plastic. "Get him!" She scrambled past him on her hands and knees and turned right, using the side of the greenhouse as a guide.

She found him and grabbed his shirt collar, dragging his massive weight an inch at a time. Her lungs filled with smoke as another set of hands grabbed Brody. She pushed as the unknown helper pulled. As he slithered past, she turned. Her foot kicked something metal. The box! Coughing and trying desperately to breathe, she patted around, found it and grabbed hold of the burning hot metal. Oh God, which way was out? The heat and the smoke seemed to be on all sides of her.

A hand slammed on her shoulder, grabbing her shirt, and she was tugged backward. She struggled to keep a grip on the box. Cradling it to her chest, she pushed with her legs, helping whoever was pulling her. A cool wall of air hit her. She curled around the box and blinked through a curtain of tears. "Brody!"

He was flat on his back, and two firefighters were on their knees, working on him. Someone tried to cover her face. She struck at whatever it was and tried to roll onto her hands and knees.

"Swanson, stop!" Terrell was in front of her. "Let them give you oxygen. King is alive. Let them work!"

She would have fought harder if she hadn't had to cough so hard, she puked. The oxygen mask covered her face as soon as she stopped retching.

"What in the hell possessed you two to go into a fucking building that was burning?" Terrell's question reminded her of the box.

She pointed at it. "Evidence." The single word caused her to cough again.

Terrell grabbed the box and muscled it open. He removed several pieces of paper. Shaking his head, he dropped the papers back into the box. She reached toward him. "Not... good?"

His eyes rose from the box; anguish showed in his dark eyes and almost took what little breath she had away. "The evidence is there, but nothing is worth my people dying." Pain ripped through his voice. He closed the box and looked across the lawn. Amber followed his gaze. The bounce of red and blue lights illuminated the lawn in an eerie dance of colors.

Oh… my… God. It looked like a war zone. There were paramedics, street cops and even neighbors caring for people on the ground. "What..." she took four shallow breaths, "... happened?"

"Peña declared war." Terrell pushed off the ground, clutching the evidence. One of the team trotted across the lawn and called to him. The captain gave Brody one last look before he straightened his shoulders and walked toward the chaos.

Brody jolted suddenly and rolled onto his side, coughing. She turned and reached her hand to him. His eyes were frantic until he saw her. He stretched his hand toward her. Yards of grass separated them, but it didn't matter. They were alive and together.

CHAPTER 22

Gage sat quietly between his grandmother and Aunt Dawn. The hard, plastic chair squeaked when he moved, so he tried hard not to move too much. He was worried, although both his grandmother and Aunt Dawn had told him both his parents were okay, but they needed to get checked out. His grandfather had called Aunt Dawn and told her his mom and dad had been taken to the hospital because they inhaled a ton of smoke at a fire. So, they got in the car and came to the hospital.

He watched a person walk down the hall. A doctor, probably. He had a white coat. All the doctors on television wore white coats unless they worked in the emergency room. Then they all wore scrubs. Only this place wasn't like the hospitals on the television. It wasn't as crowded, and the people weren't running around. There was hardly anyone in the halls. His mom always said television was filled with overly dramatic events. This place was almost vacant. He'd visited his Aunt Dawn in the hospital once when she had her appendix taken out. It wasn't like the shows on television either, so maybe being a doctor wasn't all it was cracked up to be. That hospital, where they went to see Aunt Dawn, was even smaller, and they went right to Aunt Dawn's room. Not like here.

He looked at his grandma. He could tell she wasn't happy right now. Which was strange, because she was always smiling and laughing. Maybe she was kinda worried, too. "Did Uncle Blay fight this fire?"

His grandmother jerked a little bit. "Oh, no. This fire was in another firehouse's area. He'll be here as soon as he's free." She patted his leg.

"Why can't we see them now? Didn't Grandpa say they'd be okay?"

She looked down at him and blinked before she

answered. "That is a very good question, Gage. Grandpa did say that, didn't he? Why don't I go find out what the delay is?"

"I'll come with you." He stood and glanced at his aunt. "Do you want to come, too?"

Dawn glanced at his grandmother. "No, I'll wait here."

His grandma smiled at Aunt Dawn. "Thank you. Gage's aunts and uncles will be here shortly. Could you let them know I've gone to find out why we can't see them?"

"Oh, yes, ma'am. I'd wish you good luck, but I don't think you'll need any." Aunt Dawn chuckled and checked her phone. Gage looked between the two women.

"Come on, Gage." His grandmother started walking, and he fell into step beside her. She stopped in front of a counter. "Excuse me. I'm looking for Amber Swanson and Brody King."

The woman was scrolling through something on her phone while standing behind the counter. She held up a finger without even looking at his grandmother. Gage watched his grandma lift her chin and then her eyes narrowed. "I don't know who raised you, young woman, but it *is* common courtesy to acknowledge someone who is talking to you."

The nurse glanced up from the phone in her hand. "Excuse me?"

"No ma'am, I don't think I will. I am Hannah King. I'm looking for my son, his father, and Amanda Swanson, this young man's mother. They were brought in two hours ago. The emergency room sent us up here."

The woman stared at them for a couple of seconds and slowly pocketed her phone. "We haven't had any admissions during my shift." She crossed her arms.

His grandmother leaned forward. "Would you please use the computer and tell me where they were placed?"

His grandmother smiled at the woman, but it really didn't seem like a smile, more like a throw down. He'd seen fights at school. His stomach felt the same way now, like it was upset, and he was waiting for something bad to happen. The way his grandmother was looking at the nurse, he could tell she really didn't like the woman, but she was being really nice to her anyway. His eyes bounced to the other woman.

"I'm sorry, I think it's broken."

"Do you?" His grandmother asked. "Without even wiggling the mouse, you believe your computer is broken.

"Yep." The woman smiled at his grandmother. "Maybe you should go back down to the emergency room and ask again."

"Oh. I see." She leaned toward the counter a bit. "Emma is it?"

The woman smiled at his grandma. Kinda.

"Well, Emma. My husband, Chauncey King, is the Commissioner of Hope City's Police Department. Our grandson's mother and father, a police detective and a DEA agent, were brought to this hospital almost two hours ago. Now, I can have my husband, as busy as he is, contact the Executive Director of the Hope City Hospital System and ask the exact same question I'm asking you. I'm sure he can take time out of his evening with his family to find out where they are. Of course, I'd be sure to explain the exceptional help we've received here today. I'll be sure to mention you by name." His grandmother smiled at the woman again.

The woman's eyes narrowed, and she sat down at the computer. She hit the keys hard. "What are the names again?" the woman snapped.

"Brody King and Amber Swanson."

"Mr. King is on the fourth floor. Room 412.There is no record of a Swanson being admitted."

"What does that mean, Grandma?"

She put her hand on his shoulder. "I don't know. Let's go see your dad and maybe he'll know where she is."

He swallowed hard and asked, "She's okay, right?"

"I'm sure she is, Gage. Your grandfather would have told me if there was a serious injury. Now, let's pop up and see your father." She headed away from where Aunt Dawn was waiting.

"Don't you want to tell Aunt Dawn where we're going?"

She opened a door which led to a flight of stairs. "We'll come back down and tell her as soon as we know where your mom and dad are. Up you go." She motioned to the stairs and they started walking.

"Why was she so..."

"Unpleasant?"

Gage made a choking sound. "Yeah, that." He'd call her a bitch. But not around his mom or any other adults. Around the guys, though, yeah. That's what he'd call her.

"Maybe she was having a bad night." His grandmother couldn't hide her smile.

"Maybe she's always like that," Gage countered.

"Probably." She laughed as she agreed. "Most people are nice if you're nice to them."

"Most. Some are real jerks."

"And that's a life lesson, young man. Fortunately, the majority of people you deal with will be nice."

Gage opened the door for his grandmother like he'd seen his grandfather do, and she smiled at him. "Thank you." She stopped inside the door and looked at the numbers on the wall. "All the way to the end I think."

They approached the counter and the nurse behind the desk looked up. "Oh! Mrs. King?"

His grandmother stopped and smiled. "I'm sorry, I'm afraid I don't recall your name?"

"I'm Candice. I was Brock's nurse while he was with us last winter."

"Oh, yes. Candice, so nice to see you again. My son Brody was admitted?"

"Yes, ma'am. Right this way. I thought you'd be

here sooner." The woman stepped away from the desk.

"We had a slight problem and were routed to the third floor. We've been waiting for almost two hours. I finally had to talk to the nurse on duty at the station."

"The third floor? That's for same day surgeries and by this time of night there's only an aide on duty because the floor should be vacant." Candice stopped. "She let you sit there for two hours?"

His grandmother nodded.

"I'll talk to my supervisor and see what we can do."

"Thank you so much. Could you also call down and ask the young lady, Emma, I think her name is, to be so kind as to tell his aunt and any of our family who have gathered to come upstairs?"

"Absolutely. Your son is this way." They started to walk again.

"We're also looking for Amber Swanson, my grandson's mother?"

The nurse nodded. "I'm pretty sure she's with your son in his room. Pretty lady with long golden red hair?"

As if summoned by the nurse's description, his mom appeared in a doorway.

"Mom!" Gage bolted from his grandmother's side when he saw his mom. She wrapped her arms around him and hugged him tight, almost smothering him.

"It's all right. I'm here."

He moved away and pinched his nose. "Sheesh, you stink!"

His mom laughed and hugged him again. He let her for a minute and then he backed away. "Where is Dad?"

"Right here." He looked beyond his mom and saw his dad sitting up in a bed with an oxygen mask covering his mouth. He walked to the bed. "What happened?" There were bandages on his hand. Big white strips of cloth wrapped around them, and his face looked like it had a real bad sunburn.

"Well..." His dad coughed hard and held his hand up, like the woman had earlier, but you could tell his dad wasn't being disrespectful. Finally, he said, "I was getting some evidence from a building that had caught fire. Your mom helped me to get out. We got a lot of smoke in our lungs, and I burnt my hands a little."

"But you're okay?"

"Going to be fine."

Gage stared at his dad for a long time. He'd talked to his father on the phone a lot while he and his mom worked, but he was still kind of a stranger. "Do you have to go back to working there?"

"No," his mom said as she sat down with his dad on the hospital bed.

"Well, thank goodness for small favors." His grandmother spoke for the first time. "We've been waiting downstairs for the last two hours. I didn't know you were up here."

"No worries, Mom. You didn't miss much. I just got back from x-ray. We would have texted you, but our phones didn't make the trip."

"X-ray?" His grandmother stood up straighter.

"Precaution. They'll take another one in a couple days." His dad coughed again. "It's because of the persistent cough. The doctor didn't want to take any chances, and he's playing it safe."

His grandmother nodded and then reached forward and pushed some of his mom's hair away from her face. "And you? Chauncey said you were transported here, too?"

His mom smiled and shook her head. "Treated and released. I made it up here just before they took him to radiology. I was going to try to get Dawn and have her contact you."

"She's downstairs, Mom."

His mom sent him a questioning look.

"We were told you were going to the third floor. After waiting forever, Grandma persuaded the woman to find out exactly where you were."

His dad chuckled and then coughed, but not as bad as the last time. "You persuaded the woman, Mom? A nurse? Please tell me you weren't in hover-copter mode."

His grandmother kicked up her chin. "She was an aide, not that she was of much assistance, and I was perfectly nice. Right, Gage?"

He glanced up at his grandmother and then at his mom and dad. "I don't ever want Grandma to be perfectly nice to me. Ever." He rolled his eyes, and all three of the adults started laughing. Both his mom and dad ended up coughing, but it was worth it to watch his grandma's shocked expression. "I'm ten, Grandma, not two. She was disrespectful and you put her in her place."

His grandmother sniffed and stuck her nose up in the air. "Sometimes people need a little encouragement."

He glanced at his mom. "You know that word I can't say that Nick and Simon say cops are?"

His mom narrowed her eyes and nodded.

"Yeah, well Grandma is the OG of badass."

The way his mom and grandmother sputtered and fussed at him shouldn't have been so funny, but his dad thought it was hilarious and laughed until he started coughing again.

CHAPTER 23

Brody glanced around the front room of his apartment. The setting sun filtered through the floor to ceiling window tinting the room with a golden hue. Brock, Blay, Sean, Kyle, Rory, Carter, his dad and Colm McBride sat around two nice card tables he and Blay had built. They folded and the legs collapsed so they traveled when needed. Tonight, they made the trip from Blay's apartment to his. Blay and the guys at the station had borrowed them last weekend for a marathon game of *Pokémon*. And no, he still couldn't understand the fact grown-ass men were playing a child's game *and* taking it seriously. Some shit did not compute.

The men had spent the last hour laughing at

corny dad jokes, and they tossed harmless insults around, it was a good time. What was better? Sharing this home with his wife and son. Gage's football sat in the corner of the living room along with his shoulder pads. Brody had taken him down to sign up for football as soon as registration opened up. This year, Gage was playing tight end. He was too big and not quite fast enough to be a wide receiver, but he was perfect as a tight end, even though the coach had to be convinced to give him a try in that position. Brody smiled remembering the day the coach was convinced to change his mind on where to play Gage. *His* size tended to intimidate people. His size, plus Brody, Blay, Kyle, Sean *and* Rory had unequivocally silenced any argument the coach had about where Gage would be playing. He was so glad they could come to a quick and equitable agreement. Gage had great hands, and he was growing fast. When he caught up to his body and gained some coordination, the kid would be phenomenal.

"Yo, Brody, you going to raise or you going to daydream?" Brock's voice brought him out of his musings. He glanced down at his three aces and two queens and grimaced. "What's the pot at?"

KRIS MICHAELS

"Fifty cents to you." Carter put his cards down and lifted his glass. "I'm on empty. Anyone else?"

The chorus of yeses put a pause on the games as the tables emptied and the men moved into the kitchen and the makeshift bar. Brody put his hand down, careful not to let anyone see his cards. This pot was *his*.

Brock kicked his feet under the table. They didn't get up to refill their glasses because Blay was pressed into duty even though he was sitting at the other table. When he looked at his older brother and arched his eyebrows in question, the guy smiled at him. "Welcome to the ranks of the married."

Brody chuckled. He and Amber had made a fast trip to Boston and gotten married last weekend. Boston was nearby, out of town and away from family. It was a perfect place to tie the knot. The only person they'd told was Gage, and the kid kept the secret. Much to his grandmother's dismay. Amber had handled it perfectly, asking Hannah to help her with a family reception next month.

After the Friday afternoon ceremony, they'd spent the weekend doing the tourist thing and eating tons of great food. They'd splurged on a hotel room with two master suites. Gage about freaked out, in a good way, when he realized he had a room to himself. It took about three hours of research and a ton of phone calls to secure that exact style of room. He wanted Gage with them when they were married, but he was going to have a honeymoon, too. The split masters put a living room between them, which worked perfectly for his plans.

"Where's Gage tonight?"

"Johnny's dad organized an overnight camping trip. The last one before school starts."

"How is Gage taking moving to a new school?"

"He's bummed, but they'd be changing schools moving into sixth grade anyway. He already knows a couple of the kids, the ones on his football team, so he won't be going in as a complete stranger."

"And Amber? How is she adapting to JDET?"

"God, she's a perfect fit. Rayburn and Watson have adopted her. You can't separate those three." He laughed and leaned his weight forward, glancing into the kitchen where Rory and Blay were clowning around and amusing the rest of the crowd. "I've always loved her, man. I always will. Tell me you found that with Kallie."

Brock smiled and closed his eyes for a second. "She's my perfect counterbalance."

Brody leaned back as Blay walked their way, two cups clutched in one big hand. Brody thanked his brother for the drink before he told Brock, "I know the feeling."

"What feeling?" Kyle and Carter sat back down with them while his dad, Colm, Blay, Rory and Sean sat at the other table.

"Balance. In life and at work." Brody picked up his hand and tossed two quarters into the pot. "Call."

"Who wants cards?" Kyle picked up the deck since it was his deal. Brock took two, Carter, one. He stood pat and so did Kyle.

"Balance is hard to find, but when you do, grab it," Carter said before he tossed a quarter in the pot.

"Twenty-five cents to you." Kyle was the self-appointed table monitor. He kept the game going at a good clip.

"Give me a second." Brody stared at his cards like the visual inspection would change the numbers into face cards, or at least he hoped that's what it looked like. He hadn't had this good of a hand dealt to him in years. He was going to milk it for everything he could get.

Kyle glanced at Carter. "Balance as in my sister and niece? That type of balance?"

Carter chuckled and took a sip of his drink. "I may be your brother-in-law, but I will not discuss your sister with you. Ever. I believe we've had this conversation."

Kyle narrowed his eyes at Carter. "I think that particular conversation was with Sean, but I get the gist. I'm sitting with three old married farts. Maybe I need to grab Blay and Rory and you can take Dad and Chauncey. Married men against those of us unattached.

"Speak for yourself."

"Who's unattached?"

Blay and Rory spoke at the same time.

Kyle threw up his hands. "Seriously?"

"Nah, but it was cool to see your face." Blay laughed and ducked a torpedo in the form of a crunchy cheese doodle Kyle chucked his direction.

Kyle grabbed a cheesy snack and shoved it in his mouth. The man glanced over at him and gave him a wink. Oh hell, his friend was hiding something. Did he have someone?

Rory launched another doodle, smacking Carter in the side of the face. God it was good to laugh. Things at work had been hard. Captain Terrell had aged years in the last two months. His boss, the bastard Fenton, had him removed from duty because of the clusterfuck of events which had happened when Peña's men came to clean house. It took IA three weeks to reinstate him. Three weeks of dealing with Fenton in their business every day. Dress code changes, procedure changes, reporting changes... the team had threatened to mutiny, and they'd had many meetings outside of Fenton's observation to stem the frustration. Thankfully, the captain had been reinstated without censure, and Fenton was once again behind a fence.

"Call." He tossed in two quarters.

"That wasn't a call, that was a raise." Carter pointed to the pile. "It was a quarter to you."

Brody blinked at the pile. "Damn it. Okay then, I'm out an extra twenty-five. I raise." He sighed heavily and dropped his hand to the table. He leaned back so he could see the men at the other table. "Hey, Sean, are you working the apartment fire at Juliette and 21st?" He'd heard it was started by the building owner to gather an insurance claim.

"The case was a slam dunk. The man left a trail

straight to him. There was a fatality. He's going to jail for the rest of his natural life."

Blay's head came up. "Ah, damn. The kid didn't make it?" He was the one who'd pulled the boy out of the burning building.

"No. I got the call a couple hours ago. His parents took him off life-support."

Rory tossed his hand into the pot. "What a waste."

Blay tossed his hand into the pot, too. "Maybe if I'd gotten there sooner."

"Stop. You did everything you could." Rory's words were stern, but the hand on Blay's shoulder was the connection his brother needed.

Sean sighed, "Damn, I thought you knew."

Blay shook his head. "No."

"I'm sorry, man." Sean glanced at Brock.

Chauncey took a deep breath and folded his hand, too. "The person at fault here is the building owner. He started the fire. He endangered his tenants. He is the person responsible for the boy's death. When we do our jobs, sometimes we get lucky. Most of the time we get to mop up what the worst of our city delivers to our doorstep. Moments of regret and second guessing every action happens. It's human nature. It's how we deal with those moments that define us as the men we are."

Colm McBride nodded. "If every decision we make allows an event or a person to undermine our work, erode our confidence, or lessen our effectiveness, it weakens all of us. Blay, son, you put your life on the line to get into the apartment and get the boy out. You reacted the way you were trained. It hurts, let it. Don't let the pain control what you do the next time you go after someone in the same situation."

Blay nodded and swallowed hard. "I know. I think I'm going to head down to my apartment. 'Night everyone."

Rory stood without hesitation. "I'll come with you." He put his hand on Blay's shoulder when the guy opened his mouth. "Shut up. I'm coming. Deal with it."

"Damn, I didn't mean to break up the party." Sean scrubbed his face with his hands.

"Man, didn't you hear what the 'rents just said?" Brody folded the best hand he'd had in years. "You didn't cause this. That bastard who started the building on fire did."

"Do you ever think we'll get ahead of them?"

Kyle asked. "The ones selling the drugs, setting the fires, killing the innocents?"

Quiet enveloped the room for several minutes before Chauncey replied. "I have to believe it. It's the reason I clip on my badge every morning. When I'm done, I want to look back and say I gave everything I could so people in this city were able to live without fear."

Colm nodded. "It's all we can hope for."

Brody raised his glass. "To what we hope for, to those who serve to achieve it, and the people who support us while we do it."

The men all lifted their glasses. Hope filled his chest. With men like the ones in this room, the city had a fighting chance.

Amber sat across the counter from Hannah King and Sharon McBride. The women were amazing to watch.

"Do you think they've done this a time or two before?" Kallie King, her newly minted sister-in-law, leaned in and filled her wine glass after pouring a bourbon for herself.

"You'd think it was their kitchen." The women

danced around each other as they worked to finish an array of treats.

"Right?" Kallie reached across the counter and snagged the tray containing the meat, cheese and crackers, moving it closer toward them. "I haven't eaten since breakfast." She grabbed two crackers and made a quick sandwich. "Hannah, are you sure you don't want any help?"

"You relax. Sharon and I have this. Amber, honey, where did you put the dessert box you brought in?"

"Here it is!" Sharon removed it from the bottom of the refrigerator. "Oh, Amber! Thank you!" Sharon spun as she opened the box. "I know you had to go all the way across town to get these!"

"You and Hannah adore the cannoli from De Palma's." The mini cannoli *were* fabulous, and she liked to be able to treat the two older women. "I had to go over there to drop off Gage. He's so excited about camping this weekend."

Hannah laughed. "We had a blast pulling the old tent from the garage and puzzling together a way to set it up. That boy is so smart. I'd still be on the lawn trying to make all the pieces fit."

"Thank you again for letting him use it."

"He can have it! I have reached the age where my idea of camping is falling asleep on the couch."

Sharon pointed to the living room. "Have you tried Tara's couch?"

"What about my couch?" Tara asked when she and Brianna walked in the kitchen. "Hey, can all of you come every weeknight and do the cooking?"

"Kallie is a better cook than I am." Amber volunteered her sister-in-law immediately.

"Hey!" Kallie grabbed the wine bottle she'd used to fill Amber's glass and slid it away from her.

Brianna grabbed the bottle and poured herself a glass. "Where are the princesses?"

Sharon McBride answered. "Let's see, Bekki said she was going to be a little late, and she was going to pick up Erin from the clinic on the way here. Caitlyn is out back with Colleen. What have you two been up to?"

Tara leaned over the counter and grabbed a wine glass, holding it for Brianna to fill. "We were talking about how slow the city council was in addressing any new initiatives. Brie has worked hard to address all the issues and concerns they've thrown in the way of her idea to help feed the homeless in the shelters."

Amber stopped with a cracker halfway to her mouth. "Wait, I'm lost. What initiative is that?"

Brianna sat down on a stool next to her. "At the restaurant we have excess at the end of each night. Every restaurant does. Some things can't be shoved into a refrigerator and used again the next day. So I thought a few restaurants in the area would be willing to band together and put the leftovers into disposable containers, labeling the top with the contents to avoid any food allergies. The local businesses like mine could use the donation write off, but the main reason is because we are throwing away food which could be used to provide a meal to the local shelters. If we are allowed to proceed, we could provide the template for the rest of the city. Hunger could be wiped out at the shelters."

"And if there is enough support, we could start to provide for the ones who don't live in the shelter."

"Like what?" Kallie cocked her head, questioning the two women.

Amber got it. The inherent dangers of dealing with the homeless was probably front and center in her mind, too.

"Well, for instance, the Cardboard Cottages. We

could take a food truck once a day and provide meals. Until the food ran out." Brianna shrugged. "But that's a pipe dream right now, and the first hurdle is getting the council to approve my initiative on a trial basis."

Amber and Kallie exchanged glances.

"What? What is it? I saw that look." Brianna wagged her finger between them.

Kallie nodded to her.

"Well, it's a noble effort, but if you ever do extend the service to places like the Cardboard Cottages, please coordinate security. While some of the people who live in those environments are down on their luck..." She glanced at Tara, knowing the woman was a social worker.

Tara sighed and stared at her wine. "I know. The homeless population has a problem with drugs."

Kallie nodded. "Among so many other problems. I agree with Amber. If you do ever get to that point, please consider security. Even if it is a rent-a-cop, the presence of security would keep things from devolving."

Brianna elevated her glass to her lips and took a sip of the wine. "So, to get off this depressing topic, I met someone."

Every woman in the house turned toward her. "What?" Hannah gasped.

Brianna's cheeks turned a dark rose color. "It's really new, Mom. About three weeks, but I really like him."

"What's his name?"

"What does he do?"

"Where did you meet him?"

"Is it serious?"

Brianna threw back her head and laughed as each woman asked a question at the same time. "Well, I met him at Chester's gym."

"Sorry it didn't work out." Sharon grimaced. "I didn't know he was dating anyone."

"No worries. I loved his gym, and he's a great guy who's perfect for Gretchen."

Tara whipped her head around. "Mom! Are you setting up Hannah's girls now?"

Sharon and Hannah giggled, and Sharon waved off Tara's comment. "I helped Hannah by introducing a mutual friend."

Hannah leaned on the counter and stared at Brie. "What is his name?"

"Ryker."

Amber swallowed her wine and coughed when it went down the wrong tube. Kallie whapped her on the back. *Hell, Ryker was a common name, right? Maybe?* "You going to live?"

"If you stop hitting me, yeah." Amber laughed as she grabbed Kallie's arm.

"Wimp." Kallie mumbled under her breath and then laughed. The woman's laugh encompassed her entire body and nobody in the vicinity could resist joining in.

"What's his last name?" Amber asked when she could breathe again.

"Terrell. Why, do you know him?" Brianna turned to her and Kallie. No one else could see her face. Her eyes were huge, and the face she made, well the only thing Amber could take away was a silent plea for them to remain silent on just who Ryker Terrell was.

"Ah... the name's very familiar." Amber dropped her eyes and busied herself with a cracker and cheese.

"I'm sure I've heard it somewhere before." Kallie kneed her under the counter. "Sounds like a movie star."

"What does he do?" Sharon asked.

"Ah, he's in management." Brianna shrugged. "But he's been on vacation for the last three weeks. We've worked out together and had a few meals."

KRIS MICHAELS

Amber watched Brie carefully, and if the blush rising up her neck was any indication, they'd done more than eat a few meals together. Kallie knocked her knee again. She extended her middle finger under the countertop away from everyone else's view but Kallie's. Her sister-in-law laughed again. God, she loved the woman next to her. She and Kallie were two peas in the same pod.

Hannah clapped her hands together. "Can we meet him?"

Brie opened her mouth and then closed it. She took a deep breath and faced her mom full on. "You know I love you, right?"

"Yes..." Hannah stretched the word out in response.

"Listen, I really like this guy. I'd like to have the space to see if it is going to work. No family yet. If the guys get wind of this, you know what will happen."

Tara snorted. "They ganged up on Carter. My brothers *and* yours."

"The boys?" Hannah's hand went to her necklace. "They didn't!"

"Yes, the boys did, Mom. They always do, and if either of you tell the dads, the boys are going to find out and then... I want some time, Mom. He's

412

special. I *really* like him." Brianna smiled softly. "I promise when I know he feels the same way, I'll introduce you to him. But please, Mom. No hovercopter action."

Hannah blinked and then stated, "I don't hover."

Amber and Kallie faked choking on their drinks, and Brianna and Tara burst out laughing. Hannah's eyes opened wide, and she reached for her best friend. "Sharon, I think I may be insulted."

"Hannah, sweetie. You do tend to get into your children's affairs."

"But only with the best of intentions." Hannah's eyes went wide.

"Okay, Mom. Please, I promise I will tell you everything, and I'll even go one step further. *I'll* call *you* once a day to let you know how I'm doing. But please, give me the space to see if this is what I think it could be."

"I can do that, honey." Hannah embraced her oldest daughter. Amber and Kallie sniggered behind their glasses when Hannah crossed her fingers behind Brie's back.

"Oh, and for the love of God, don't tell Bekki. He does not need an investigative reporter shoving a mic up his——"

"Brianna!" Hannah scolded before Brie finished the sentence.

Brianna huffed, "I was going to say... nose."

Amber and Kallie laughed again. Brie sent them a withering glance which made them laugh all the harder. When Kallie was able to control her laughter, she tipped her glass toward Amber. "Welcome to the insanity, my sister. We are in for one hell of a ride."

Amber clanked glasses with her sister-in-law and took a drink.

Hannah King flashed her a smile and winked before she took a drink of her own wine.

She'd already been on one hell of a ride, but she'd take another trip around the park with these women. Anytime.

CHAPTER 24

By the time he heard Amber come inside, he had the kitchen cleaned and the tables folded ready to take downstairs in the morning. He remained where he was, facing the harbor and watching the lights. She slipped up beside him, and he wrapped his arm around her. "Did you have a good time?" He dropped a kiss to her hair and smiled at the smell of alcohol on her breath.

"We had a great night."

"Tell me you didn't drive home."

"Nope. Kallie and I shared an Uber." She stepped in front of him and wrapped her arms around his waist before laying her head on his pec. He wrapped his arms around her. "She's crazy."

"Kallie?"

"Yep. They're coming tomorrow night."

"Who? Brock and Kallie?"

"Yep." Amber nodded against his chest.

"When?"

"What?" She looked up at him.

"When are they coming over?"

"Who?"

"Brock and Kallie."

"Oh, yeah, they're coming over. I told you that, didn't I?"

He smiled and put a finger on her nose. Her eyes crossed trying to follow it. "How much did you have to drink?"

"I'm thinking... enough." She smiled up at him.

"I think you are correct."

"Brianna is in love." She slipped from his arms and slid her shirt off.

He caught the material when she tossed it to him. "Damn."

Amber ran her hands up her waist and higher where he saw the leopard print of her bra. That was new... and sheer... so damn sheer he could see her nipples poking against the shimmer of leopard print.

"Brianna."

"What?" He blinked at her face but dropped his

eyes immediately when her hands dropped to her jeans. The button unanchored and the zipper peeled down. He could see the very top of her panties. Shit… they matched. She shimmied from her jeans, and he laughed. Her socks had a lace cuff and were the same leopard print. "Come here."

She moved toward him; her eyes dropped to the buttons of his shirt. "You are wearing too many clothes, Detective." Her fingers popped the buttons out of the holes easily. She pushed away the fabric and tongued his nipple. The feel of her velvet soft tongue on his skin aroused his already hard cock. He shrugged out of the button down and held on to her waist as she unbuckled his belt, unfastened his jeans and pushed the zipper down. Her smaller hand reached into the denim and sweet merciful heavens he saw stars.

She purred, "I want you."

"Here?" He shoved down his jeans and boxers, snagging his socks as he stomped out of the clothes. His cock strained, hard and ready for his wife. Damn, he loved the phrase. His. Wife. She was his until death do them part, and death was the only thing that could tear him from her.

"Yeah. The lights are out, and the harbor is so pretty. No one is going to see us. She urged him to the window and turned around, placing her hands on the glass. She arched her back and looked at him. "Come and get me, Detective."

The wanton smile would have sealed the deal, but no... Amber stepped away from the window while keeping her hands planted on the glass. She arched harder and damn, that ass of hers had magical powers because his feet moved as if commanded by another force. His hands traveled up the outside of her thighs, and he bent over her, nipping her shoulder. Her small gasp added fuel to the torrent of sensations, visual and physical, which inundated him. He trailed his fingers through the crease of her sex. She was hot and wet. Her hips bucked back into the touch. He stood straight behind her and traced the small elastic band of her panties. Too bad the tiny strip of material wouldn't be used again. He curled his fingers around the fabric and rent the panties into scraps. Amber gasped and then threw back her head in a sexy as hell laugh.

He dropped to his knees and spread her legs a bit more. He trailed his tongue up the inside of one thigh as his fingers found the top of her sex and started a slow assault on her clit. He licked a stripe through the heart of her and was rewarded with a low moan. Catching her as she pushed back, he doubled his efforts. Her thighs shook around him as he stimulated and teased. He wanted her to finish, because there was no way he was going to last. He reached down and tugged his balls away from his body. She bucked again and then seized repetitively. Her low, sexy sounds of need and release surrounded them, and it was a music he'd never tire of hearing. He stood behind her and gathered her away from the glass, wrapping her arms around his neck.

She threaded her fingers through his hair and when he bent his knees to position himself, she moaned and rose onto her toes. His shaft slid into her slick hot body and he had to stop moving or he'd be done before he started. He kissed her shoulder as his fingers pushed up the almost-there bra and rolled her hard, pebbled nipples. They said the '*I love yous*' and the '*I need yous*' every day. They worked on saying what they meant, never wanting another disaster to cost them time.

But words weren't necessary here. They'd be wasted. The communication between them at this level was the most basic and most intimate. They were one. He slowly retreated and then pushed back in. Her body moved with his, her hips moving as he slid forward and her back arching as he withdrew, trying to hold him inside her. He held her against him, her back against his chest. The softness of her curves enticed and enthralled him. Her softness a perfect foil to the hard muscles of his body. He moved forward and she pushed back. Yes, God yes. She was his counterbalance. His stability and equilibrium against the world outside the window.

As he stared out the window, he saw their reflection, no... her reflection. Amber's face was soft and lost in their love. Her beautiful full lips were parted, and her pleasure was there for him to see. He lost the battle against his desire and erupted inside her. The urgency of his body's need countermanded his want to make the moment last. He managed to keep himself, and her, upright through one of the most intense orgasms of his life by bracing an outstretched arm against the glass.

"Wow." She chuckled and dropped her hands to the arm he had wrapped around her.

"Yeah, that was..."

"Wow." She repeated.

"Yeah." He panted a little longer before she moved, and he slipped out of her. He stood up straight. "Have I told you today how much I love you?"

Amber turned around and stretched her arms up and around his neck. "Several times, but I could hear it again."

Brody swung her up into his arms. "Then I'll tell you again, and again, and again."

EPILOGUE

R yker Terrell stared at the computer screen. The indictments from the Edelman and Desoto collar had netted them Rubio, but Peña had fled the country. The Jacksonville contingent had moved on the nursery and netted the production point of Gray Death, plus enough elephant tranquilizers to put down a herd of the majestic beasts. His counterparts in the FBI and DEA were watching the borders for Peña, not that the surveillance would stop the cartel boss from crossing the border again. The man ghosted in and out of the country like the borders were made of Swiss Cheese.

He'd cleared the debacle of paperwork nightmares Fenton had caused and was ready to call it a night. Finally, his team's plate was clean, and they were able to concentrate on the information Masters had provided the DA about the shipments of drugs via Treyson Enterprise's vast global shipping company. Most of the grunt work would be on their end, here in Hope City. The rest would be on the alphabet agencies.

He glanced down at his cell when it vibrated on his desktop. A smile automatically lifted the corners of his mouth. He slid his finger across the face and leaned back in his chair. "Hey, you. How did the night with your family go?"

"It went. I actually told my mom about you." Brie's soft voice caressed his ear.

"Did you? How much?"

"That you were in management and that I really liked you and would appreciate her letting us see where it is going before she shifted into hover-copter mode."

He laughed at the saying. "Seriously, your mother can't be that bad." His mom had passed years ago, but he *could* remember her being very curious about his brother's girlfriends.

"Oh, but she is. It's a good thing she's doting on her grandson now. He's got all of her attention and it is easier for the rest of us."

Brie had told him she had a big family. He did too. He had four brothers and he was the oldest, but definitely not the most successful. His brothers had run circles around him in that category. Not that he cared, he was happy and enjoyed his job, when Fenton could be held at arm's length.

"What is she going to think about the age difference?"

"I'm thirty-three! If I'm okay with you being ten years older than me, she isn't going to say a word."

"Fourteen years older." He was forty-seven this December.

"Thirteen and a half." Brie chuckled. "Besides it isn't my mother you need to worry about. It's my brothers. The idiots. They think they need to approve all of my boyfriends."

Ryker smiled and softened his voice, "Is that what I am? Your boyfriend?"

"Is that too juvenile? How about my sexual machine?"

"Yeah, I bet your brothers would love to hear that." He could just imagine meeting her family with that label. *Whatever*. He'd never met a woman like Brie before. She was smart, independent, engaging, sexy as hell, and damn it, he really liked her as a person. She was devoted to helping the homeless and worked almost as many hours as he did.

"They won't need it. When the Kings and McBride brothers get together, they lose sight of the fact they are detectives and firemen. They act like barbarians. I'm warning you now, so you won't be intimidated."

Say what now? "Brie?"

"Yes?"

"Your brothers are police officers?"

"Yeah, but they're detectives. Didn't I tell you that? I'm sure I did. My sisters-in-law are too, and they seemed to recognize your name when I mentioned it tonight. They won't say anything. You're a captain, so it figures that your name would be kind of recognizable." She sighed happily. "I'm looking forward to tomorrow."

He closed his eyes and dropped his head back onto his chair. *Holy fuck.* Brie King. *King, as in Brock, Brody and Commissioner King.* He was so screwed.

"Ryker? Is everything okay?" Worry made her voice waver.

"Yeah, fine. I'm looking forward to tomorrow, too." He opened his eyes and stared at the fake fire-retardant ceiling.

She was silent for a minute. "Are you sure? Did I screw up mentioning us to my mom?"

"No, it's fine. I promise, and you didn't screw anything up." He sat up and squared his shoulders. "I can't wait to see you. Wear the dark blue dress for me?"

"I could, or I could wear something that I just happened to pick up today."

He growled and adjusted himself, "Okay then, surprise me."

That soft sexy laugh filled him. "I will. Until tomorrow."

"Good night." He disconnected the call and stared sightlessly at the computer screen. Brie King had just complicated his life a hundred-fold. A smile crept back to the edges of his lips. Not that it mattered. The Kings could recruit help from their powerful cousins, and he wouldn't back away. Not unless Brie told him to, and he was pretty damn sure that wasn't going to happen.

For the next Hope City Books, Click Below!

Kyle

Ryker

Continue on for a sneak peek of Kyle, Chapter 1!

SNEAK PEAK OF KYLE!

CHAPTER ONE

BY: MARYANN JORDAN

"Jesus."

The word was whispered, and Kyle McBride shot a glance toward his partner sitting on the passenger side of his pickup truck. Alex Tilson's gaze was pinned on the scene through the windshield. Both detectives for the Hope City Police Department, this was not their first rodeo. But seeing this level of poverty never gets easier.

Having exited off one of the main highways that cut through Hope City, he maneuvered along several streets and ramps, finally turning onto a pothole-strewn road. The word 'road' was a gift... more like packed dirt, crumbled asphalt, and craters. Nestled under the Highway Thirty-One bridge, the Cardboard Cottages created a city under the city. Cardboard Cottages was the moniker given to a makeshift neighborhood for the homeless, mentally ill, runaways, social outcasts, and drug addicts. And that was probably it's good points.

The neighborhood was constructed from an amalgamation of cardboard, tarps, plywood, and corrugated tin. At one time graffiti had covered the concrete walls of the underpass, but now only glimpses could be seen between the homemade structures.

Occasionally, a real tent was erected between the other homemade shelters. That was a new improvement... tents. The city had been working to clean up the area and disband those living there, but they always came back. So several churches and those working with the homeless population had donated cold-weather sleeping bags and small camping tents in an effort to provide a more hospitable environment.

Hospitable. *Fuckin' hell.* All it accomplished was splash color on an otherwise dreary scene.

He parked his truck at the edge, near the first burn barrel he came to. Both men sat, their gazes scanning over the area. It didn't pay to act in haste in a place where suspicion was in the eyes of everyone looking back, some with an added heavy dose of malice.

The weather had turned warm, but men still congregated around the burn barrels scattered about the area. A few tents were placed around the edges where the families lived. Grass was a distant memory, and several children kicked a ball along the hard-packed dirt outside the tents.

A memory flashed through his mind of warm evenings spent playing ball in his family's large backyard. Because it was connected to their neighbor's yard and the children of the two families played together constantly, they joked that it was hard to grow grass between their houses. In reality, their yards were lush and well-tended compared to what he was viewing now. The cheers and laughter from times gone by were not known by these children. Desolation, hunger, cold, and fear were what these kids knew best.

The children had stopped their play, and several women alighted from the tents, gathering the children close. Knowing they feared whoever was sitting in the truck, he said, "Let's go. With the morning they've had, they're going to wonder who the fuck we are."

A call had come in early. Three men were found dead near one of the burn barrels. The medical examiner had already examined the bodies and had them transported to the morgue for autopsies. Crime scene techs had searched the area for evidence and homicide detectives had already come and gone. By the time Kyle was called in, the initial cause of death was suspected to be an accidental overdose.

Recognizing two of the men standing near one of the burn barrels, he stalked over the litter-strewn dirt, his senses heightened. The bleak area was known to him, as well as many of the long-time residents. But he would be a fool to not keep his wits about him. Poverty and hunger often led to desperation. And the police were not seen as friends.

To a casual observer, he might not appear much different than the men he was approaching. His hair was longer on the top, slicked back away from his face. Tats peaked out from below the sleeves of his shirt. His jeans were worn, frayed at the bottom, although clean. His black T-shirt had seen better days but still fit tightly across his chest. His blue denim shirt helped to hide his body armor, but to the residents of the Cardboard Cottages, his casual-rough appearance did little to hide that he was with the police force. Of course, the light blue gloves he wore on his hands were a beacon, but he wasn't about to go without the protection. Not here, where illness ran rampant.

The men standing around the burn barrel stayed in their place, stretching their fingers out toward the warmth of the fire. He and Alex slid in amongst them. "Hear you had some excitement this morning."

Two of the younger men he didn't recognize shot gazes between themselves. One was caked with dirt and the body odor emanating was potent. Another one looked as though he might have had a shower within the last few weeks… or maybe took a dunk in one of the ponds at the Hope City Park, something the city council complained about often. The older man sighed. "Not much exciting happens here."

"Whatever happened, happened right here." Kyle tilted his head in a nod toward one of the large boxes. "I know that's where you lay your head. You didn't see anything that happened twenty yards away?"

"I was sleeping."

One of the younger men decided to jump into the conversation. "Yeah, we was sleepin'."

"Shut the fuck up," the first man said. Turning his gaze back to Kyle, he shrugged. "Shit happens. You know that."

"Yeah, what I want to know is how you slept through all three getting rolled?"

"When I sleep, I sleep hard."

Alex snorted, and Kyle's lips twitched as he cut his eyes toward his partner. "So you wake up this morning to three dead, naked men around the burn barrel and aren't surprised?"

"Nothin' much surprises me around here," the older man said.

With a chin lift acknowledging he knew exactly what the man meant, he stepped back from the burn barrel and began walking toward the darker areas under the bridge. Here, the early morning light didn't penetrate so brightly. The cardboard of some of the structures was deteriorating… time for some of the residents to go dumpster diving for more boxes, as well as food.

A slight breeze blew, unable to sweep away the stench of unwashed bodies and refuse. His stomach clenched, and for a few seconds, he regretted the strong coffee he had downed on the way to pick up Alex.

Hastening his steps, he glanced to the side, seeing a woman relieving herself behind her shelter. She jerked her pants up and stumbled along, her gait unsteady. As she swung her head around, he recognized the glaze in her eyes and wondered what drug of choice had helped her sleep.

A glance inside a few of the structures, revealed some residents still asleep, curled up in their sleeping bags, blankets, and a few tucked in tightly with their dogs. The animals eyed him as warily as the humans.

Another burn barrel stood nearby, this one's flames burning higher. Recognizing one of the men, he nodded. "Manny."

Manny grinned, exposing his tobacco-stained teeth— what few he had left. "Dee-tective," he greeted. "I wondered if you might show up."

"Well, me and Alex just figured we'd take a little early morning stroll around the cottages."

Manny began to chuckle, which immediately rolled into deep-chested coughing. Alex pulled out an unopened bottle of water from his pocket, untwisted the lid, and handed it to Manny.

Manny's thin fingers reached out and curled

around the bottle, and he drank deeply. After several long gulps and more strangled coughing, he finally sucked in a ragged breath. Lifting the bottle slightly, he nodded. "Appreciate it."

"Yeah, well, make sure you put the empty in a recycle bin when you're finished."

Manny grinned again, shaking his head. "You know it, Dee-tective. Don't want to do no pollutin' around here."

More men closed ranks, moving toward the barrel, each looking as rough as the next. A couple of the older ones had sleep creases down their faces, their gazes pinned on the fire warming the area. Several younger men wandered over, their eyes alert as they stared at Kyle and Alex.

Turning his attention back to Manny, he asked, "You got anything for me?"

Manny scrubbed his hand through his scruffy beard, his eyes darting all around before landing back on Kyle's face. "A lot of shit going around. Far's I can tell, same ol', same ol'."

"What about those three stiffs from last night?"

Lifting his shoulders, Manny shuffled from foot to foot. "Talk this morning was old dinosaur." Shaking his head, he muttered, "Dumb fuck."

He had wondered if they'd all been using heroin. "And the younger ones?"

"Didn't know 'em. Probably crank."

"Anything else you can give me?"

"'Fraid not, Dee-tective. Didn't see nothin' and don't plan on asking about it."

The others shook their head, a few with slight grins.

Casting his gaze around, Kyle asked, "Are you sure?"

One of the younger ones replied, "Nobody saw nothin'. Not a damn thing."

Manny's gaze shot behind Kyle and he took a step back. Kyle glanced over his shoulder and spotted a friendly face walking their way. Not surprised that the residents scattered like roaches when a light went on, he lifted his chin as Detective Brody King stepped closer.

He and Brody had been best friends since birth and the King family was the neighbors he was thinking of earlier when remembering his childhood home. The three men fell into step as they walked toward the fresher air in daylight now flooding the outskirts of Cardboard Cottages.

"Amazing how three people end up dead by this

BY: MARYANN JORDAN

burn barrel, in front of all these people, and no one saw a thing."

"Safer for them not to get involved," Brody said, glancing around. "Who has the death scene?"

"Homicide detectives were here and did the initial canvas. Crime scene techs got what evidence they could, but the bodies had been rolled. No shoes, clothes, nothing of value left on them. It sucks. So many people, so little resources to help."

"Hey, people like Tara and Brianne are doing everything they can."

Kyle nodded, acknowledging their sisters' work with the homeless. Snapping off his latex gloves, he dropped them into the burn barrel as they passed by. "True, but what brought you here?"

"We've got good intel that Peña's cartel is bringing in Gray Death. Two OD's are suspected already. Was there any indication that these three were using GD?"

Kyle shook his head. "One died with a dirty needle in his arm. H is my guess. The other two men were meth heads. If they had the money, they'd buy more crank."

"One of GD's primary components is heroin, but they cut it with elephant tranqs."

"Are you serious?" Kyle blinked up at him. "I've heard about GD, but I haven't seen it on the streets. Not here at least, thank God."

Brody nodded. "Do me a favor and keep your eyes open. When the tox comes back on that H user let me know what it says?"

"Yeah. I got a good working relationship with Miller and Tripp. I'll give them a call and give them a heads up."

"Thanks, but keep it quiet for now. We don't need anyone talking. If Peña gets wind of us working to close down his suspected pipeline, we're screwed."

"Gotcha. I'll call and make an inquiry then. Casual."

"Perfect. You have much business in the Cottages?"

Kyle noticed Brody shoving his hands into his jean pockets and didn't blame him. The stench alone would make him crave a shower, but that only made him feel sorrier for the residents. "Always. Cheap drugs cut with everything from baby powder to drain cleaner tend to eliminate the poor suckers that are hooked on the shit, but I'm tracking an anomaly out here. Prescription drugs."

Brody's brows raised to his hairline. "No kidding?" His gaze jumped between Kyle and Alex.

"Yeah."

Brody nodded slowly and Kyle knew his friend understood. Kyle's sister, Tara, had unwittingly become entangled in prescription fraud and illegal distribution to the homeless shelter she worked out. Several months ago, she nearly lost her life when trying to ferret out the information. Kyle had watched as someone held a gun to Tara's head before her now-husband saved her. Her husband, Carter, was also a detective and he wondered how Carter slept at night having witnessed that scene. *I sure as fuck can't get it out of my mind.*

Brody clapped him on the shoulder. "Let me know if I can help. We can put out feelers if you have anything to go on." He started to walk away, then stopped. "Oh, and thanks for coming to the 'rents.'"

"I'll take you up on that offer and, dude, mini-you is a great kid. Sorry I couldn't stay longer." He jerked his head to the side toward Alex and added, "We had a call out."

"No worries. I'm glad you made it over."

"Hell, I wouldn't have missed it. You were getting pretty close to Amber. That on again?"

Brody had reconnected with a girl from his past and they were all shocked to find out that he had a son.

"It is."

"Be careful."

"Man, not you, too."

Shaking his head, Kyle chuckled. "You're my best friend. Yeah, I'm going to tell you to be careful, but I'm also going to tell you to go for it because that woman and that kid are worth the effort. I tried to kick your ass into going to see her after the accident."

"Yeah, I remember. Wish like hell I'd taken your advice then."

Brows raised, Kyle shot a glance over to Alex before turning his attention back to Brody. "So… you're saying…"

Brody huffed. "Fine. You were right."

"Damn, that hurt, didn't it?" Just as he was finished ragging on Brody, a flash of color to the side caught his attention.

"It did. I'm leaving now." Brody tossed a wave to Alex and turned toward his vehicle.

Kyle glanced around, his brow furrowed. "Yeah, okay."

"What did you see?"

"Someone that doesn't belong, which makes me edgy. Let's go to the Celtic Cock this week. You owe me a drink or ten for being right."

"Deal, take care."

Attention now zeroed in on what captured his attention, he tossed a wave toward Brody and said, "Alex, circle around to the other side and see if you see that woman who just passed by over there. She's either fuckin' nuts if she thinks this is a place to cross through or there's something in that backpack that we need to check out."

It was not hard to follow the girl as she skirted around the outside of Cardboard Cottages. Her red, sweatshirt hoodie stood out like a beacon. Dark jeans and flat, leather shoes were another giveaway that she didn't belong. As he approached from behind, it was evident the small backpack slung over one shoulder was a leather purse, and his suspicions heightened at the idea of what she carried in that bag.

Another gust of wind snapped the hoodie back, allowing tendrils of long, honey-blonde hair escaping a sloppy bun to whip about her head. Her steps hastened and he glanced ahead seeing a small car parked near the end of one of the exit ramps leading back up to the highway.

She held a cell phone in one hand, talking low and steady and didn't appear to hear him approach as he gained ground. "Stop! Police."

She screeched as her hand jerked up when she whirled around, eyes wide, shooting pepper spray wildly into the air. Her aim sucked, but before he could duck, the wind whipped it around both of them. It wasn't a direct hit, but enough that he felt the sting in his eyes and burn in his throat.

"God dammit!" he yelled, rushing toward her. Their bodies collided, and as she flailed about, he wrapped his arms around her and maneuvered her to the ground. "Stay down!"

He had not taken a direct hit from the irritant, but his eyes teared and he sucked in a ragged breath. He pinned her to the ground with one hand on her back and swiped his hand over his eyes and nose, blinking to clear his vision. Hearing rapidly approaching footsteps, he looked up and saw Alex approaching, weapon drawn.

The girl continued to wiggle and sputter, and he flipped her over. A streak of dirt mixed with a trail of tears on her cheek marred her otherwise flawless complexion. Coughing, trying to catch her breath, she blinked rapidly. Finally, her eyes stayed open, and he gasped when staring into their familiar green orbs. A familiar green he had been looking for but wasn't sure he'd see again.

For a few seconds, the underbelly world of Hope City disappeared as the two stared at each other. "You?" he growled, recognition hitting him, barely aware that she had uttered the same word in equal disbelief.

Passages: The Kings of Guardian Book 13

A Backwater Blessing: A Kings of Guardian and Heart's Desire Crossover Novella

Montana Guardian: A Kings of Guardian Novella

Guardian Defenders Series

Gabriel

Maliki

Guardian Security Shadow World

Anubis (Guardian Shadow World Book 1)

Asp (Guardian Shadow World Book 2)

Lycos (Guardian Shadow World Book 3)

Thanatos (Guardian Shadow World Book 4)

Everlight Series

An Evidence of Magic (Everlight Book 1)

An Incident of Magic (Everlight Book 2)

STAND ALONE NOVELS

SEAL Forever - Silver SEALs

A Heart's Desire - Stand Alone

Hot SEAL, Single Malt (SEALs in Paradise)

Hot SEAL, Savannah Nights (SEALs in Paradise)

ABOUT THE AUTHOR

USA Today and Amazon Bestselling Author, Kris Michaels is the alter ego of a happily married wife and mother. She writes romance, usually with characters from military and law enforcement backgrounds.

Made in the USA
Monee, IL
29 August 2020

40355041R00246